Book Five, *Dear Noah,*
The Conclusion

"Having lived in Lake Arrowhead for many years, Chrysteen Braun's books continually remind me of just how wonderful it is to live up here. It's been fun figuring out places both real and fictional. Her storytelling skillfully blends relationships, rich characters and unexpected endings, all set in our delightful mountain towns."

—Angela Yap, Editor, Mountain News,
Lake Arrowhead, Ca.

"Braun continues to skillfully weave love, loss and resilience into the conclusion of Annie Parker's story. Book Five, *Dear Noah, The Conclusion*, continues the story of friendship and new beginnings set in the quaint mountain town of Lake Arrowhead, California. Well done."

—Elizabeth Conte, award-winning author of
Finding Jane, and Chosen Mistress.

The Guest Book Trilogy
Book One, The Man in Cabin Number Five

"For those looking for a complex, engaging novel you won't be able to put down, this book is for you."

—Review by Book Excellence
(www.bookexcellence.com)

The Guest Book Trilogy
Book Two, The Girls in Cabin Number Three

"This book takes up where *The Man in Cabin Number Five* left off, with plenty of intrigue in an idyllic mountain locale."

—Susan Denley, former Associate Features Editor,
Los Angeles Times

The Guest Book Trilogy
Book Three, The Starlet in Cabin Number Seven

"Braun's a top-notch story teller; Book Three, *The Starlet in Cabin Number Seven*, is well plotted with clearly defined and relatable characters. Her research is exemplary."
—Kate Osborn, formerly with the Mountain News, Lake Arrowhead

The Guest Book Trilogy (Now a Series)
Book Four, The Maidservant in Cabin Number One
The Beginning

"The series keeps growing! In Book Four, Braun weaves in the story about the woman who originally owned the cabins before Annie bought them. What a great story."
—Kate Osborn, formerly with the Mountain News, Lake Arrowhead

"*The Maidservant in Cabin Number One* offers a rich historical tapestry interlaced with the personal growth and perseverance of its protagonist. It's an engaging exploration of a woman's journey through several pivotal decades of American history."
—Literary Titan

THE GUEST BOOK SERIES   BOOK FIVE

DEAR NOAH

THE CONCLUSION

CHRYSTEEN BRAUN

Available now on Amazon, or through your local bookstore.

ALSO BY CHRYSTEEN BRAUN

The Guest Book Series

The Man in Cabin Number Five, Book One
The Girls in Cabin Number Three, Book Two
The Starlet in Cabin Number Seven, Book Three
The Maidservant in Cabin Number One, Book Four, The Beginning
Dear Noah, Book Five, The Conclusion

COMING SOON

Family Portrait
The Storyteller
Table for Eight

Copyright © 2024 Chrysteen Braun

All rights reserved.

No part of this publication in print or in electronic format may be reproduced, stored in a retrieval system, or transmitted in any form or by any means, electronic, mechanical, photocopying, recording, or otherwise without the prior written permission of the publisher.

This is a work of fiction. Names, characters, organizations, places, events, and incidents are either the products of the author's imagination or are used fictitiously. Any resemblance to actual persons, living or dead, or actual events is purely coincidental.

Design and distribution by Bublish, Inc.

ISBN: 978-1-64704-908-9 (paperback)
ISBN: 978-1-64704-909-6 (hardcover)
ISBN: 978-1-64704-907-2 (eBook)

*For my husband Larry; my Noah.
Always the wind beneath my wings.*

Part One

Noah

NOAH

You might wonder how, after so many years, I can still recall the first time I laid eyes on Annie Parker. It was a Monday, and I was on my way back from the lumberyard when I stopped to check in on Sam. He'd been like a second father to me after my parents died, and now it was my turn to look after him. The door to one of the cabins was open and I could tell by the extra car in the drive that he had a guest.

The air was so still, my boots crunching on the gravel echoed as I made my way down there.

"Hey, Sam," I said, leaning on the doorjamb.

A suitcase was sitting on the bed, and Sam and a young woman turned to look in my direction. My heart turned over and I couldn't take my eyes off her. In that split second, I took in her large dark eyes and her pouty mouth. There was something about her that drew me in. Tight jeans and a red knit sweater completed the picture—and I lost my train of thought.

"Oh, Annie," Sam said. "This is Noah Chambers. He's a local, and since my wife died, he seems to think he has to check in on me."

"I heard that," I said.

Sam shook his head but chuckled. He then opened a cupboard, took out some towels and set them on the bed. "But I do appreciate it," he whispered with a crinkled smile.

They both stood there as if waiting for me to say something else, but it was hard for me to focus on what to say next. What I wanted to say was, 'I can't believe you're so incredibly beautiful.' But the woman turned her head back to her task at hand—unlocking her suitcase—and I lost my opportunity to say something profound.

She grabbed the towels and turned toward the bathroom, and Sam just stared at me. He raised his eyebrows, and I knew he could read my mind. When I saw it was obvious she wasn't going to talk to me, I dumbly said to Sam, "Well, it looks like you're in good hands for now, so I'll get back to work. Nice to meet you, Annie," I called out.

She either didn't hear me, or just wasn't in a friendly mood. I turned and headed back to my truck, listening again to my boots on the gravel, the sound roaring in my head.

All the way back to the job site, I couldn't help but think about her; the way her long dark hair fell onto her face when she bent over, and then how she brushed it back with her hand. And those eyes. I couldn't put my finger on it, but they were so out of the ordinary—almost seductive.

I knew I was going to have to figure out who she was, and then my mind went into overload as I wondered how I'd see her again, much less find out if she was interested in me. Even though I knew it probably wouldn't go anywhere, I had a hard time trying to focus on my work.

At around one, my stomach started growling, and I was at a good stopping point to grab a bite for lunch. I hadn't been to the Sports Grill for a while, so after my guys said they wanted to stay on the job and work, I drove into town by myself. Because I was on my own, I planned to eat at the bar. I walked in and let my eyes acclimate for a few seconds, and when I looked to my right, Annie Parker was sitting by herself at a table watching one of the televisions.

My plan to eat at the bar changed, and I cleared my throat as I walked over to her table.

"Hey, there," I said.

Dear Noah

Boy, did she give me a look. I almost said to myself, forget it, but instead, I raised my hands in mock surrender and said, "Hey, I'm Noah. I met you at the cabins, with Sam."

She looked down at my work boots, and her demeanor completely changed. Her face softened and something like a smile surfaced.

"The sun was in my eyes, so I didn't get a good look at your face," she said. "But I recognize your boots."

"Mind if I join you?" I asked.

"Sure."

I sat across from her.

"Are you by yourself?" I asked, and then realized how dumb that sounded—she was by herself when she checked into the cabins.

"Yes, I am," she said.

"Where are you from?"

"Long Beach."

"I'm originally from up here. Never did like it down the hill. How long are you up for?"

She sighed. "A week, or maybe two. Depending on how I feel. I'd forgotten how beautiful it is here, and I need a break."

Suddenly, her dark eyes took on a sad look, and I was curious to know more about her.

"What break, if you don't mind me asking?"

When she didn't immediately answer, I thought for sure I was hitting a brick wall. I continued. "I didn't mean to be so blunt. It's just not usual to see a single woman come up here."

I could tell my face colored.

"I mean, there are single women here, but not many come up by themselves."

She bit the inside of her cheek, then said, "Well, I'm not really single. My husband's on one of his business trips, and I'm tired of sitting at home. So, I decided to break out and do something for myself for a change."

I gave a slight nod. "I admire that."

I was studying her when she asked, "What about you? What do you do up here?"

I tilted my chair onto the two back legs to try to relax, and every time I did that, I couldn't help but think about my mother reminding me not to.

"I'm a carpenter by trade. I also build homes now and then. So I stay pretty busy."

"Have you lived up here your entire life? I wouldn't have thought there were a lot of business opportunities up here."

"Yup," I said. "I tried moving down once when I was seeing someone, but it didn't work out very well for me. I wanted to be up here and she wanted to be down there. And my work was up here."

I shrugged my shoulders, which I often did when I couldn't think of anything else to add.

"Even if I was over the moon in love, I knew I'd never really be happy if I moved away."

I wasn't sure why I even added that.

"I'm sorry," Annie said.

Her lunch came, so I said, "Well, I've interrupted your lunch, so I'll let you go."

I stood, then said, "If you find you need something to do at night, there's a local cowboy bar just across the street. It's very casual, and you don't need to wear boots."

I could see the beginning of a smile form, and I smiled back.

"Thanks. I'll keep that in mind. I'm sure I'll be looking for things to do."

Then I looked down at her heeled shoes and said, "I *do* suggest that if you're going to be here for a while, you get out of those *city* shoes and put on tennis shoes. Or mountain boots."

"I'll keep that in mind, too."

I took a chance and gave her a big grin. And when she smiled back, I knew at least I hadn't completely struck out. That just made it harder for me to not think about her all night.

Most mornings I stopped at Ginny's in town before I headed for work—I'd found a good breakfast kept me going without a break until early afternoon. I wore my hair long and after my shower, I pulled it back into a short ponytail. I felt like a new man in a clean shirt and clean work jeans. When I got to Ginny's, an older man was trying to open the door and I could tell he was struggling a little bit, so I held it open for him and his wife. Over the years, I'd seen a number of older people in town, and I was always curious if they came up here when they were younger and now they were too old to move back down. Seeing this couple now, I couldn't help but wonder how they got along when it snowed...

The smells of breakfast quickly reminded me why I was there, and then I looked for a place to sit. It was surprisingly busy for a weekday, but I headed to the back of the restaurant, where I could usually find a place to sit.

I stopped dead in my tracks—I would have recognized her anywhere. There in a booth sat Annie, looking at one of the home magazines from the racks outside the door. As soon as I approached her table, she held up her empty glass of iced tea, no doubt thinking I was one of the waitresses. It caught her by surprise when she saw it was me, and I swore I saw a patch of pink color her cheeks.

"You need to quit following me," I said. She looked pretty as a picture sitting there in a black sweater. I couldn't help myself, and I grinned like a Cheshire cat, thinking I'd caught her again.

"*Me* following *you?*" she said, putting her hand to her chest. "*You're* following *me*," and she broke into an open and friendly smile.

"Mind if I join you?" I asked as I slid into the booth across from her. I'd pushed the envelope by assuming she'd be okay with it.

"I guess you already did," she said, raising those eyebrows again.

"Hey, Molly," I called to the waitress. "I'll have the Hungry Man breakfast and a strong cup of coffee."

"What else is new?" Molly said, cracking a wry smile.

"I guess you're a regular here?" Annie asked.

"Yup. If you live up here long enough, you're bound to become a regular just about everywhere you go."

"I have that at home, at some of the restaurants I go to a lot."

Why would a woman like her go to restaurants by herself, I wondered, and before I could ask, she said, "My husband is always working and my schedule is all over the place, so I end up eating on my own a lot."

I wanted to know what kind of husband let this beautiful creature wander about by herself, so I asked, "What does your husband do?"

"He's an attorney. He refers to himself as a 'slip and fall' guy."

I was sure I wrinkled my forehead in thought, for she answered my next question without me even asking it.

"He's kind of a jerk, but if you need something done, he's the one to do it."

Annie's breakfast came, and I watched her eat.

"How long have you been married?" I asked.

"Almost nine years," she said, watching my expression turn to surprise. "I was a child bride," she said with a smile.

"Wow," was all I could think of to say. "Do you have kids?"

I knew I was asking for the full lowdown on her, but I figured I might as well ask as long as she was willing to share. She didn't seem to mind my questions..

"No. Kids weren't on the menu. But I knew that when I signed up. He came with a family. And you?"

"Nah," I said. I'd already told her about my one failed romance, so I figured I might as well tell her about the other one. "It's another sob story," I said. "We never officially got engaged, but we talked about marriage. Eventually she said she wasn't ready to settle down, and looking back on it, neither was I. However, she wasted no time marrying someone else not long after we split up."

Molly set my breakfast down, and I spread butter on my pancakes.

"So I guess that's two for two," I said. "I wasn't meant to be with either lady."

"It doesn't look like you're very lucky in love," Annie said.

Did she look amused?

We ate in silence for a few minutes, and when I looked up, Annie was concentrating on adding more powdered sugar to her French toast. Her eyes mesmerized me and I was still trying to think what it was about them that captivated me.

"You're exotic," I blurted out like a fool, and I caught her by surprise.

"*What?*"

"I've been trying to figure out what it is that's so different about you, and you're, somehow, exotic."

Then I noticed powdered sugar on her upper lip.

"Plus, you have powdered sugar on your lip."

"I do? Where?"

I desperately wanted to wipe the sugar off myself, but I didn't dare to. Instead, I mirrored my own face and said, "Here," pointing above my lip.

She tried to lick it with her tongue, but missed it. I took a clean napkin and started to reach across the table, but I thought better of it. Instead, I used it to show her by wiping my own mouth.

"Did I get it?" Annie asked.

"No, not all of it. One more try."

"Now?"

"Yup."

She grinned.

"*What?*" I asked.

"We used to come here for breakfast when we had our cabin on the lake, and I was in love with the young man who cleared the tables. One morning he pointed out I had syrup on my chin and I knew when he winked at me, he liked me."

As she talked, I couldn't help but study her lips, and when she looked up at me, I felt an instant jolt of electricity pass through me. It took me by surprise. Was I the only one who felt it?

Annie wiped her mouth again, then said, "I was only ten at the time, and my sister Loni called me a dork."

I knew I was pushing it again, but I was profoundly drawn to Annie, and if I'd been truthful with myself, I wanted to spend more time with her. My brain told me there was nothing that could come of it, but my heart said, '*Why not?*'

"What's on your schedule for today?" I suddenly asked.

I could almost see the wheels turning in her mind before she answered, and I would have given anything to know what she was thinking. Her brown eyes narrowed slightly, possibly trying to figure me out, and then she sat back and relaxed.

"I thought I wanted some time to do nothing up here but think, but I really can't picture myself sitting outside my cabin and reading all day. I believe that's also called procrastinating. What do you have in mind?"

Inside, I sighed a huge sigh of relief. Outside, I kept a straight face.

"I have a light day today if you want to check out some of my job sites. Plus, I can drive you around the lake?" I realized I'd asked that last part as more of a question.

"You're on," she finally said.

I grinned like a kid getting a candy bar, and then I immediately felt like a fool. And when Annie smiled back at me, I was sure it was with amusement.

We left her car at the coffee shop, and we took my Jeep. I held the passenger door open for her, but it took her a couple of tries to jump in. I laughed and said, "I can see you'll need a step stool."

"Don't pick on me," she teased back.

Our first stop was a small home built in the 1920s, and while I'd never counted them, there must have been fifty steps from the driveway up to the front door. Half way up, I could tell Annie was getting winded, but she tried her best to hide it. When we got to the front door, she bent over to catch her breath.

"You okay there?" I asked, knowing full well she needed a few minutes.

Once I could see she was all right, I gave her some space and said, "We're doing a kitchen remodel here, and as you can tell from all the steps up, it's a challenge getting the materials inside."

"Whew," she said, finally following me into the kitchen.

Dear Noah

"That's what happens to city folks," I said, joking. "Can you imagine getting up here when it snows? The perfect house is one where you drive up and are on the same level as the house. They call it level entry, but since most everything here was built on the hilly mountain, it's not always an option."

Annie went immediately to the bay window, and her eyes brightened in amazement.

"What an incredible view," she said. "I can see the shoreline and all the boats on the lake. I see why the steps didn't keep them from buying this place."

"The style and age of this home make it a charmer," I said. "It's one of the original homes on the lake. They're usually on the smaller side since they were built as vacation homes, but they have a lot of personality. The trick is to remodel them while trying to keep that charm and character intact. To do it right, everything needs to be custom made."

I left her to go to the table I'd set up in the dining area, where I checked out some of the paperwork. I made a few notes and when I was satisfied, I asked, "Ready to go to the next job?"

"Can I finish looking around?" Annie asked.

"Sure, go for it. We're not doing anything in the rest of the house yet."

"Do they live here?"

"No, they mostly come up on the weekends. They could still stay here while the remodeling is going on, but I haven't seen them much since we've been here."

I waited at the front door, and in a few minutes, Annie came out.

"The steps going down won't be so bad, but you'll probably get winded doing that, too. It takes a while to acclimate to the higher altitude up here."

I drove the long way around the lake so Annie could see all the homes along the highway.

"It's too bad you can't see much from the road," she said.

"That's because the houses sometimes are two to three levels above the lake and the trees take up a lot of the views. But maybe we can go out in the boat while you're here, and you can check it out from that perspective."

"I remember being on the lake in our boat, but back then, I didn't really appreciate the houses." Annie chuckled and then said, "The first time my mother learned to drive our boat, she took off like a crazy woman and she quickly learned she liked the speed."

Our second stop was the cabin in Sky Forest. Also built in the 1920s, it was painted a blue green color with red window trim and shutters, and it was on over an acre of land. We drove around the circular gravel driveway, which had a roundabout set up with a lifeguard chair, and an old red boat. Painted red strips of wood were laid in the dirt to look like a dock, and four large round logs were sunken into the ground to resemble pilings.

"Wow," Annie said. "This is magical. And look at the fences. They're actually branches tied together like split rail. It looks like the B&B, with the gravel and rocks lining the flower beds."

"That's where I got the idea," I said. "Let's go in."

I opened the multi-paned glass front door which opened into the mudroom, then unlocked the thick heavy door leading into the sunroom. I watched as Annie took it all in; the walls of windows and the brick floor in the sunroom, and then the hardwood flooring throughout the ground floor. She looked up at the newly installed skylights, which had totally transformed the dark rooms, and then she made her way into the kitchen. I'd installed white cabinets and black granite countertops, to contrast with the old O'Keefe and Merritt stove with the red knobs. She ran her hands over it as she checked out the room.

"What a great blend of old and new," she said. "I see the wide pine floor is taped off in squares. What are you doing there?"

"Truthfully, I wasn't sure what I was going to end up doing. I'd like to paint the floor, but I'm stuck."

Without thinking about it, Annie said, "Why don't you paint in black and white squares on the diagonal? Like diamonds."

I rubbed my beard in thought.

"I *am* a designer, after all," she said, "and I love coming up with unique ideas."

"I didn't know what you did," I said, giving my shoulders a shrug. I loved the surprised and pleased look on her face.

"Well, you never asked."

We went on a tour of the rest of the house—three bedrooms and three newly remodeled bathrooms. Then we made it back through the dining area of the kitchen, where French doors opened out to a side deck that overlooked more of the property.

"This is so charming, Noah. I'll take it," Annie exclaimed, clapping her hands.

"Whoa there, this place isn't for sale—it's mine."

That stopped her in her tracks.

"What? You're kidding. It's wonderful."

"Thanks."

I would have been lying if I said I hadn't had an ulterior motive behind bringing her there. Of course, I wanted to show her my workmanship, but after her comment about wondering what someone could do up here, deep down, I wanted her to see what I was capable of doing.

"I could live here," she said as we made our way back to the sunroom.

I wished.

Subconsciously, I was still strutting when I saw Annie go down. She somehow missed the step down to the sunroom, and she lost her balance and fell. My heart raced fiercely as I reached for her.

"Are you all right?"

I helped her to her feet, and she rubbed her elbow.

"I guess that's a step I should warn people about," I said sheepishly.

"I guess it's a step I should have remembered and seen." She took a step and said, "Ow."

But once she crinkled her face and laughed, I knew she was just being dramatic.

"Are you sure you're okay?"

"I'm fine, just embarrassed."

Her face had turned red, and she rubbed her elbow again. I couldn't take my eyes off her.

"I have another job site we could go to, or I could drop you back off at Ginny's."

Annie looked up at me with those beautiful dark eyes, and I could tell she was pretending to think about my offer. I wondered if I'd pushed it by asking for more of her time.

"It's not like I have any time constraints," she said wistfully, and for a minute I felt like she was having to make a decision about choosing me over spending the rest of her afternoon sitting outside her cabin and reading.

"I mean..." I started.

"Let's keep going," she said. "It's nice to have company."

Annie made her way outside while I locked everything up. I stood and watched her as she stopped to straighten a rock on the path to the roundabout. She moved a few more with her foot before she got to the Jeep.

"Wait," I called out.

I unlocked the door to the laundry room off the garages and found a plastic crate, then steadied it on the gravel so it would be easier for her to step up.

"Here you go, shorty."

Her grin told me my humor pleased her.

"Don't pick on me," she said.

Even though I tried to keep my eyes on the winding mountain roads, I found myself constantly turning to see her looking at all the houses or basking in the sun that radiated through the passenger side window as we drove. I had no particular thoughts when I said, "You're awfully quiet."

"I'm just daydreaming," she finally said.

I let her be.

We were only at the next site for a few minutes while I updated more notes. I'd found that by being detailed, I saved myself a lot of time having to go back and remember later what we'd done.

"Hungry?" I asked.
"I can't believe I am," Annie said.

While pretending to study a menu I knew by heart, I noticed the rings on her left hand, the way she twisted her hair while trying to decide what to eat, and then when she looked up, I felt as if I had been caught staring at her, which I had. It wasn't the first time I'd lost my train of thought with her.

"So," I said, nonchalantly putting my menu down. "Any decisions?"

"I'm a club sandwich girl, so that's what it'll be, I guess."

We gave the waitress our order and then we sat for a few minutes in a comfortable silence, with only the sounds of the busy restaurant filling in for conversation.

"Tell me about down the hill," I said.

Annie sighed.

"I'm an interior designer and I have my own business. You already know that my husband is an attorney. I love where we live, not far from the beach, and I've lived in Long Beach my whole life."

I wanted to know more, but I couldn't just ask personal questions like, why are you here? What's wrong with your husband that he has a beautiful wife who is unhappy?

Instead, I asked, "What about your family?"

"My sister's married, and my parents are talking about retiring soon..." She bit the inside of her cheek, and then added, "My father is Taiwanese."

Before I could catch myself, I said, "That explains what's different about you."

Annie bit her cheek again, and I felt myself redden.

"You're beautiful," I said, now feeling myself turn beet red.

"What about your family?" she asked, as though she hadn't heard me. "Are they up here?"

I couldn't think of any way to talk about my parents other than to say, "They were killed in a head-on crash on Highway 18."

Chrysteen Braun

I knew I should have chosen my words more carefully when I saw the look on Annie's face.

"I'm sorry. I should have added that it was a long time ago, and I don't mind talking about it."

Our lunch came and for a few minutes, Annie just picked at her French fries.

"Eat," I said. "It's all right."

I picked a fry off her plate and ate it to show her I was okay. Boy, was I a numbskull.

I dropped Annie back at Ginny's and as much as I wanted to, I resisted asking her if she had any plans for that evening. I had no idea what we'd do, but even *I* knew I was overstepping my bounds. She was not only out of my league, but married.

"See you around," I said like a fool.

My father was a deputy sheriff. We lived in Lake Arrowhead, and for years, every day, he'd make the trip up and down the hill to the San Bernardino central station where he worked patrol. My mother was a nurse at the hospital in town. As a kid, I thought it was cool to have two parents who could talk to my classroom about their careers. When my father talked about keeping the community safe, he handed out shiny plastic badges, and when my mother spoke about saving lives, she gave everyone a sucker with the hospital's name on the wrapper. It was like getting a treat from the doctor if you promised not to cry.

When I was younger, growing up with a father in law enforcement wasn't as bad as some of my friends thought. I'd brag to them about his job, making up stories about how many tickets he'd written lately. One day when I came home and asked my dad about it, he laughed at me and said, "Son, I barely write a ticket a day. Someone's got to be doing something pretty drastic for me to pull them over."

As I grew older, his stories changed, and became more serious. I figured he was telling me things so that I'd learn from other people's experiences, and I can truthfully say that as an adult, I still think of some of the things he used to tell me. Like how some men left their families to fend for themselves while they were off drinking or doing drugs. Or how most people were honest, but how people would tell stories full of contradictions. And how it was always best to tell the truth, so you didn't have to try to remember what you'd said. He and his fellow officers quickly learned to tell when someone was lying, and when that happened, they'd just look at each other and shake their heads.

"So that means don't lie to either me or your father," my mother used to say. And I believed her.

Before I went into high school, my dad was transferred up to the mountains, which meant he wasn't away from home for so many hours a day. I know my mom was relieved, for life in the mountains was much safer than it was down the hill. We didn't have a lot of crime and there weren't a lot of calls in the middle of the night to come to the aid of one of his fellow officers.

Mostly, life with a cop was good. On the days when my dad had a bad day, my mother would put her forefinger to her lips as her way of telling me to give him some space. They never really fought like some of my friend's parents did, but sometimes words could get heated—and my mom rarely fought back. She'd take a deep breath and walk away. My dad would then silently watch her before he either headed for the stool in his workshop or for the wooden bench that circled one of the trees in our yard.

I took after my mother. I wasn't a fighter; I was a placater.

I always loved the changes of the seasons, and the December I was twelve, it was the coldest I'd ever remembered. It snowed on and off for days, and my mother talked about people coming into the hospital almost frozen because their heaters weren't working. One mother who'd driven up from somewhere down the hill actually died in her car with her baby in her arms because she'd run out of gas. She got stranded on an out of the way road. It was days before anyone saw her car buried under the snow. My dad complained about having to be out on patrol 'freezing his ass off,' as he liked to say, even with the car heater on and a warm cup of coffee in his hands.

But it was also Christmas, and I wasn't too old to get excited thinking about what I might find under our tree. We had an area on our property where we let white fir trees grow so we could cut them down, and in a way, that always made me feel like I was taking a part of nature off our land. But we continued to cut our trees rather than go out into the forest, which was illegal. Once my father pointed out that our trees often provided shelter for small animals, and when I saw them myself, I began bringing extra fruits and vegetables for them to eat.

"I understand why you want to feed them," he said once he and my mother realized what I was doing, "but technically leaving food for them is illegal, and feeding them can make them become reliant on unnatural food sources, which actually hurts them in the long run."

It didn't stop me from doing it; the way I figured, if I was going to get into trouble for either taking trees from the forest or feeding the animals, I'd rather break the law by taking care of the animals. I just learned to be more careful; I made sure there was no evidence when the time came to find a tree suitable to cut down.

"Hose it off before you bring it into the house," my mother would remind us, and my father would look at me like, duh. Once we let the tree dry out, we'd nail it to a stand and set it in the front window where it would go every year.

Because she'd want the ornaments hung a certain way, she'd never let me hang any, but I'd climb up on the ladder and put the tree topper on before she got started. One year, I'd done it after the tree was decorated, and I knocked the whole thing over, breaking some of her favorite ornaments. I think it was the closest I came to getting a licking, although I knew for certain there were other things I had done that were worse than that.

What I really wanted that year was a dirt bike. I had a regular bike, but I was feeling like it belonged to a kid, and not a soon to be teenager. I wanted something with bigger tires so I could ride it along the trails and "commune with nature," I told my parents. The problem was, dirt bikes were expensive, and if I got one and my friend Josh didn't, we wouldn't be equal out there on the trails. He was certain he'd never get anything like that for Christmas. His parents had split up a few years back, and his mother constantly complained about not having enough money, although his father also complained about how much he was having to pay her in child support.

Depending on my parents' schedules, it was a miracle if we ever celebrated Christmas or birthdays on their designated days, like most families did. Until Josh's parents split up, it wasn't unusual for me to go to his house for holiday dinners, and I quickly learned I had an advantage over my friends; I got to celebrate holidays twice.

Everything seemed to fall in to place that year when my parents both had Christmas Eve off. Josh's mother had a date with the local bar, and his father was spending the holiday with his new girlfriend's family in northern California, so my parents invited him to spend Christmas with us. Josh and I helped in the kitchen, which was something my father suggested we do, and I actually enjoyed cutting up vegetables and peeling potatoes. Josh mostly kept up with the pots and pans, and when dinner was ready, we were both starving.

We each got to open something that night, so Josh and I got new PJs, my dad got some gun cleaning tools, and my mother got a new perfume she'd wanted. Josh and I stayed up most of the night playing the radio and talking about nothing, and yet in the morning we were up at daybreak to see what else "Santa" brought.

"I don't expect anything, but it'll be fun watching you get your presents," Josh said before we came downstairs.

There, parked in front of the tree, were two bikes with huge red bows. One was electric blue, and the other was aqua, both with white decals.

"You two are going to have to fight over who gets which one," my dad said.

I was thirteen when my father said, "Son, meet me in my workshop. We need to have a talk."

The shop door stuck as he tried to open it, so he gave it a quick kick, and all the while, my mind went in a hundred directions. By the time we sat at his bench, I thought for sure he wanted to talk to me about the birds and the bees. When my buddies shared stories about how their dads tried to have this awkward conversation with them, we all cracked up. We figured we already knew all there was to know. But I'd been dreading that conversation; even with my dad, I knew I'd die of embarrassment.

Instead, he wanted to tell me about his childhood. Over the years, he'd talked about the farm where he grew up, and he'd told me how the mountains reminded him of the land and forest he loved. I remember nodding at him, not quite bored but taking it all in, when he told me point blank, he was adopted.

He'd caught me off guard and I raised my eyebrows in surprise, but I didn't say anything.

"I wanted you to know," He said. "I never had a problem with it. I probably could have looked into my birth mother later, especially after my mom died. After having a child, I don't know how she had the courage to do it, but I always thought if my birth mother felt it was what she needed to do, for me and for her, then it was the right thing to do."

The only thing I could think to say was, "But could you try to find her now?"

My dad gave me a half smile and said, "Son, there's no need. I'm good with it, but I wanted you to know."

"Then if you're okay with it," I said, "so am I."

And that was the last of it.

Before my dad got transferred up, if their work schedules permitted, every Christmas, we'd all go down the hill for the station's party. It was informal, and because I was fourteen, I could go too. Most of my memories were of the men drinking too much. As the night went on, they slapped each other's backs and talked about all the crazy close calls they'd had; part of me wanted to hear their stories, but another part of me didn't want to know about dead bodies and abused women and children.

"If we can joke about it, it doesn't make it seem so real," my father said.

On the way home that night, my dad told us the story about a call he got down in San Bernardino. Neighbors called in to report that a baby had been crying for hours. My dad and his partner went to the house and followed the sounds until they found the baby upstairs. His arms had been duct taped to his crib and there was no sign of the mother. My dad cut the baby loose and brought him downstairs, just as the mother was walking up to the house. He handed the baby to his partner, and then he handcuffed the mother. The baby had stopped crying, but the mother sobbed all the way back to the station.

"Why on earth did you have to tell him that story?" my mother asked.

It was the first time I'd ever heard my mom chew out my dad, and I didn't like it.

I also didn't like that story.

By the time I was in high school, I never would have told my dad this, but it wasn't always cool to have a deputy as a father—especially if he dropped me off for school in his cruiser. If he was in a good mood, sometimes he'd whoop his alarm, and everyone would turn to see what was going on. When he did that, I wanted to slide down on the front seat and hide.

My dad would just look at me and ask, "*What?*"

Guys that were trouble makers went out of their way to avoid me, I'm sure thinking I'd rat on them if I knew they were up to no good. But I didn't need to, for my dad already knew most of them, anyway. Sometimes I felt like a badass, since almost every adult I knew was in law enforcement. I knew that in a way, I had a second family that would look out for me if something happened to me, or if I did something stupid. I have to say, though, that on more than one occasion, when I was tempted to do something that could get me in trouble, I thought about how my dad would feel if I got caught. It was a surefire way for me to keep on the straight and narrow—for the most part.

I'd had rheumatic fever when I was young and my doctor told my mother then I'd never be able to play any sports. But football was my passion, and *I* thought I was healthy enough to sign up and play. I brought the parental approval form home, but I never took it out of my notebook; I forged my mom's signature and brought it back in to the coach the next day.

We were well into the season when the newspaper ran a photo of the football team, and there I stood, smiling like a moron. My mom saw me in the paper, and she called the coach. He had no choice but to pull me.

It was the only time she said, "Wait until your father gets home."

I thought for sure I was going to catch holy hell, and when my father sat me down, I started sweating.

"Son, if you're ever going to do something dumb like that again, make sure you're not in any photographs."

I still followed all the games, and the coach let me sit on the bench with the team. It wasn't quite the same as playing, but just the same, it caught the attention of the girls.

I'd had enough money stashed away to buy that truck in my junior year. It needed a lot of work, but I took auto shop from Sam Jackson and throughout the semester, I worked on it as my class project. The summer before I became a senior, it was ready for the road, if you didn't take in to consideration it still needed a paint job, and my dad finally let me drive it to school.

In my senior year, my mother convinced me to go to the homecoming dance and to my senior prom. For both occasions, she drove me down to San Bernardino to rent my tuxes, and she then had the local flower shop make up my boutonnieres and corsages. She took a ton of photos of me and my dates standing in front of my old 1951 Chevy truck.

Years later, when I packed up all my parents' things, I found all my baby pictures along with the cards I'd given them both over the years. My mom saved it all, including the photos of me, the truck, and the pressed boutonnieres. I considered tossing them all, but for some reason, I didn't. I just put them in to a box marked photos and took it all to storage.

Normally, my mother worked day shifts at the hospital, but when they were shorthanded at night, she volunteered to alternate shifts to help out. Sometimes there'd be an emergency, and she had to get patients ready to be airlifted down the hill to another hospital. She told me when that happened, the adrenaline was what kept her going. Once the patient was on their way down, all she could think about was them and their family.

More than once, my dad would escort someone in to the hospital and run into my mother. When that happened, they passed each other like ships in the night, as she'd say. It was all business when they were on duty, but when they got home, my father would give her the lowdown. I heard stories about old Chester who'd had too much to drink when he fell off a curb, cutting his head. More than once, my father escorted couples in on their way to have their babies, and once a couple named their son after my dad. On the opposite side of the coin, he brought a woman in who'd been a victim of her boyfriend's assault. Usually, it wasn't the first time there'd been an incident, and as it often happened, when he'd answer another call for the same victim, he admitted he wanted to beat the crap out of the boyfriend. But his first obligation was to take care of the woman.

When he told my mother about worse stories, like car accidents before an ambulance arrived, or a robbery gone bad, my dad tried to keep his voice lowered, but I could always hear what he was saying.

As was the custom, my father attended funerals for law enforcement officers plus firemen, even if he didn't know them. We attended more deputy sheriff's funerals than we had family members. In fact, we didn't have any family left except my mother's cousins, who lived in the Midwest.

Both my parents were from northern California; his adoptive mother was a woman named Rachel Keller. When she married the man he always knew as his father, a man named Samuel Chambers, he became Benjamin Joseph Keller Chambers.

"It's important you know your history," my grandmother told him.

They lived on a farm where they grew crops and raised livestock to eat and sell. When my father was twelve, Samuel was killed in a farming accident, and suddenly, the burdens of the farm and ranch went to my dad as the man of the house.

Even though my father always dreamed of becoming a police officer, when he married my mother, he knew they'd have to stay on the farm to raise their family. But not long after their wedding, his mother died. Since my mother's family had already moved back to the Midwest, there was nothing keeping them on the ranch, and my father saw this as an opportunity to move to Southern California and fulfill his dream.

When they sold the ranch, they had enough money for my mother to go to nursing school in Los Angeles, where I was born; and then they discovered Lake Arrowhead.

From my mother, I learned compassion and patience, and how to sew up a wound if I needed to. I knew how to shop and cook a basic meal, and I always said please and thank you. I learned that not everyone was as fortunate as we were; a lot of families were raised with only a mother, and that a lot of families went without a proper dinner.

From my father, I learned how to handle a gun, how to clean and hand load it, and how to keep my work area neat and orderly. I learned never to shoot anything unless you had a use for it, and how to protect myself and my family if need be. I learned it was okay for a man to feel love, sadness and appreciation for whatever he had.

From both my parents, I learned to stand up for what I thought was right, to listen to others in case their point of view had merit. While I'm sure I could have learned all that from different parents, I think I learned it best from mine.

My parents served the community, and they took their jobs seriously. I learned that was the only way to be.

When my parents were killed in a head on collision on Highway 18, and I realized I would have to continue learning to be an adult without them, I didn't remember them ever telling me I'd be able to do that without them if I had to.

Until the department told me, I wasn't aware that it was customary for an officer to include written directives for their memorial in the event of death, so that the department would know how to plan their funeral service. When the Sheriff came to see me at Sam's, he had my father's file with him. His requests were simple; he wanted his closest friends there, but he didn't want the fanfare or the procession with everyone and his brother making a big deal about it. I knew my parents ultimately wanted to be buried in the mountains where they would be surrounded by the seasons and the sounds of wind whispering through the tall trees, so Sam and I made all the funeral arrangements. I should say I mostly went with Sam while he made the decisions. I didn't have a preference which caskets they were going to be buried in, and at first, I told him I'd never be able to stand up and talk at their service.

At first sight of the caravan of his fellow officers coming into town, I nearly burst with pride. My body went cold, and I attributed it to the adrenaline shooting through me. Even though my father had dismissed the idea of fanfare, I knew even he would be impressed with the sight of all of them, and the small local chapel was filled to standing room only. I did my best to keep a stiff upper lip as I greeted everyone, and I was grateful Sam and Josh stood by me. A few times during the service, I would have sworn the ground moved from under me, and when that happened, one of them would push me up straight. Sam, Trudy, and Josh sat with me in the front pew.

As much as I swore I wouldn't be able to do it, Sam pushed me up off the pew when it came time for me to get up and talk. He and Trudy had helped me write something up, and it was short and simple.

"Thank you all for coming today. Even though my dad didn't want a lot of fuss, I know he'd be really impressed with you all coming to see him and my mother off. I'm afraid if I say too much, I'll break down and cry, and you all know that young men don't do that."

Everyone chuckled, and I somehow relaxed a little as I looked down at my notes.

"I'll just say that you knew my parents, so you knew the kind of people they were. Not perfect," I paused, "but pretty close to it. It's hard for me to tell right now just how much I'll remember when it comes to making all the right choices in life, but I *do* know that having had them for parents will help me make those choices easier."

I sighed, willing the tears to stay inside when I turned to face their coffins, and then I said, "I love you both."

Later, when I was older, I always thought what I said that afternoon wasn't really adequate, but it was all I could do at the time.

Sam insisted we observe some traditional department services, so I was presented with an American flag, and a bagpiper played *Amazing Grace*. The only way I survived the service was to constantly tell myself this wasn't happening to me. My heart was hammering in my chest the whole time, and the first chance I got, I left the chapel. Sam held Trudy's arm as she tried to stop me, but I couldn't breathe. It felt like my throat was closing up, and I thought for sure I was going crazy.

Away from everyone, I bawled my eyes out.

I eventually joined everyone at the gravesite, but I stood back and watched silently as first my father, then my mother, were lowered into the ground. Sam waved me over and encouraged me to throw the first handful of dirt onto their caskets.

Josh made his way to where I was standing and grabbed another handful and tossed it in.

"They were like parents to me too," he said.

I knew he was heartbroken as well.

Flags at the station and throughout town flew at half-mast to honor my parents.

And that's when Sam and Trudy took me in, and I saw the same goodness in them I'd seen in my parents.

I moved into the second bedroom at his cabin and Trudy bought me a new pillow and bedspread to make me feel like the room was more mine, but I preferred my old one and asked if I could use that instead.

I'd done work for him and his wife for years, but living with them was still a little awkward at first. It felt good to have a woman around, but I missed my parents. I was surprised; it didn't take long for us to function as a family. I think in some ways, I felt like I was the son they'd never had. Life was figuring itself out.

Before my dad died, he'd bought me a Smith & Wesson Model 29 six shot double action revolver like Dirty Harry owned, and even though it was a bit large back then for my smaller hands, I grew into it. I took it out every time we went shooting. I showed Sam how to reload bullets, and when Josh and I would go to the gun club, Sam would bring his beloved shotgun out and shoot with us.

For a long time, Sam kept telling me things would get better, and while I knew he was telling me all the right things, in my heart, I didn't think I'd ever get over losing my parents. But he was right, and eventually I did start feeling their loss a little less.

Eventually, Sam and I started packing up my old house. Except for my things, I'd left everything the way it was before my parents were killed, I'm sure I was secretly hoping I'd never have to go through it all and could just move on. We boxed up some personal papers and a few kitchen things I thought I might want some day, and we stored everything else in cabin number five along with all the other junk in there. Trudy had a yard sale once we were finished. I couldn't stand the thought of watching people dicker over my parents' things, and I didn't want to be there while people went through everything and took it away.

I knew I'd never be able to live in that house again, so Sam helped me list the property for sale. It didn't take long for someone to make an offer on it, and before I knew it, it was sold. Sam helped me open a savings account in town, and it was bittersweet knowing my childhood home was forever lost to me, but I now had a nice chunk of money in the bank.

When he needed a break from his mom, Josh would sometimes spend a few nights with us, and Sam and Trudy welcomed him like they did me. If his mom was going to be out of town, I'd go spend some time at his house. Sam and Trudy made me toe the line, but they gave me freedom enough that I wanted to stay with them and not get myself into trouble.

Like Sam said more than once, "Just let things happen, and everything will fall into place."

And a few years later, I was ready to spread my wings, so I rented a place of my own—a cabin on some land, and I got a dog.

I thought I was in love a couple of times, but things didn't work out with the gals I was attracted to, and I'd resolved myself to the fact that there probably wasn't anyone for me out there. So when the cabin I was renting came up for sale, I bought it and started remodeling it. It was a mess, but being by myself meant I could stay there while I worked on it. I could finally see light at the end of the tunnel, and it wasn't another train coming at me.

I'd be lying if I said I hadn't thought of anything else but Annie for the last day and a half. I tried to stay away from seeing if she went to the Cowboy Bar like I'd recommended, but sure enough, the next night when I walked through the door, I could see her and Laura with their drinks; Laura with her beer and Annie with a glass of wine. Laura was a local hairdresser, and they'd become quick friends. The minute Laura got up to get them another round of drinks, I was there at their table.

"What are we drinking to?" I asked.

Then I saw Annie wipe away tears. She tried to look away, but I pulled out a chair.

"Make yourself at home," Laura said, giving me a punch in the shoulder when she brought back their drinks.

When someone asked her to dance, I saw my opportunity to strike up a conversation. But I could see Annie wasn't the chipper self I'd met the two days before.

"Hey, what's going on?" I asked.

"A lot," she said. "I don't know where to start."

"Start with the beginning?" I asked, and without thinking, I reached for her hand.

She didn't pull it away.

"I'm going back down tomorrow, and I think I'm divorcing my husband."

All I could think of was getting her into my arms, so I pulled her to the dance floor, and under the guise of dancing, I was able to draw her near to me. The minute I did, I felt a spark between us. I knew I was asking for trouble, but I couldn't release her.

"I need to talk to you alone," I whispered in her ear. "I need to know what's going on."

"We can go to my cabin," Annie said.

Laura was still on the dance floor, and I caught her eye as we left the bar.

The gravel beneath our tires as we both drove in to the parking area seemed to echo in the silent night, and I hoped Sam wasn't able to hear us as we pulled in and parked. For some reason, I felt guilty, like I was doing something I shouldn't be doing. When Annie opened the door to her cabin, the camp cat greeted me.

"Hey Jezebel," I said, reaching down to pet her. "Won't Sam be looking for you?"

I sat on the sofa while Annie opened a can of cat food.

"I've always had dogs," I said. "I hadn't had one for years, but once I bought the cabin, I got one. I have plenty of room." I was babbling. "So, what's going on?"

She sat on the sofa next to me.

"You've talked with your husband?" I asked.

"Well, the short version is that before I came up here, I found out my husband was having an affair."

I leaned forward and said, "Are you kidding?" I realized that was a dumb thing to say, and I sat back again.

"I've had a few days to sort it through, and when I'm not angry, I think about us and how we really haven't had a relationship for a while. I think we just grew apart."

I could see the beginning of tears welling up in her eyes again. My first response was to find her husband and kick his ass, but then I realized that wasn't a very good idea. So instead, I tried to think about this logically.

"Do you love him?"

I wanted to know.

She wiped her tears.

"I don't think so. I believe I still care about him, but I'm not in love with him." Annie looked miserable. "It's obvious he feels the same about me. And that hurts."

Although she forced a smile, I understood. I couldn't help but open my arms to her, and when she scooted closer, I put my arm around her.

"I'm kind of overwhelmed right now," she said. "Can we just sit like this?"

She shivered.

"It's getting chilly in here. Should we light the fire?"

"That would be great," she said and tucked her feet under her.

She watched as I got the fire started, and I looked back at her, I think just to make sure she was still there. Jezebel had already jumped up and taken my place.

"She has three babies," Annie said, bringing her up on her lap. "We bought a house a couple of years after we were married, and I was really happy. I thought I had everything I wanted and that we'd live happily ever after."

She laid her head on my shoulder, and I couldn't resist touching her cheek. The electricity was back.

"I think I never realized what I didn't have until I started looking at other couples who looked and acted like they were in love—and they didn't look like us. I saw romance everywhere I went, and I wondered why I didn't feel that way about our relationship." She looked up at me and said, "I even thought about having an affair. I've never said that out loud, so I guess that makes me as bad as him. I know that sounds awful. I would never have had one, but I thought about it and over the years, and I'd had opportunities. I could tell when men were interested in me. But I was determined to make a success of my business and my marriage. Marrying David was the one thing that changed my life for the positive."

I didn't know what to say.

"Have I made you disappointed in me?" Tears still shone in her eyes. "I don't know why I told you all this." Annie sighed. "I need some wine."

She got up.

"I think I have a beer if you'd like one."

"You're certainly a complex little lady. What will you do now?" I finally asked.

Part of me wanted to hold her and solve all her problems by loving her, but the logical side of me knew I was getting into some pretty deep water here, and if I wasn't careful, I just might get in over my head. But knowing that, and thinking I could save her, were two different things.

I reminded myself she was not only out of my league, but she was married. Her life was in shambles, and I could only complicate things.

"What do you want to do now?" I finally asked.

"Right now?"

"Yes."

Then she said something I would never have expected.

"Right now, I want you to kiss me."

Wow. I hadn't seen *that* coming.

I'll never forget that first kiss. If I was honest with myself, I'd wanted this since the moment I first saw Annie Parker. I wanted to know what it would feel like to kiss this woman who had turned me upside down the minute she tucked her brown hair behind her ears when she started unpacking her suitcase.

When I opened my eyes, I could see I'd had the same effect on her. She opened her eyes, and right then, her beautiful brown eyes were only on me.

I confessed, "I've wanted to do this since I laid eyes on you."

"I think I've wanted it too, although I just didn't know how much," she whispered.

We kissed again, and then the reality of where we were heading stopped me dead in my tracks. I would have given anything to go down that path, but I didn't want her to use me as a revenge tool, to pay her husband back. That was as bad as what he'd done to her.

I pulled away from her, and she started to cry. I felt totally miserable, and I wasn't sure what to do.

"I think you need to go," she said. "I need to let Jezebel out, and I need to go to bed."

I knew then there was never going to be any way she would end up being mine. Even if her husband was a fool, he would never let anyone like her go. And it was obvious we lived in two different worlds.

The next day, I thought of nothing else but Annie and that powerful kiss. When I went to the lumberyard, I had to go back through my notes because I knew there was something else I needed, but I couldn't put my finger on it. I knew if I ran into her again, I wouldn't know how to act or what to say, but that night, the Cowboy Bar lured me in; I just couldn't stay away. I finally broke down and drove over there, and when I walked in, I saw only Laura at the bar, no Annie. I hitched my head over towards a table, indicating I wanted her to join me. I was hoping she could tell me where Annie was, but I didn't want her asking me about the other night with Annie. I was fidgety and kept turning my beer glass around, just staring at it.

After my second glass, Annie burst through the doors almost like a whirlwind. It only took her a few seconds to scan the room, and then she found us.

"I made up my mind. I'm getting a divorce, and I asked Sam if he'd sell me the cabins," she said, before she sat down.

"*What?*" Laura and I both asked at her the same time.

"Yup, I did it. I asked him before I came here if he'd sell me the cabins. They need my love and it would be a lot of fun restoring them."

What happened to the Annie I'd been with the night before? The one who was trying to decide what to do?

"What did Sam say?" I asked.

Laura just looked from me to Annie.

"He said he'd think about it. I kind of sprung it on him, and I think he thinks I'm a little crazy."

"I do too, Annie," Laura finally said. "You've obviously made some decisions about what's going on?"

"In fact, I have. I'm moving up here no matter what. And if I get the cabins, I can run them while I establish my new design business. "

I had no clue what to say. My brain was still processing what she'd just said.

"You can close your mouth now," Laura said to me, and then to Annie, she said, "I don't know what to say. Congratulations?"

"I'll have another beer," I said, getting up from the table.

"Can you get me some wine?" Annie asked.

"I'm good," Laura said, although I hadn't asked her.

I turned to see the two of them huddled together talking, and my brain went in to overtime wondering what they were talking about while I was gone. I was hoping I could get Annie back up on to the dance floor so we could talk. I only gave her time to take a few sips of her wine before I took her hand and led her out there. When I held her, we gently rocked back and forth to the music, and she rested her head against my chest. My heart was thundering, and I wondered if she could feel it. I sensed that same sense of excitement and danger I'd felt between us the night before, and I ached to hold her close to me.

"I've made some decisions," was all Annie would say. The music was too loud for us to say much more.

She didn't invite me back to her cabin that night, which was probably for the best.

I didn't want to be the first one to make the next move, so I gave Annie my phone number and said, "Call me if you want to." With someone like her, I knew I needed to give her some space. A few days later, she left a message on my machine telling me she'd be at the Cowboy Bar that night if I was around. I didn't want to appear too anxious to see her, so I waited until around eight before I left my cabin. My stomach sank as I drove up, thinking maybe I'd pushed it when I didn't see her car right off. When I checked across the street, though, there it was, and I parked next to her.

I could tell by the empty dishes on her table she'd already eaten, which I hadn't thought about. I also hadn't thought that waiting so long to get there might make her upset with me, but there was only one way to find out. I acknowledged her with a head nod and went to the bar to get a beer. I held up my glass to see if she needed more wine, and she nodded back.

I hadn't sat for more than a few seconds when she said, "Sam and I have come to an agreement."

I'd tipped my chair back, and I choked as I swallowed a drink of my beer.

I leaned back towards her and she said, "I didn't think you'd be that shocked."

"Holy cow," I said. "You do work fast." I coughed again to clear my throat.

"Am I freaking you out?" Her eyes sparkled in the bar lights. "Do you think I've gone crazy?"

The corners of my mouth turned up, and I said, "A little. I'm just surprised at how quickly you move."

"We sign papers tomorrow. I can't think of a better way to get my life back together than to jump in. It's what I do." Her smile twisted, and she said, "Sometimes I do move pretty fast."

I wasn't quite sure if Annie understood how much her life was going to change by moving up to the mountains, but she didn't seem fazed by it at all. We took it easy between us the next few days, but then she caught me by surprise when she called and asked if I'd go with her up to the furniture market in San Francisco in two weeks. She'd already started taking measurements and drawing floor plans of the cabins, and when she showed me a list of furniture and décor she wanted to buy, I didn't know how she was going to get it all done. I guessed it was like me knowing what I needed from the lumberyard when I started a new project. It was instinct. I knew what to do.

One thing was for certain: I took it as a sign *my* life was going to change too, but I tried to not let my wishful thinking run away with me.

Two weeks later, Annie flew up on Friday afternoon so she could wake up early Saturday morning and get a head start. I flew up Saturday afternoon, in time for plans to have dinner. We'd decided it would be more cost effective for her if we shared a room, and it was clear I was sleeping on the pull-out sofa. When I got there, the room was stuffy from being closed up all day, so I turned on the air conditioning and unbuttoned my shirt. I tried to find something to watch on the TV and since I didn't want to pay for a movie, I turned it off, and after looking at my watch, decided I had time to take a quick nap before Annie came back to get me. Her key in the door woke me, and when I realized I'd fallen asleep with my shirt open, I jumped up to button it back up.

I detected a gleam of interest in her eyes, and I felt my stomach flip. Her slight blush confirmed it, and I realized how spending the night in a room with her wasn't going to be as easy as I thought it would be.

"Hungry?" I asked to break the spell.

Annie set her samples and bags down on the desk and, averting her eyes, said, "I have a great place for dinner, so I hope you don't mind that I made a reservation. They said we didn't need one because it was early, but I wanted to make sure we could sit in a booth. It's one of the oldest restaurants in town."

"Sounds great," I said. "I'm starving."

"Like a lot of restaurants in San Francisco, it's off the beaten path, but the cab driver will know exactly where to drive us," Annie said as a cab pulled up to the hotel entrance. "Alfred's," she told the driver.

I'd never taken a cab before, and when we pulled up to the restaurant, I think I successfully hid my surprise at how expensive the ride was. But I paid him and then rushed to open the front door for Annie.

It took us a moment for our eyes to adjust to the interior of Alfred's Steakhouse with its dark red walls, red leather booths and low lighting. This was another first for me; I'd been to the Saddleback Inn up in the mountains many times, but I'd never been in such a formal old school restaurant like this one before. I casually squared my shoulders to illustrate my ability to adapt to my new surroundings. I knew as long as I didn't do anything dumb, I'd make it through the evening.

Annie checked in with the maitre d' and they headed into the restaurant while I stood fascinated by the refrigerated glass case with all the hanging slabs of meat. She turned and pulled on my sleeve to keep me moving.

The first thing we ordered was wine. Annie lifted her wineglass, and I did the same. "To a very exciting project and to someone whose friendship I really appreciate."

Before I could think, I said, "To more than a friendship, I hope."

When she didn't object, I set my wineglass down and reached to run my finger down her cheek, ending at her lips. It had been years since I'd touched anyone like that and it felt electric. Annie closed her eyes, and I wanted to kiss her right then. I knew she cared about me, and that in itself was arousing.

Then playfulness got the better of her, and with my finger still on her bottom lip, she made a growling sound and opened her mouth like she was going to bite me.

We both jumped in surprise and then we laughed.

Throughout dinner, I followed Annie's lead, using all the knives and forks as she did. We had more wine, Caesar salad, New York steaks, and cheesecake for desert. Dinner was incredible, and I was stuffed.

It was the perfect ending to a perfect dinner.

When the bill came, I reached for my wallet, and I must have turned ten shades of red when she brought out her credit card to pay.

"Noah, it's on me. Not only did you make time to come help me, but I can deduct it," she said, pushing my hand away.

I expected our very proper waiter to raise an eyebrow with that exchange, but he acted as though that it happened every day; without a comment, he took her card and nodded before walking away.

When we were ready to leave, Annie asked our waiter to have the maitre d' call us a cab, and the first thing Annie did when she got in was kick off her shoes. I knew she was exhausted, and she leaned her head back against the seat and closed her eyes. I watched as the streetlights lit her face, and, for most of the ride back, we were both silent.

Once we got up to the room, she took her shoes off again and started sorting through her orders. Over her shoulder, I looked on at images of furniture and bedding, and I found I naturally shared her excitement about all that she'd accomplished so far. The next day, we'd work on artwork, then fly back home. I used the word *we* loosely, for it was obvious she certainly didn't need me along to help her make decisions.

"I'll shower tonight since I'm assuming it'll take me longer to get ready in the morning than you," she said, as she grabbed some things and closed the door to the bathroom.

She came out with her hair in a towel and she had a one piece nightgown on under a matching robe. I'd already changed into sweatpants and a t-shirt, and I was pulling pillows off the sofa to get my bed ready.

The question now was, had it really been a good idea for me to agree to stay in the hotel room with her? I could sense she was thinking the same thing when she twisted her mouth in thought. If her life was settled, everything would be different.

She climbed onto her bed and said, "Are you up for a movie? I don't think I can sleep yet."

"Sure," I said.

"If you promise to behave, you can sit here with me."

She patted the spot next to her on the bed and looked for something to watch.

We started *Ordinary People* and about ten minutes in, she fell asleep. I moved her and put my arm around her so she could comfortably lean on me while I finished watching the movie.

"So much for the movie," she said after about an hour.

I could have sat with her like that forever.

"Stay where you are," I whispered.

I raised her chin to meet mine, and I kissed her; first nibbling on her lower lip, then her top lip, then brushing my lips with hers, teasing us both. They tasted like wine. Then I covered her lips with mine, enveloping her with my kiss. I was breaking the rules, but I didn't care.

Slowly and seductively, I continued to kiss her, and I gently discovered where to find the part of her body that ached for mine. I knew this wasn't a good idea, but I also knew it was what we both wanted.

"Noah, I don't have protection," she whispered.

"There's more than one way to skin a cat," I said.

I could feel her heart pound against me as I slowly lay down on top of her. I leaned on my elbows and kissed her, my breath eventually slowing.

"You're beautiful, Annie," I said, and then touched a tear that had filled her eyes. "Are you crying?" I asked gently.

"No," she said as I rolled off her. She whispered, "Will you hold me tonight? Even though we promised Laura you'd sleep on the sofa?"

And I smiled, knowing we'd have a hard time convincing Laura we hadn't been together after all.

We both took quick showers, and by the time I was back in bed, Annie was sleeping soundly. It took me a while to go to sleep, my mind continually playing back at how amazed I was at the passion Annie had drawn from me.

That morning in the hotel restaurant, I couldn't help looking at her, remembering how I touched her the night before, and I actually felt my face growing warm. I didn't remember ever feeling that electricity with anyone before, much less being with someone like Annie. I reached across the table and took her hand, and I played with her fingers while I looked at the menu. She'd taken another quick shower, and she smelled so fresh.

I called valet service to help us bring everything down from the room; we'd take our luggage and her sample bags to the mart and check them in there until we were ready to leave for the airport.

There were two showrooms she wanted to go to and between them, she made a list of everything she needed. At first, I felt self-conscious chiming in, but I soon felt comfortable expressing my opinions, especially if I really didn't like something. Several times, we touched hands and caught each other's eyes. I, for one, felt like a schoolboy with a crush. It was incredibly sensual.

I watched her as she looked at everything, and it mesmerized me to watch her flip through the wings of framed prints, making notes of images she wanted photocopies of. I was amazed how she felt so comfortable talking with the sales representatives, not hesitant to let them know if something was perfect or if it didn't fit with her overall plan.

By around one, we were ready to leave for the airport.

I'd been embarrassed to ask Annie how much cash I should bring for the trip, and I was really glad I'd gone to the bank. Cab fares ate up most of my money.

It was hard not to look at Annie's profile as she drove back up the hill. Being with her made the time fly, and I wanted this time together to last as long as it could. I loved watching her, and when she suspected I was looking at her, she'd look my way and give me a crooked smile, sometimes touching my thigh and leaving her hand there.

"Tell me what you'd like me to know about yourself," she said.

"Well, I've already told you I've lived here all my life. I graduated from the local high school and instead of college, I opted to learn to become a carpenter. I eventually took over the construction company when my boss retired."

"Tell me about your parents."

I rubbed my beard in thought. "My mother was a nurse at the mountain hospital, and my father was a sheriff. When I was twenty, they were coming back up the mountain, and a driver coming down was going too fast. He lost control of his car, and they all died in a head-on collision."

I could feel the warmth rise in my face as I talked.

"I used to wish the guy hadn't died, so I could have killed him myself."

Annie didn't say anything for a few minutes.

"I'm glad you didn't." She touched my arm. "And that's when you met Sam?"

"I knew Sam before. He helped me rebuild my old truck in shop class, and I'd do odd jobs for him and Trudy around the cabins. When my parents died, they took me in."

Once we got back up the hill, we had an early dinner and then headed over to Annie's cabin.

"I had a great time," I said, leaning in and kissing her cheek.

"I'll bet you did," she laughed. Then she grew serious. "So did I. I'd love to just go to bed, but I'd like to lay everything out so I can get it ordered on Monday."

"If I promise to behave," I said, raising an eyebrow, "I'd love to see how you decide what goes with what."

"If you really want to, and promise to stay on your side of the bed this time, then fine. I could use some final thoughts on what I've chosen."

I set her bags of samples next to the sofa while she fed the cats, then she changed into a sweatshirt and flannel sleep pants. She emptied all her samples onto the bed and laid everything out by cabin; first bedding, then rugs, then artwork. I sat relaxed in one of the chairs and watched. She chewed the inside of her cheek as she sorted and then rearranged her choices until she had everything coordinated the way she wanted it.

"What do you think?" she asked, chewing her cheek again.

"You're amazing," I said. "Would you help me with some of my projects, too?"

"Really?" she turned to face me. "You seem to do a pretty good job by yourself."

"Yes, but you'd add the finishing touches. When you finish the B&B, we can talk about it."

"That'd be great, Noah. I need to start developing my client base up here. I'll focus on it later." She turned back around and picked up one of her finished layouts, taking it to the small table.

Dear Noah

Annie started numbering each sample to match the cabin number where it would go and then listed what she wanted to order by vendor. There was a method to her process, and again, her organizational skills amazed me. I could tell she was totally in her element.

The sun had gone down by then, and it was completely dark outside.

"I need to get back to my place so I can get ready for work tomorrow," I said. "I'll leave you to your paperwork."

"Okay," she said, distracted by her work. "Talk with you later."

Over the new few weeks, I saw Annie almost every day either for breakfast or dinner, but she was preoccupied with plans for the cabins. We'd gone over everything she wanted me to do, and like her, I made a material list for each cabin. When she gave me the heads up, we'd start working on them. I would have been lying if I said I wasn't disappointed that we hadn't taken our relationship to the next level—whatever that really was. I knew she had a lot on her mind, and I also knew we had to take things slowly if it was going to work between us.

I'd offered to drive her down in my truck when she was ready to pick up the rest of her things, and when she took me up on it, I immediately regretted it. She'd asked her husband to give her time at the house, but if he was there, I wasn't looking forward to meeting him.

I knew I could stand my ground, but all I could think of was he'd been the man she'd once loved. And what was worse, she'd given herself to him. The side of her I'd not yet seen. The closer we got to her house, the more my stomach tightened, and although I rationalized it was just jealousy I was feeling, I caught myself gripping the steering wheel. My knuckles had turned almost white. Plain and simple, I wasn't nearly as confident as I'd convinced myself I was. And when I looked over at her, I saw her fidgeting and I knew she was nervous, too.

When we pulled up to her house, she said "Crap."

David's car was there.

"It'll be all right," I said, more confidently than I felt. I put my hand on her shoulder before I turned the truck engine off. "We'll get in and out, unless you two need to talk."

"Promise me you won't let him get under your skin," she said.

"I'll just be a fly on the wall," I said, hoping I sounded more fearless than I felt.

Annie went in to the house first, and David stood at the kitchen island unwrapping the newspaper. I would have sworn I saw a spark of something in his eyes, as he smiled at her tentatively; was it love? Or regret.

And then he saw me.

"Oh," he said. "You'll need to change your mailing address," he said dryly. His entire demeanor changed. "Here's your mail."

He gave me the once over and said, "I see you found yourself a cowboy."

His comment caught me off guard, and if I was a ruthless killer, I would have...what? What would I have done? I could see the anger in Annie's eyes, but she said nothing, and I stayed in the entry unclenching my fists and trying to remain a neutral party.

Even in casual clothes, David carried himself well, with his freshly pressed pants and penny loafers. And while I'd always prided myself on not judging a book by its cover, I understood the attraction, and I instantly detested him. He'd given me the once over and probably felt the same about me.

"Well, aren't you in a mood?" Annie said wryly.

I followed her out to grab some boxes.

"I'm sorry for that," Annie said. "I can't believe he's acting like an asshole."

Tears welled up in her eyes, and I wanted to grab her right there and hold her, but I knew if David saw us, he'd know he'd pushed Annie and won round one.

"He's just lost the best thing he ever had," I said, without looking at her. "And he's taking it out on you. Let's get you packed up and out of here."

We went to the bedroom first, where a few partially filled boxes sat over in one corner, and then Annie continued to show me what she was keeping from the rest of the house. We wrapped the larger pieces

Dear Noah

in blankets and put them in the truck's bed first, and then we filled in around them with boxes and bags. When we'd finished, David was still sitting at the island, and I waited back in the entry.

Annie walked up to him and said, "You've got to be kidding, David. I can't believe you're acting like a total asshole. And it's none of your business if I have a cowboy or not. I'm done, so the ball's in your court."

She slammed the front door behind her.

"*Yes*," I said to myself, then realized I was acting like a juvenile.

I waited until we'd been on the road a while before I tentatively asked, "Want to talk about it?"

"Not really," Annie said, her face still red. "He can be such a complete and total prick."

Without thinking, I said, "I agree."

Annie took me by surprise when she just stared at me.

"Whoa," I said.

I'd made her even more angry, for she said, "Don't *whoa* me."

Tears filled her eyes again, and I turned to the road.

"There are napkins in the glove compartment."

"Thanks," she said somewhat resentfully.

Even at the risk of making her more angry with me, I said, "He cheated on you and now he's jealous because I thinks you have someone in your life; someone who can make you happy. And you deserve to be happy."

She started crying, and I left it at that. We were almost at the storage yard before she said, "I'm so sorry, Noah."

"We're good," was all I said. I didn't want to be unkind, but I felt distant, and I knew it came out that way.

We unloaded the truck in silence.

"I'm actually hungry," Annie said with a mock smile. "Can we eat before you drop me off?"

We didn't say a word during our meal.

"You okay?" I finally asked when he pulled into the parking lot at the cabins.

"Yeah," she said.

"Then I'll head for home," I said.

The next day, when the rancher I did work for in Colorado called to see if I could make a quick trip out to work on the stalls in the barn, my bravado said yes. If I was honest with myself, my ego had been bruised and it wouldn't be a bad idea if Annie and I spent some time away from each other. However, the minute I hung up, I wanted to call him back and tell him I couldn't come out, but I'd already made the commitment and I couldn't renege. I knew I was free to do what I wanted, but apprehension knotted my stomach. I had a sinking feeling I hadn't made the wisest of decisions. Dreading telling her, I left Annie a note at Sam's telling her I'd call her when I got back into town.

The minute I pulled away from the cabins, I was miserable. I'd made the two-day drive out there many times, but this time it was grueling. I drove until I couldn't keep my eyes open and stayed in the same flea-bag motel I always did when I made the trip out—and seeing that the bar next door was still open, I went inside and had a beer. But tired as I was, sleep evaded me.

I finally dragged myself out of bed the next morning and took a quick shower before I got back onto the highway. I figured I'd stop for something to eat when I got hungry. There was a Mexican restaurant I'd eaten at before, but when I pulled into the parking lot, it was empty. The place had been literally boarded up. I was dying for something to drink, so when I stopped to get gas a few miles on, I bought chips and a Coke in the convenience store. It would have to tide me over until I could have a real meal in Colorado.

Once I got to the ranch, I checked in with Don, the owner, then unpacked my bag in the bunkhouse. I made a list of what I needed to get the stalls back in shape and then headed out to the lumberyard. I probably wouldn't get much work done that afternoon, but I'd be able to get an early start in the morning. Don's wife made dinner for me and a couple of the other guys, then at their urging, I joined them at the local bar.

I called it an early night and headed back to the ranch, hoping I was tired enough to sleep. And somehow, I did. The next morning, I awoke to snores, and took my shower before I went into the house for breakfast.

I had plenty to do, but I couldn't focus on my work; I was hoping Annie was just as miserable as I was. Somehow I made it through the week, and then I made the long trek back home. I'd been gone long enough, I figured we'd get caught back up and see where this was all heading.

But I was the one who was surprised. I'd driven by the cabins and when I didn't see Annie's car, I drove into town and there it was, parked in front of Ginny's. It was a perfect time for lunch, and I figured we'd start the ball rolling again over food.

When I walked in the door, I saw her at the back of the restaurant, and she was with an older man going over fabric samples. My first impulse was to turn around and walk back out the door, but then I thought, why do I need to do that? He looked like he could be a client, which was super for Annie. I did my old rooster strut and started walking back to where they were sitting. I didn't have to get too close to them to see the way the man was looking at her, and I got the feeling he was more interested in her than the fabrics she'd laid out.

"Hey," I said.

Surprised, Annie looked up at me and her face widened in a big smile.

"Oh, Grayson...this is my friend, Noah. I didn't realize you were back," she said to me, touching my arm.

"Pleased to meet you, Grayson," I said, as I comfortably extended my hand.

"As am I," Grayson replied, acknowledging me with his hand and a nod of his head.

"Grayson is the new client I told you about. We've been going over floor plans and fabrics." She picked up a fabric sample, though I didn't look down at it. "Noah is a local contractor and has a job he's working on in Colorado..."

"Well—I don't want to interrupt you," I said. "I didn't realize you had an appointment. I saw your car as I was headed to Sam's. I'm literally on a quick turnaround and will head back to Colorado tomorrow." I nodded at them. "So I'll leave you two to it. Call me later."

Grayson extended his hand to me. "Again, very pleased to meet you, Noah," he said, graciously.

"You, too." I turned to leave and felt all eyes upon me.

"Boyfriend?" I could hear Grayson ask. I was dying to turn and look back at them. Annie hadn't told me about a new client.

I couldn't just leave her there, so I waited outside in my truck, burning with jealousy and feeling ridiculous.

"Hey," I said, surprising her when she finally came out. I'd clearly caught her off guard. "Sorry, I didn't mean to scare you. I stopped at the grocery store across the street and then saw you were still here, so I waited," I lied.

I reached for her.

"I feel like we've been strangers," I said.

"I have to say I do too, especially with you leaving. But I've also been really busy, so it's worked out okay," Annie said.

"Looks like you have a great new client. Just what you need to help you get established up here." I paused. "I hope he stays just a client."

The minute it escaped my lips, I knew I'd made a big mistake.

Annie looked at me incredulously.

And if it was at all possible, I made it even worse. "I can tell the way he was looking at you when I came in..."

"Noah, you're kidding me, right?"

I'd hit a sore spot.

"He's a client. A handsome one, but he's not interested in me."

"I'm just saying—I'm just watching out for you."

"Like I'm not able to take care of myself?" she asked defensively.

"I know you can," I said, touching her arm again, but for some reason, she quickly pulled it from my grasp.

"Annie," I started, but she didn't let me finish.

"I need to get back and put this all together so I can get it ordered," she said and she got into the car.

"I really came over to tell you I'll be at the Cowboy bar tonight. I'll buy you dinner."

"I'll think about it," she said, closing her car door.

She pulled out, leaving me standing there wondering what had just happened.

It was eight when Annie came into the bar. I was sure I'd mentioned dinner, and I was starving. I could tell she had a hard time finding me, so I stepped away from the bar and waved her over.

"Hey there," she said as she approached me.

"Hey, back," I said, turning to face her. "Are we good?"

"Yes, we're good. I'm such an idiot. I wanted to apologize for over-reacting. I just think you caught me off guard."

"Let's drop it, okay?"

"Sounds good to me."

"Wine?"

"I was thinking we could just go back to my cabin and sit by the fire. I have some beer and wine at home."

"I'm in," I said.

She kissed me lightly and said, "See you in a few?"

When I drove in, Annie had left the door to her cabin open, and I leaned against the doorframe and watched her for a few moments. I could tell by the look on her face she was happy to see me, and I was hoping this would be the night to get our relationship off to a better start.

"I'm sorry for the way I acted today," I said. "I didn't know you had a client and I should have figured that out and respected it. I was hoping to apologize tonight."

She offered me a forgiving smile, and before I could say anything, she pulled me into the cabin by my jacket, and kissed me...

My hips pressed firmly into hers, and then she started unbuttoning her blouse.

I whispered hoarsely, "I need you tonight."

Annie finished the job of taking her blouse off and then she unhooked her bra. She slid off her shoes and then her jeans, and finally she stood before me. She took my breath away, and then I took off my shirt and jeans and I pulled her down onto the bed. I knew tonight we would make love, and I'd finally be able to show her what it felt like to be with a man who truly cared about her.

I was leaving for Colorado for another week, and I was going to miss Annie terribly. She said she'd be busy checking orders for Grayson's job, and then she'd see her doctor down the hill before stopping at the design center to pick out some more fabrics. When I returned, I was looking forward to starting work on the new vanity and kitchenette she'd designed for the cabins.

My week in Colorado away from her was almost as unbearable as the last time I came out. Being with her was all I thought of. I called from the gas station down the hill to let her know I was on my way back up, and the minute my truck hit the gravel drive, my heart raced. She'd obviously heard me drive in, for when I got close to the cabin, the door was open and she stood there wearing only a robe that barely covered her breasts.

"God, I've missed you," was all I could say, before I pulled her to me, my mouth starving for her.

In between making love, we nibbled on cheese and crackers, wine and beer, and then Annie made us sandwiches. We both agreed it wasn't the most romantic of meals, but neither of us wanted to leave the cabin. We could eat again tomorrow.

I was like a teenager in love. The last few weeks with Annie in them made it impossible for me to stop thinking she might be the one—the woman I wanted to spend the rest of my life with. We were like the actors in a movie who were madly in love, and you'd see glimpses of them doing things together, like going on a picnic, laughing, or dancing to slow music—even making love. It was difficult for me to focus on anything but how she made me feel, and how beautiful she was. If she wasn't in my bed, I felt lost. In my heart, I knew no one could ever be perfect, but Annie came close.

Every day I woke to the thought that I didn't see how our time together could get any better. And then Sam called to tell me David was at Annie's cabin.

"Keep an eye on him," I yelled.

Thoughts of him being there froze in my brain. I should have brought my gun, I thought on the way over, but quickly realized that it would have been a big mistake. Shooting David wouldn't solve anything, and it would have been the worst thing I could do. Instead, I drove like a wild man, recklessly taking the turns and curves with only the thought of me getting there in time.

"What the fuck is he doing here?" David hollered when he saw me. His face was so red I wondered if he was going to have a stroke.

I rushed over to Annie and took her arm.

"Are you all right?"

"Fuck off, *cowboy*," David said.

"Hold on now," I tried to calm him down by taking both his hands.

"*Did you hear me? This is not your business!*"

"I don't know what you two are talking about, but it looks like it's getting out of hand," I started, and then David lunged for me.

What had just happened?

I hit the ground and then David went after me, but my age and strength worked in my favor as I pushed him off me.

"*Stop it, both of you,*" Annie screamed.

David lunged for me again, and this time I jumped away and he went down. He stayed there for a moment, and I thought he might actually cry. This was unbelievable! I could see how people were murdered in passion and outrage, for that's exactly how I was feeling. I was so worked up, I thought I could have killed him.

Instead, I bent over, with my hands on my knees, just to catch my breath. David was still down on the ground and he had his hands over his face.

Sam stepped up with his shotgun, as if he was going to make everything right by shooting someone. If it wasn't so serious, it would be comical. The newspaper headline would read, **"Old mountain man shoots soon to be ex-husband while he fights with wife's new boyfriend!"**

"For god's sake, David, *get up*," Annie said. She looked like she was actually going to kick him. "And how did *you* get here?" she asked me.

For a minute she looked at me like I was the one who was crazy, and then Sam piped up, "I called him."

"*Get up*, David," she said, "and go home before I report you to the Bar. Your behavior is appalling. And it will change nothing. In fact, it makes me wonder what else you've lied about...but I want this to be over. I want the divorce to be finished."

By this time, the cats had inched their way out of Annie's cabin to see what the commotion was.

"And I need my money, now," she added.

David stood and brushed himself off. Desolation drained all his color as he stood and brushed himself off, but leaving his hair disheveled. He rubbed his hand on his shoulder and I was glad he hurt himself. We watched as he painfully made his way back to his car, all traces of rage left behind. Sam followed him back, to be certain he was truly leaving.

Annie stood there, trembling, and I realized this could have gone much worse. I went to her side and touched her arm again.

"Are you okay?"

She suddenly stepped back from me, like I'd been the one who'd gotten out of control, and she winced. Her look cut me to the bone.

"Jesus, Annie," was all I could say before I turned to leave.

At that moment, I made a decision; if Annie wanted to talk to me, she knew where to find me.

Then, just when I thought we were back on track, our lives took another sharp turn.

When Laura called me from the hospital, it felt like the ground beneath me cracked open and I was falling in. And then I was numb. How could this have happened? I hadn't even known she was pregnant. I felt the blood drain from my face and then I froze.

I didn't bother to hang up the phone, but instead, I just ran to my truck.

Annie had just lost our baby. How was she doing? I thought she was on the pill. Had she known she was pregnant but hadn't told me? It didn't help that I'd eventually get the answers. I tried to keep my thoughts in some sort of order, but I wasn't very successful.

When she woke, I was sitting by her bed. I pulled her to me and held her in my arms, and she started crying.

"I'm so sorry, Noah. I had no idea."

They finally released her with instructions to take it easy for the next few days, and she insisted on going home to her cabin. The minute I opened the door, Jezebel and her kitten, Socks were there and I could tell just seeing them lifted her spirits.

"Hi, my girls," she said.

Annie changed into her PJs and climbed into bed. It wasn't cold, but I started the fire anyway, and just listening to the crackling sounds the wood made relaxed us both as it always did. I told Annie Sam and I would go pick up her car and get it back on to the grounds. I offered to bring something to eat when I returned.

"Oh, god, Sam will know I was pregnant," she said. "That's so embarrassing!"

"I just told him you had some female problems. Nothing serious." Her face was drawn, and I could tell this whole mess had overwhelmed her. "Are you okay?" I asked again.

"I am...I haven't really digested it all yet. I didn't even know I was pregnant, so I'm still unable to think clearly. I know I dropped a bomb on you, Noah. And I can't believe I'm crying again." She took a few minutes to compose herself. "I'll be fine. And I'll be hungry when you get back."

Both the cats climbed on her bed and laid next to her. She petted them, then went back to sleep. I envied her peacefulness.

I was back in a couple of hours and knocked quietly on her door.

"I'm up...come in."

The cabin had darkened in the afternoon sun, and Annie sat wrapped in a blanket, staring into the fire.

"I brought nourishment," I said, setting turkey sandwiches and iced tea down on the small coffee table.

"I'm famished," she said. "It feels like I haven't eaten in days."

After a few bites, she asked, "Will you stay with me tonight?"

"I wouldn't leave you for anything."

"Even though I can be annoying?"

I thought, more like sometimes cutting me through my heart.

"Yes, even though," I said.

I slept on and off, waking to every move Annie made. I woke once, and Annie had curled up next to me, cuddling her back into the curve of my body. We slept until almost nine the next morning, and it surprised me how good she looked. When we finally decided to face the day, we were both hungry, so after showers, we dressed and left for Ginny's.

"Are you okay?" I asked as we parked.

"I feel really good. I'm surprised. And since we're speaking again," she said somewhat sheepishly, "can we get back to work on the cabins? I need to do something to fill my time."

"But I think you need to rest," I said, stopping her as we walked.

"I can rest and work. I'll just take it easy if I get tired. I can't really say I feel like they did anything, which is weird; I should feel something," she said pensively.

She'd just lost our baby, and it didn't sound like she was going to give herself any slack.

"Are you sure you're ready to get back to work?"

I know I looked at her like she was a madwoman for even thinking about anything but what had just happened, but the whole ordeal had taken a toll on me.

"I'm good. I just need to slow down for a couple of days, but you guys do all the hard work. I just supervise," she answered with a timid smile.

"You just never stop, do you?" I asked, almost as a plea.

A pain squeezed my heart as we sat there, but there was nothing I could say. During breakfast, she could tell I was not happy with her, but it was more than being upset. From across the table, I took her hand and just shook my head.

"I was hoping to have an open house and ribbon cutting before Christmas, but I don't think we'll be finished in time," she said.

"When are the new signs going to be ready?" I asked, trying to shift my mood.

"Next week, so once those are up, people driving the highway will be able to see where we are. That itself should help our bookings."

She played with her straw wrapper for a few minutes, and then said, "I'm okay to stop by the grocery store on our way back to the cabin. We need something we can make sandwiches with and I could use more water with electrolytes. I'm still totally dehydrated. I do know I'll want to take a nap today, so if you have something else to do, you won't offend me," she said.

After shopping, I carried the groceries in and put them away while Annie changed back into her pajamas and climbed under the covers. I used the wood in the basket to add to the fire, then went outside and gathered more. Soon she was sleeping.

I left to check on a few jobs, but came right back. I hated to leave her, although I knew she was fine and just tired. We hadn't talked about the miscarriage all day, and I'd tried not to dwell on it. After dinner, though, sitting in front of the lit fireplace, I brought it up.

"How are you feeling about all this?" I finally asked.

"Honestly, I'm trying *not* to think, but when I do, my thoughts are mixed." She sighed. "Part of me says that since I didn't even know I was pregnant, *that* part of me says this definitely isn't a good time to even think about having a baby. And I *strongly* believe that if there was a miscarriage, then something was wrong with the baby, and the pregnancy needed to end."

The way she said it made perfect sense, but I was still at the part where we lost a baby. I popped the lid off a bottle of beer and brought Annie a glass of wine. I watched her face as the fireplace cast a glow on it. She was tired, but still so beautiful.

She thought before she spoke again.

"I do eventually want children...I think...but for so long, they weren't in the equation. So I'm not even sure how I feel about that either. My mind hasn't gotten to that point yet."

She took a sip of wine.

"What about you, Noah? Do you want a family?" she finally asked.

I studied her for a minute, then said, "Down deep I've always thought, or wished, I'd find the right person to settle down with. And I guess that means having a family. In a perfect world, I think that if it's meant to be, then it'll happen and it'll be the right time, too."

Her eyes were beautiful in the fire's light, and I watched them as I traced her face with my fingers.

Eventually she said, "Even though this whole thing has made me sad, I'm pretty practical, and I know I'll be fine. It almost doesn't feel that it was a pregnancy, if that makes any sense."

Jezebel wove her way around my legs and I reached down to pet her.

"I know everyone deals with miscarriage in their own way," she continued. "I think I'd feel differently if we were planning on having a baby. I may still be in shock, but I'm not sure what I feel. I feel detached; like it hasn't really happened. Does this make me a terrible person?" she asked, I knew, hoping she hadn't disappointed me.

I pulled her to me so we could lie on the sofa and watch the fire.

"I don't think you're a terrible person, Annie. I think all this needs to settle in. For both of us."

I stared into the fire, watching its dancing flames, and said, "I've never come close to becoming a father, so I think I understand how you feel. And just so you're aware, I think you're the strongest person I know. *And* I think you'll be just fine."

I turned to look at her with mischief in my eyes. "If I could, I'd show you how much I care about you by making love to you all night— but I'll just have to wait and show you when you're ready."

"I'd love that too, Noah. And I'll let you know just as soon as I know myself." Then she kissed me.

In the coming days, Annie talked very little about losing the baby, and while she said everything was okay, I, who am not an expert at feelings, could tell she felt stronger about it than she let on. The whole thing ripped my heart out, and I hated that she was able to at least pretend that nothing had happened. In a way, it was as if she built up a small wall; one that let her pick up what had just happened and tuck it deep behind it.

I tried to use her logic. This wasn't a planned pregnancy and if it was meant to be for us, we'd have another chance.

November was crazy for Annie. She had a booking for Thanksgiving weekend and she was in seventh heaven. We planned on having dinner with Sam and Ginny, and then we were going to drive out and see Annie's parents in Prescott. I had to admit I was a little nervous to meet them. After all, Annie and I had been in our relationship for a while now, and it was obvious we'd been sleeping together. I knew we weren't teenagers, but thinking her parents would know I'd made love to their daughter made me feel like it.

As if Annie read my mind, she periodically reached over to either touch my arm or pat my thigh as we drove.

"They'll love you," she said more than once.

Even though Annie had told me Prescott reminded her of the mountains, once we got out of the desert, I could see why. The elevation and landscape began to change, as did my growing apprehension. Almost the moment we turned into the park with where their home was, I knew that with all the surrounding trees and greenery, if they loved living here, I had nothing to worry about.

Even though Annie told me to call them by their first names, I referred to them as Mr. and Mrs. Chang, and her father shook my hand with both of his. After a quick assessment, he offered me a slight nod. I could tell from the look on his face, I'd passed the initial test. Her mother greeted me with a warm hug and said, "We're so glad to finally meet you. And, for goodness' sakes, call us Victor and Lisa. After you two make yourselves at home, I've made something simple for dinner."

"Which room's mine?" I whispered to Annie as we walked down the hall.

"This one," she said, passing a small bedroom/office crowded with a twin bed, a dresser, a small desk, a chair and a filing cabinet.

When we came back into the living room, her mother joked, "I hope your feet don't hang over the bed."

Annie and her mother put platters and bowls out on the table, and once they sat, her mother said, "Don't be shy."

We passed around meatloaf, mashed potatoes, green beans, and coleslaw.

"This doesn't look like a simple dinner," I said, serving myself a little of everything. And after a few minutes, I added, "And everything is delicious."

Annie's father asked about my work in construction and I told them if they needed anything done around the house while we were there, I'd be happy to work on a project.

"Oh, no," her father answered, "we could never have you work while you're on vacation."

Even though I knew a little bit about their story, I asked her mother how they'd met. Her mother reminisced about the lake house when the girls were younger, and then her face clouded over. I knew she must have been thinking about Annie's sister Loni. Annie changed the subject and told them about the work I was doing on my cabin.

"We have a rule here," her mother said, clearing up the dishes. "No one under fifty-five is supposed to stay here, so you two will have to keep it down." She turned and laughed. "We don't want the neighbors reporting us!"

We watched her father's favorite TV programs for an hour or so before I said, "I don't know about you, but I'm beat."

"Me too," Annie said, taking the dessert plates to the sink and rinsing them. "What's on the agenda tomorrow?"

"We were thinking of taking you on a tour of the area, and ending up at Goldwater Lake," her mother said. "We'll pack a picnic lunch and watch the boats go by," "Exciting, huh?"

Once Annie and her mother made sandwiches, we packed the cooler with drinks and ice and put it in the trunk of their car. Her parents were both pretty good guides, telling me about the town, the rodeos, and how Arizonians were beginning to complain that Californians were moving in, causing home prices to go up. Once we got to the lake, we brought the cooler out and each had a soda. Annie's father and I took a walk while the girls sat and read from books they'd brought.

"Do you fish?" I asked her father.

"No. Not really," he said. "And you?"

"I like to fish, but I don't eat much of it, so I end up tossing everything back."

"What kind of fish do you have in Lake Arrowhead?"

"Let's see. I know we have bass, trout, and catfish."

Her father nodded at me and said, "I think that's what we have here, too."

"I used to eat a lot of fish before I came to America. Lisa doesn't like to cook it, so I only get it when we go out for dinner. You know, the store in town named after the old Mayor? Mr. Goldwater? He died in the 30s. This lake is named after him too. When we moved here, Lisa looked it up."

Before we headed back, we drove to Mount Union Lookout and I couldn't believe all the evergreen trees; I wished there were ways to see them like that in Lake Arrowhead.

All that fresh air made us hungry, and Annie's parents wanted to take us somewhere special for dinner that night. While we waited for our steak dinners at The Palace Restaurant and Saloon on Whiskey Row, Annie's father and I checked out the displays throughout the restaurant floor, filled with images and memorabilia of two of its most famous customers, Wyatt Earp, Doc Holliday.

Then, after another long day, we headed back to their house and crashed. Once we all finally had our turn in the bathroom the next morning, we went out for breakfast and then continued with our tour of the Prescott area. We toured the Smoki Museum of American Indian Art and Culture, The Sharlot Hall Museum, and finally had burgers and malts. It seemed like all we did was eat and sightsee, but I couldn't have asked for anything more.

The next morning, we headed for home.

"See, I told you they'd like you," Annie said once we were out on the highway.

I would never tell Annie I had worried her parents would compare me to David, but negatively. More than once I'd gritted my teeth, preparing to defend myself if need be. But when I reminded myself how David had shown his true colors the couple of times I'd seen him, I realized I'd wasted my time and energy even thinking about it. When my self-confidence wavered, even for a few seconds, I took a deep breath and reminded myself that, at least for now, Annie had chosen me over him.

After our trip, even though we hadn't made official plans for the future, we were serious enough to start thinking about the next steps of our relationship.

Work on the cabins progressed, and once Annie put her finishing touches on them, they looked incredible. She had an opportunity to work part time at the flooring store, and I took on a nice job that Annie could consult on. Bookings increased for her, and by Christmas, two families had reserved cabins between Christmas and New Year.

Just before the holidays, it snowed, but it hadn't taken long for the ice to melt from the trees and rooftops and by Christmas Day, the few icicles that were left had just turned into drops of water falling from the eaves. There was still plenty of snow on the ground, but I knew it was disappointing for her.

Annie and I spent Christmas Eve at my cabin with my dog Rufus, and after we drank wine and opened a few gifts, we made love. On Christmas Day, we slept in and had muffins and orange juice before heading over to Ginny's, where she made a delicious brunch for the four of us.

Annie got me a buck knife in a leather shield, and we got Sam a Swiss pocket knife with a chain, since he was always losing his knives in the middle of a project. Annie got Ginny two personalized aprons she could wear around the coffee shop. The three of us chipped in and bought Annie a metal branch coat rack for the lobby, so everyone had a place to hang their coats.

On Christmas Day, Annie's disappointment lingered, as we didn't have a fresh snow dusting to wake up to. No matter what they say, everyone who comes up to the mountains for the holiday wants it to be a white Christmas.

I wanted that as well.

The week after Christmas, Annie got the strangest phone call from a woman named Alyce Murphy, who wanted to know if there was any record of her father staying in the cabins years ago. Annie checked the old guest registers and no John Murphy had registered.

"I see a John Smith for the dates you gave me," she told the woman. And then she noticed he'd stayed in cabin number five. "That cabin has been used as storage for years."

She explained she was restoring the cabins but hadn't gotten to that one yet, but there was something about the woman's plea that convinced her that Alyce Murphy needed to come up. When they hung up, she asked Sam if he knew anything about that cabin.

"John Smith's name is here in the guest book, all right," he confirmed, "but I have no idea why she wants to see that particular cabin." He shrugged.

"It's the oddest request," Annie said, "but I couldn't say no."

A few weeks later, Alyce Murphy came into the office.

Two of my guys were scheduled to meet Annie and Alyce at cabin five, so they could start emptying it out. I was working on a big project, so I couldn't make it. Piece by piece, they checked everything that came out; they took drawers out of furniture, they rummaged through every box, and they looked in every nook and cranny for anything interesting. Of course, there was no way of telling how long any of it had been in the cabin, and at the end of an exhausting day, the cabin was empty of everything, including the carpet and any hopes of finding clues to unravel the mystery. At least Annie came away with a clean slate to start restoring the cabin, but Alyce was no closer to learning about what happened to her father.

"Most of her life Alyce thought her father had died of a heart attack," Annie said that night. "It turns out he killed his business partner, and then committed suicide."

Sam took his old hat off and scratched his head when she told us.

"Her husband warned her she might never find out why he did it, and after today, I think that's probably what she's going to have to live with. I'll see what she wants to do in the morning."

Alyce stayed the night and went back down the hill in the morning.

There was always something about Annie that made me feel like she was moving on, with or without me. Like when she originally decided to move up to the mountains and buy the cabins. Where had that strength and determination come from? Or, later, when she bought the flooring store, when the opportunity presented itself. And then when the space next door came available, she wanted to expand. I knew it was impossible to never doubt yourself, but it was like she jumped in first, and then figured out how to swim afterward.

I would have been lying if I said her drive didn't sometimes throw me off balance. That drive was one of the things I loved and admired about her, but I also had to come to terms with it if I wanted to be a part of her life.

And when I finally came to realize I could be happy being that supporting partner—one who brought their own strengths to the table—I was determined to make a life with Annie happen. I didn't have an exact plan, but once I realized that the more freedom I gave her, the more she gravitated towards me, I just waited for the right time.

And then, that next summer, my world imploded. And the cause of it all was Grayson Underwood.

Annie was still working on his lake house, and now she was bursting with excitement to tell me he'd asked if she was interested in redecorating his ranch in Montana. They'd fly out on the next Saturday, make a list of what he wanted to do, spend the night and then fly back on Sunday.

It was a perfect opportunity for her to land another large job, but my gut caught fire just thinking about how Grayson would try to weasel his way in to her life. We were at her cabin when she told me she was interested in the project.

"I can use the additional income to make an extra payment on the cabins," she said. "Plus, it'll be wonderful for my portfolio."

If I told her what I really thought, that this was a perfect opportunity for Grayson to make a move on her, she'd shrug it off like she'd done when I said something about him before. I was a guy, and I knew how some men operated.

"We'd get started on it right away, and I've never flown in a small plane—that's kind of scary. But I'd love to tell him yes," she said, giving me a weak smile. I knew she was silently asking for my blessing.

It was as if I could see myself through her eyes, and neither one of us liked what we were seeing. I knew I was possibly risking everything when I said, "I don't like it, Annie. I really don't feel comfortable with you going off with him like that."

"Come on, Noah. He's just a client," she argued. "And a really good one at that. I don't know why you're so worried about him. And *me*, for that matter."

I heard a warning voice in my head, but I only half listened.

"Annie, I don't trust him."

Even to myself, I sounded desperate, but in my mind, I was watching her inevitably leaving me for someone who could provide her with a life filled with everything I couldn't offer. How had I gone from the man she said she loved to the one who was expecting her to leave?

"I'm trying to respect your opinions here, Noah…"

The tone of Annie's voice caught me by surprise, and I just looked at her.

"But I also know this is exactly what I've been hoping for. I feel better about everything since I've moved up here, and this is just a stepping stone to getting established again. I understand how you feel, but I just don't see it."

I was at a loss for words as she seemed to read my mind.

"I'm not interested in Grayson's lifestyle. I need normal. And this is a great opportunity for me."

I knew I could be making the biggest mistake of my life when I took Annie by the arms and said, "If you take this project, then you're disregarding how I feel."

I could tell she was speaking to me with as reasonable a voice as she could manage when she said, "Then you're pushing me into making a decision I already wanted to make. I'm trying to work with you on this, but you're ultimately making me want to take the project even more."

"Then you've made your decision and I'm not part of it," I said.

I grabbed my jacket and left.

Sleep eluded me that night as I alternated between feeling sorry for myself and regretting my behavior. In my mind, Annie had given me no choice but to push her into making a decision, and it wasn't the one I'd hoped for. Throughout the night, Rufus inched closer to me in bed and his constant whimpering kept me from falling asleep for even a few minutes at a time.

"We'll be fine, boy," I said, wishing in my heart it was true.

The next morning, I called my customer in Colorado and told them I was available to work if he had something for me.

"There's always work," he said.

I called Sam to let him know I was leaving, and I was grateful he didn't ask why.

"I'll let you know when I'm back," I said.

My helper, John, could finish up my projects in town. I called him before I packed Rufus up and we took off before lunch.

I spent five weeks in Colorado, working more on the barn and raising hell with the other guys at the local bar. I thought if I drank enough, I wouldn't miss her, but that only worked until I came home to the bunkhouse and tried to sleep. There were only two other guys staying there, but their snoring made me wish I could just sleep in my truck.

For being a small town, there never was a lack of women, and one Saturday night while I was sitting in the bar at my regular table, a couple of ladies saddled up to the bar, ordered drinks, and then checked out the room. The music had already started, and several couples were out on the dance floor. I just stared at them, *the lovers*, and my heart broke thinking about how Annie and I would dance and I'd hold her tight.

I was so focused on them that at first, I didn't notice that one of the ladies appeared at my table, and was just standing there.

"Care to dance?" she asked.

Her strong perfume preceded her. I wasn't in the best frame of mind, and without thinking about it, I waved my hand in front of my face, as if I could clear the air around me. My gesture obviously offended her, for she squared her shoulders in indignation and abruptly walked away.

It was just as well. I wasn't interested in meeting anyone, anyway.

I turned back to watch the couple on the dance floor, but by then, they'd left, and I was ticked off. I tried to find them in the bar, and eventually caught sight of them at a table, laughing, and when they kissed, I thought I was going to lose it.

Just then, one of my bunkmates found me and suggested we go back to the ranch. The minute I stood, the room swirled, and I knew I needed to make it outside before I puked. Rufus was waiting for us in my truck, and I gave my buddy the keys.

"You need to drive," I said before I barfed again.

Thankfully, I had the next day off so I could get myself back in better shape, but that next Monday, I found myself drinking the minute we were done for the day. When I woke up Tuesday morning, I was still drunk, and I knew I should have stayed in the bunkhouse and slept it off. I thought if I worked, it would make the time pass quicker, so I went back to work on the barn.

I still had wood to cut so I could finish repairing a wall in the tack room, and the minute the skilsaw nicked me in the knee, I thought for sure I'd almost cut my leg off. Blood gushed everywhere, and I was lucky one of the guys was working in there too, for when I cried out, he tore off his t-shirt and tied it around my knee. He drove me in to the emergency room where, from the sight of me, it looked like I was badly injured. But once the nurse unwrapped the wound to get me ready for the doctor, she said, "It looks like you'll live. Plus, you have enough alcohol in you to kill any germs in there."

I knew I needed to get home, so I laid off the beer for a couple of days so I could make the trip back up the mountain without killing me or anyone else and find out just where Annie and I stood. Me being in Colorado wasn't solving anything.

When I got back up the hill, I drove by the flooring store first, and when I didn't see Annie's car, I headed for the cabins. She wasn't there either. I knew I looked like shit, and probably still reeked of beer, but I wanted to also see if Sam was okay.

When I walked in the door to the office, he took one look at me and said, "Well, aren't you a sight? Things that good, huh?"

I could tell by the way he hemmed and hawed, he wasn't wanting to be the one to say anything, but he told me Annie had gone back up to Montana to decorate the house, and that she'd be back after the weekend. I felt the bile rise in my throat, just imagining what she was doing right then, and I turned and headed back out without closing the office door.

I had no one to blame but myself, and the minute I made it to my bedroom, I fell into bed. All I could do now was wait for Annie and get back to work on my own projects.

Monday morning, Annie called.

"Hey," she said.

I let the line go silent, and then finally said, "Hey."

"So I'm back and the project is finished," she said. "Thank goodness."

Visions of Grayson wooing her into his bed ripped me to shreds. I should have had more faith in her, but the sound of her voice was so tentative, I knew my worst nightmare had come true. And when I didn't say anything, she continued.

"I figured if I waited for you to call me, it'd never happen, so here I am."

And there she was.

"I've missed you," she said, and I could tell she was crying. "I'd like to see you."

"I've been busy too," I finally said.

"Can you come by tonight?"

It was up to me now, to either let her back in or to go on without her. And I knew going on without her wasn't going to work for me. I was now trembling, but I took a deep breath to still my breathing.

"Yeah, sure," I said, calmly. "I'll come by after work."

I wanted her to think I was unshaken, but I was hanging by a thread. And there was no way I was going to be able to work with my mind as messed up as it was, but I went to the job site, anyway. I was so preoccupied I couldn't focus, so I ended up driving around the lake. I wound up back home, sitting in one of the Adirondack chairs on the cobblestones out in front, petting Rufus, watching the wind rustling through the trees, and staring at the pine cones on the ground. My mind started playing games on me; I'd loved and trusted her, but what if, when I saw her, her beauty had faded? Or what if I was so disappointed in her, I no longer loved her? And what if she actually told me what happened? Would I believe she hadn't secretly wanted to sleep with Grayson Underwood? I was broken, and I knew a door had closed.

I was mistaken in thinking a hot shower would wash away some of my anxiety, but I could smell myself from the day's stress. At five, my

Jeep pulled up in the parking area of the cabins, and my heart raced so fiercely I wondered if I was going to pass out.

I tried to calm my breathing as I walked down to Annie's cabin, but it was the most difficult thing I'd ever had to do. I had to face her. But before I got to her door, she opened it and just stood there like she had so many months before, in a robe that barely covered her, and even though my heart was breaking, I didn't feel any differently about her, and I couldn't imagine living my life without her.

I could tell she knew I'd figured out what she'd done, but I also knew she saw the forgiveness in my face.

"Thank you for not making this harder than it is," she said, beginning to cry.

"I don't think you realize just how hard this is..." I said.

My eyes met hers, and then my fingers caressed her cheeks. There was a long and empty pause, and the silence was heavy. She waited until I'd seen what I wanted of her, and then she dropped her robe and I almost broke the door down to get inside.

She saw me limp and, alarmed, asked, "What happened?"

Instead of answering her, I brought her body to me, and I covered her mouth with mine.

"Why did you go away?" she asked.

"Shh," I said, touching her lips with my fingers. We moved to her bed where she welcomed me into her body, and afterward we both cried.

At that moment, I knew I had her forever.

Until I realized forever wasn't really forever.

But the rest of the story was always Annie's to tell.

Part Two

Annie

Part Two

CHAPTER ONE
1982

Noah's cabin in Sky Forest sat on one and a half acres, most of it flat and accessible—and that's where we were married. Technically, it wasn't in Lake Arrowhead proper, or Arrowhead Woods, as it's called, and it's right off Highway 18 as you head east to go to Big Bear. Until 1928, its residents referred to it as the Forest of The Sky, which, since Native Americans had originally inhabited the mountains, I assumed was the Indian translation. *I* believed it was because when the clouds from the San Bernardino Valley below reach the side of the mountain, the covering is so thick, you feel you could step off the mountain and walk across the surface.

The cabin sat back off a gravel entrance, just beyond a circular driveway so it wasn't visible from the street. In the center was a roundabout with a rock border, where Noah had set up a lake scene, complete with a red dinghy with a singular mast, a six-foot tall red lifeguard chair, and a faux dock made from old pallets. He'd sunk old tree trunks along it and connected them with nautical rope to look like pilings. Blooming spring vincas with lavender flowers, which had come back from the winter snow, blanketed the ground. We'd planted wildflowers around the perennial daffodils in the stone lined flowerbeds on either side of the gravel driveway and our dogwood tree was in full bloom.

Off to the left, there was a clearing between a cluster of trees, where years ago, old flat granite cobblestones had been laid. Somehow, Noah found more aged stone and extended the area to make it large enough to accommodate us and our guests. I'd found an old iron gazebo frame that we covered in a fresh flower garland and we set it toward the back of the stonework, where we would stand and say our vows.

It was the end of April, when the threat of snow wasn't likely, and when the weather had begun to warm up. My dear friend Sarah was my maid of honor, and Noah's friend Josh was his best man.

My parents drove in from Arizona and stayed in my old cabin, now called Wood Haven. When I finished restoring the cabins, we gave them names, although we still referred to them as cabin number one or cabin number two. My old hairdresser, Laura, made arrangements at her old salon to do our hair and I had the local florist make a wreath of baby's breath that she clipped to the top of my hair. I'd met her when I first came up here, and not long afterward, she moved back down the hill when she found Mr. Right at our old stomping ground, the Cowboy Bar. He'd come up for a guy's weekend and they'd hit it off. She and Jason, who had a boat servicing business in Newport Beach, made a quick trip up, and it was great to see her.

Even though Noah and I now lived together in his cabin, I stayed in one of my cabins to observe the old-fashioned tradition of not seeing the groom until the wedding day. I'd decided on an off-white knee-length backless dress with matching pumps, and as I was getting ready, my father placed a bronze Chinese coin in my shoe like he'd done when I married David so many years ago. Originally from Taiwan, when he came to America and married my mother, he quickly adapted to the American way of life, but we still celebrated a few of his older customs. One was Chinese New Year, and the other was giving the gift of money in a red envelope.

"This one is the right one," he said as he gave me the envelope and kissed my cheek.

"I think so too," I said, and kissed him back.

Dear Noah

When I finally walked up onto the cobblestones and saw Noah, my heart skipped in my chest. He had on a black long-sleeved western shirt, open at the collar, with the cuffs rolled up, black jeans and new cowboy boots. When he saw him, I thought he was going to burst; he always wore his feelings on his sleeve, and I could tell he felt the same electricity I did. Marrying Noah was so much different from marrying David; when I met David, I knew he was going to be the man I married, but I never loved him the way I love Noah.

They say all brides are beautiful, and that's how I felt that day. I had no second thoughts about Noah, and while my *happily ever after* dreams hadn't come true before, the romantic in me knew this time everything would be different.

I took a moment to look at those gathered there, and it was everyone who was important to me; my parents, Sarah and Josh, Sam and Ginny, Laura, the girls who worked in the store and one of Noah's friends and clients, John Crosby and his wife Sally. I felt tears stinging my eyes. Suddenly, a great white owl swooped down from one of the tall trees above us, and I saw it land in a tree off in the distance. White owls represent good luck in many cultures, including Chinese, and seeing one fly near you or your house meant it would bring happiness and wealth. Noah saw it too, and even though I was sure he didn't know the traditional belief, he turned to look at me, and I knew I was marrying the perfect man for me.

Normally, Ginny cooked for all our get-togethers, but I didn't want her to be overwhelmed with all the work of the wedding, and I was determined she would enjoy the day. We'd talked about having our reception at the country club overlooking the greens, but we'd never joined even as social members. When Noah mentioned it to his friend John Crosby, he offered to host us as his guest. We jumped at the generous opportunity. There was an intimate area off the main dining room floor where smaller, private events were held, and there, two tables were decorated with flowers and lit candles; it was perfect for us. We sat at one table with my parents, along with Sam, Ginny, Sarah, and Josh.

When my father rose to toast us, he first squeezed my mother's hand, and while she'd never said anything, I knew she'd thought about my sister Loni's wedding and how her marriage was doomed from the beginning. Being an anxious bride, I hadn't really thought about my sister until my father spoke. My mother reached for my hand, and now I saw her eyes brimming with tears.

"Your sister would have loved to see you married again," she said.

I knew that wasn't necessarily true, but I said, "It would have been nice to see her."

I was momentarily at a loss, trying to remember how long she'd been gone. I'd been so busy with my own life, I hadn't thought of her for some time and it troubled me.

"You shouldn't be frowning on your wedding day," Noah said.

My father was finishing his speech, and he toasted us.

"Your mother and I are so happy for you two."

We spent our honeymoon night at the resort, and in the morning, we met Sarah, Josh, and my parents at Ginny's Coffee Shop for breakfast. Even though my parents knew Noah and I were living together, I still felt like a self-conscious young girl being with her husband for the first time. I think I blushed.

Laura and Josh said their goodbyes and headed back down the hill, and my parents drove up to Big Bear for the day. When we went back to Noah's cabin, we once more set the Adirondack chairs back out onto the cobblestones, and spent the rest of the morning with Sarah, Josh, and the dogs. In the late afternoon, the four of us had a quiet dinner at the Saddleback Inn in town.

On Monday, we met my parents for breakfast before they headed back to Prescott.

"It was a beautiful day," my mother said, hugging me as my father loaded their car.

"Yes it was," I said.

And then it was back to work for the rest of us.

Dear Noah

I'd opted for a white gold wedding band with a diamond in the center and I continually caught myself admiring it. I couldn't believe I was married again. For days, I kept looking at my left hand, surprised to wake up feeling differently than I did the day before—but life with Noah had grown so comfortable, the only *real* change I felt was that we'd made it official.

On Thursday, Sarah and I played hooky, and we went down to a large antique store in Redlands, where I found a wonderful pine dining room table with mismatched chairs that would work perfectly in our kitchen.

"Where there's a will, there's a woman," I told the man who scratched his head as he helped us take the table base off and load everything into my Jeep.

"I didn't think you'd get it in there," he said.

"Well, now you know how it's done," I said.

That afternoon, I had Noah help me unload it all. We set the table on a drop cloth so I could oil it and bring its luster back. Someone had already painted two of the chairs, so we repainted them black, and then I oiled the other natural oak and pine chairs. Back at the store, I went through my fabric books and I picked a red and white check fabric for new chair pads, and I found a red and white floral pattern for valances over the kitchen sink and at the large back window. I used the same floral pattern for a pillow for the dark green overstuffed rocking chair that sat in front of the window and that gave me an idea for making placemats. Sarah drew a pattern for a large scale leaf and I had placemats made of green felt.

I found a white vase and made a floral arrangement with vibrant red asters with their bright yellow-gold center. As a rule, I preferred real flowers, but it was impractical to even consider continually replacing them, and these looked so real.

Prior to our marriage, Noah and I consulted the attorney who oversaw my purchase of the cabins from Sam, and we discussed combining our properties and businesses.

"It's a big step," he'd said.

"We know," I said, "but we've agreed we're in this marriage for the long haul, and it only makes sense to be prepared if something happens to either of us."

"How do you feel about drawing up a trust, then, too?" the attorney asked.

Neither of us had thought about that, and we both nodded in agreement.

"Why don't we do it the week after the wedding?" I said. "We might as well get it on the calendar."

The morning of the appointment, Noah got the deeds and business paperwork out of the safe in the closet, and asked, "Are you sure you're good with this?"

"I am," I answered, just as sure as I'd ever been.

It looked cool out, so I grabbed a lightweight sweater off one of the dining room chairs just to keep myself warm. When I opened the front door, I instantly felt the cool rush of morning air reminding me how fickle our spring weather was. It looked like it was going to be a lovely day, but I put my sweater on before I got in my car.

"Love you," Noah called out as he climbed into his truck.

"Love you too," I said.

We drove two vehicles so Noah could head to a new remodeling job after our appointment and I needed to stop at the market to buy paper goods for both stores.

We met with the attorney and notary; Noah added my name to his cabin, and I added him to the B&B and the stores. I couldn't have been surer of our marriage, but as we finished signing the documents, my stomach did a quick flip. I'd just signed my life away and I couldn't help but think of signing my divorce papers not so long ago. And when Noah grabbed my hand, I wondered if he'd felt the same way. Within seconds, the feeling went away just as quickly as it had come. We were doing the right thing. This marriage was different.

That night, we brought a left over bottle of champagne to Ginny's and toasted the milestone.

"There's no turning back now," I said.

On our one-month anniversary, I swapped out the red asters for a gorgeous red rose bouquet Noah brought home. He also surprised me with dinner reservations at our favorite restaurant, the Saddleback Inn, and throughout our meal, every time his gaze met mine, my heart turned over. It seemed like every day, my love for him deepened and when he suggested we skip dessert, I felt a familiar shiver of awareness. I knew what he had planned for the rest of the evening.

CHAPTER TWO

May was a good month for me. Before the wedding, I'd picked up an interesting design client from Europe who bought the old Liberace home in the gated community of Hamiltair as a second home, and the project was well underway. His estate had cleared the house of any memorabilia, but the over-the-top wall coverings and carpet were still intact, along with crystal chandeliers. At first, the couple considered working around the opulence, but ultimately decided to gut everything and make the house their own. I'd introduced them to Noah, who got the job of remodeling the kitchen and bathrooms.

"How often do you think you'll come to America?" I'd asked.

The husband and wife looked at each other, and then the husband shrugged. "Probably once a year for a month," he said.

"So, are you comfortable with me working on the house while you're in Spain?"

"Yes. We have a home in Italy also where we can stay until we return."

No matter how many wealthy clients I'd worked with in the past, it never ceased to amaze me how some people had so much disposable income.

I agreed to host the Memorial Day Festival again, and unlike the previous year, the Chamber of Commerce allotted more time for us to advertise and organize it. So far, the weather had remained warm, and the

Dear Noah

forecast promised clear and sunny skies. The local stores all chipped in to help cover expenses and we put together an enormous basket to give away to one lucky winner. We set up a sale table outside the store, and we hired a high school student to watch it for us.

We had live music, vendors, some carnival games, the town's fire engine, and an old sheriff's car with a siren. Sam, Noah and Josh donned yellow vests and were our crossing guards again. Ginny set up tables outside the coffee shop and she served iced tea, muffins, and cookies. They must have been just as busy, for when she brought over sandwiches, cookies and drinks for lunch she swiped at stray hair from her ponytail and said, "I needed to get out of there. It's been a madhouse."

Both the design store and the At The Cabin stores were jumping and by the amount of new mailing list entries we got, I guessed we had almost three hundred people come out for the day. That night, we walked down to Ginny's, and I treated everyone to dinner. I could tell the weather was changing; the air felt damp and chilly.

"We had a great day," I said. "Thanks to everyone, and sorry for the sore feet and aching backs. And I am beyond grateful the weather cooperated."

"It did, but it feels like things are about to change," Noah said.

His prediction proved right; that night as we drove home, the fog had rolled in and by the time we got to his cabin, it looked like we were inside an enormous cloud. We pulled about ten feet into the driveway and walked the rest of the way to the cabin so we wouldn't drive into the roundabout or the flower beds.

During the night, the sound of heavy rain woke me, and I was indebted to the weather god for giving us a warm fire and a perfect day for the festival.

We started June with cloudy overcast skies in the morning—hence the perfect nickname, June Gloom—and most days, the sun broke through to warm up the afternoons. The unpredictable weather added to a tumultuous month for Sarah; her divorce became final, one of her sisters eloped, and then her mother died unexpectedly.

She took two days off and drove out to Barstow for the funeral. When she returned, we had breakfast before opening the stores. I wanted to talk to her about the funeral and about an idea I had for the store, but as she walked into the coffee shop, her slow and heavy steps matched the grim look that told me things hadn't gone well for her.

She plopped herself down in the booth.

"I don't know why it surprised me there were so few people there," she said. "There was only her husband, my sisters, and a few customers from the coffee shop where she worked. Not that I expect hundreds when *I* die, but it made me realize how unimportant she was to others."

Lately, I hadn't given funerals much thought, but when she said that, it made me think of my sister's funeral and how few people attended that, too.

Her eyes filled with tears.

"My father didn't even come."

"Did anyone contact him?"

"No one knows where he is."

She sighed, and I nodded in support. Her normal good spirit had measurably dimmed.

"I'm so sorry, Sarah," I said, feebly. I reached across the table for her arm and said, "If it makes you feel any better, I'll come to your funeral."

The minute I said it, I realized she might not take it as light-heartedly as I intended it.

She crooked her mouth and looked at me, then raised her eyebrow.

"That's only if I die before you," she said wryly.

The weak smile she gave me was better than none.

I asked her if she and Josh would join us for dinner, hoping she'd have a good enough day at the store to cheer her up.

We hadn't been to the Cowboy Bar in a while, so we met there, and she and I shared a steak. I told her I was thinking of renting a warehouse to store all the furniture and accessories I'd been buying for the staging we were doing. There were two realtors who used us exclusively to decorate homes they listed, and I could see an opportunity for that part of the business to grow.

Noah had found us a low-mileage box truck, and it was in the shop being painted. Sarah said she would do the logo and signage on it once we got it back. I knew she loved going on appointments and overseeing the installations, and when I asked her if she'd like to become our staging manager, her entire demeanor changed and her face brightened.

Once the truck was on the road, seeing it filled me with a sense of pride. I wanted to stop anyone who saw it and say "That's our truck!" Mostly I kept my enthusiasm to myself.

Somehow, Noah and I found time to go to estate sales and yard sales to buy things to sell in the store or use for staging. And customers began asking us if we could take some of their nicer furniture on consignment. We already had more furniture than we could handle, but one day I said in jest to Noah, "I need a bigger store."

"Over my dead body," Noah said, raising an eyebrow.

I'd promised him when we bought the truck I would stop taking on more projects. While he was just giving me a hard time, I also knew how he felt about me and my venturous personality. I gave him a silly smile.

June Gloom gave way to a July that topped the heat chart. Everyone in town was open on the Fourth, and customers came in fanning themselves. Every year I bought inexpensive folding fans and gave them out to anyone who commented on the heat, and by the end of the weekend, we were out of them.

Noah, Josh, Sarah, and I took the boat out to watch the fireworks again from the lake. Typical of the celebration, revelers dropped anchors around us, but unlike last year, when unruly partygoers were cited and escorted back to the landing, this year, there were no issues.

A local stunt pilot we'd met through my design clients, Hudson and Candace Fisher, flew aerobatics over the lake, and afterward, we attended a party at the Fishers'. Candace introduced me as her designer, and several people took me aside to ask about decorating challenges they were facing.

Sarah and I helped clean up after most of the guests left, and I munched on chips and salsa.

"Take some home," Candace said.

"No. If it's in sight, I'll eat it," I said, putting the rest of the chips back in their bag and clipping it shut. "The best way to keep from eating this stuff is to not have it in the house. I noticed you hung some new pieces in your office," I said. "They look great."

"We were in Sedona and I couldn't pass them up. I almost felt guilty buying them without you being there."

"Don't be silly," I said sincerely. "You have great taste, and you don't need my approval for anything you do."

"I swear we don't have room for one more piece," she said.

"What's so unique about your home is that you've incorporated everything you two love. Not everyone can make that work."

"Thanks, Annie. Coming from you, that's a great compliment."

"Thanks for inviting us," I said. "We really enjoyed ourselves. Let's get together for dinner when you have time."

"Sounds good. Thanks for your help cleaning up."

"I'm exhausted," I said to Noah as we got in the car.

"We'll be home in a few minutes."

Once he started the engine, I couldn't keep my eyes open.

CHAPTER THREE

One Saturday in August, Noah said he'd been looking forward to a day off so we could hike up at the Arboretum. The day promised to be warm and breezy as he loaded the dogs into his Jeep. We first stopped by Ginny's so she could pack us a lunch basket, and as she tucked some dog biscuits in a bag, she said, "Here are some cookies for the pups."

After about an hour of walking, we stopped at a rest point where there was a faucet and Noah filled water bowls for the dogs. I brought out their cookies, and they devoured them.

"So much for chewing your food," I said to them.

We spread a cloth on top of one of the picnic tables, and I unpacked our sandwiches, bottled waters, and people cookies. The dogs rested at our feet as we sat across from each other—and Noah played with the fingers on my left hand.

"So, I've been thinking..." he started. "Have you thought any more about starting a family? I mean, one other than adding more dogs...?"

I knew now we were married, he'd be thinking about it more, and while I'd rehearsed in my head what I'd say when the subject came up, the only thing I could think to say was, "I guess the clock is ticking, isn't it?"

I'd made room in my heart to have children of my own, and I knew I'd make a good mother. But if I were honest, my life with Noah and my businesses were perfect as they were. While I'd seen a lot of women juggle babies and working, I loved being able to do whatever I wanted, and I'd grown so comfortable with that freedom I'd become selfish.

The first time Noah and I made love, it was without protection. Those who say you can't get pregnant your first time together are liars! I did. Fresh out of my marriage, I wasn't really prepared for the dating game, and I'd never had to think about motherhood since my former husband had eliminated any likelihood of him fathering more children after his third child was born.

I went on the pill after being with Noah, but I didn't know I was already pregnant, and the pregnancy ended. They attributed the miscarriage to bad timing. Then, I never really felt I'd lost a baby, I think, because it wasn't something I planned for. But it devastated Noah. My way of dealing with the whole thing was to push it out of my mind and pretend nothing had happened, which included not talking about it. I realized later I'd forced Noah to do that, too.

No time was going to be any better than now, so I asked, "Are you sure you're ready to try?"

His whole body seemed to wait for my response, and I sensed his apprehension.

"I am," he said, with no hesitation.

"Okay, then, let's do it."

His tight expression turned in to the familiar warmth of his smile, and it drew me in like it always did. He tenderly pulled me into his arms and held me like he was never planning on releasing me.

"I love you, Annie Chambers, and you'll see; we'll make the best parents ever," he said, gently rocking me side to side.

Six weeks later, I could tell my body was changing—my breasts were sore, and I'd started feeling queasy. I was certain I was pregnant.

Noah was beside himself with happiness, but I wanted to wait another month before we announced it. When I started my period a week later, I was disappointed, but it turned out to be just spotting, and in a few days it stopped. I made an appointment with a doctor in the mountains and he confirmed I was indeed around seven weeks pregnant.

I don't know why, but I still wanted to wait before we told anyone the news, and within two weeks, I was having pelvic pain and vomiting and my heart filled with familiar dread. It instantly brought back memories of my first miscarriage, but this time it was different. I was going to lose a baby I wanted, and I began crying.

"I think I'm losing the baby," I said to Noah when he came home that night.

He froze, and then his face turned ashen. It was as if his body sank into itself when he said, "We need to get you to the hospital."

I was frightened for me, but also for him. I knew he was trying to be strong for me and it broke my heart..

Then my teeth started chattering, and my body trembled.

"I need to go now," I said, overwhelmed.

With this miscarriage, I felt different. I'd finally agreed to start a family, and that's what we wanted. My body had rejected this new baby. Through another ultrasound, they diagnosed me with an abnormal uterus, which meant I would probably never have an easy pregnancy. Suddenly, at least in my mind, trying to have children was back to not being in my plan. I didn't want to go through any procedures or risk another miscarriage, so my solution to my problem was to go back on the pill.

I was foolish to think there'd be no difference in how we acted around each other after I closed that door. At first, Noah treated me like an invalid, like a fragile princess, not letting me get up to do dishes, or reach to put something back in to the cabinets. He babied me, and at first I soaked it up. He would come up behind me and hug me—sometimes even patting my stomach. He'd kiss my cheek and more often than not turn me to face him.

"I love you," he said, oftentimes bringing my hand to his lips.

"I love you too, Noah," I would tell him, knowing how hard it was for him to deal with our loss.

At first I'd add, "I'm so sorry this happened," but soon I figured he already knew that.

Eventually, we went back to normal; I was no longer fragile.

People would tell me later I'd put up a wall to handle my pain—but I attributed my logic to my pragmatic personality. And three weeks later, Noah found a release and went to Colorado. He had worked on a project there when we first met, and all it took was one phone call from them to see if he could come out and work for a couple of weeks.

When he told me, I hated to admit I felt a measure of relief he was going. In the past, when things weren't working out the way he wanted them to, he'd left to blow off some steam. With him away, I stayed at work a little later and got a lot of things done that I couldn't do when customers were coming in and out during the day.

I had the dogs to myself, and once they got in bed with me, I hardly noticed Noah wasn't there. But every morning while he was gone, I felt the emptiness in my life and the cabin was silent. I constantly expected to hear him doing something in the kitchen, and at night, I anxiously awaited the sound of crunching gravel in the drive and the slamming of his truck door, letting me know he was home. I knew I didn't want to live by myself, and if Noah had been thinking the same, hopefully he'd come back, welcoming my company.

A couple of weeks later, I had my head buried in paperwork, so I didn't see his truck pull up in front of the store. When he stood in the doorway to my office, I couldn't help but think back to the first time I'd seen him standing in the doorway to my cabin when Sam was showing it to me, and my heart danced.

Just as it was so long ago, his jeans were nice and tight and his boots were dusty and scuffed.

"I remember you," I said. "Are you home for a while?"

I stood to greet him, and he took me in his arms.

"I've missed you," he said.

That night, instead of having dinner, we made love with the urgency we hadn't had in months. Afterward, I cried as I used to do when we first made love, and afterwards, as we laid there with our bodies still entwined, I knew then we were going to be all right.

CHAPTER FOUR

In no time, it was April again, and I wanted to make our one-year anniversary special. I remembered Candace Fisher mentioning Sedona at their July 4th party; I thought it would be the perfect destination. We could have made it there in one day, but we wanted to see Flagstaff, so I made up a quick travel plan for the four days we'd be away.

Noah was in charge of packing an emergency kit, so he made up a box with everything in it from first aid to water. We left the dogs with Sarah and headed northeast. He'd filled the tank before we left, then once again as we made our way onto the warmer, more desolate highway. The long drive through the desert reminded me of my trips to Prescott; lots of red earth and succulents. It surprised me he knew some of the plant's names, like the Ocotillo Cactus with its red flowers in bloom, and the Firesticks Cactus that reminded me of pencils.

We took a detour to Oatman to see the burros. I'd never heard about them, and when we drove through the small quaint town, free-roaming burros greeted us. Noah found a place to park and a woman who seemed in charge gave me a handful of treats.

"Please don't feed them anything but this," she said. "Just hold your hand out there and they'll eat from it."

The burro's lips were soft on the palm of my hand, and I called to Noah, "Look at this," like a child would.

Suddenly, a momma and her baby came up to us.

"The baby's only seventeen days old," the woman said. "You can feed Mildred, but don't feed Baby Hank."

"Oh my god, they're so cute," I said.

We stopped at the Saloon for a quick soda and learned from a brochure that Oatman was a small mining camp dating back to 1915. It was named after a young girl named Olive Oatman who'd been captured and enslaved by an Indian tribe. She was eventually sold to and adopted by the Mohave people who tattooed her face. In the 1850s, they released her at Fort Yuma.

I'd reserved a room at the three story Victorian style Weatherford Hotel, built in the late 19th century in the historic downtown area of Flagstaff. The new owners were in the process of updating the hotel, and storyboards showing the slow and painstaking progress they'd made were placed around the lobby. Some of the old wallpaper was still up in the lobby and when we checked in, I asked if we could possibly have one of the older rooms.

Our room was definitely pre-renovation; the red pattern wallpaper was sun faded, the loose boards of the wood floor squeaked, closet doors needed to be oiled, and the bed creaked with every movement. Instead of being annoying, I found the unfamiliar sounds comforting.

We'd brought a couple of bottles of champagne to celebrate, and we chilled one of them before we filled the hotel room's glasses. They weren't befitting a celebration, but in a way, they went with the charm of the old room.

Noah joined me in the tiny shower, and slowly and seductively, he dried me off and led me to bed. The moment we climbed on to it, I worried the creaking would distract me and annoy any neighbors we might have next door, but soon I was oblivious to any sounds but Noah breathing in my ear.

"Happy Anniversary, babe," he said.

The next morning, we checked out and made our way to Sedona, and I was surprised that for being such a well-known town, it wasn't very large; in fact, it only had two stop lights. It was a mixture of old and new, rundown and sparkling. Stalls lined the road in with signs that read, "Find your Vortex", "Self-Discovery", "Indian Jewelry" and "Tours".

I'd read Sedona was known for its red sandstone formations that glowed a brilliant red and orange when the rising or setting sun illuminated them, and some claimed its vortexes produced a range of emotional, spiritual and physical effects. Everywhere we looked, we saw a combination of red rock formations, red dirt, and junipers of all shapes and sizes. It was quite a sight.

We checked in to our hotel, the Arabella, named after Arabella Miller Schnebly, the pioneering wife of Theodore Carlton (TC) Schnebly in 1901. Called the Sedona Lodge in the 1940s, it was the first hotel in town built for Hollywood directors, and actors like John Wayne, Jimmy Stewart and Marlon Brando.

After lunch, we walked through an art colony called Tlaquepaque. Built in the 1970s in a sycamore grove, it was a living art community—a winding road village where artisans could create art and live on site. There were wonderful shops filled with paintings, sculpture, hand-woven rugs and handcrafted turquoise jewelry. I'd never given Southwestern décor much thought until I saw how easily some pieces could blend in with the traditional mountain look.

I fell in love with two bronze statues; one of a bear, and another of an Indian warrior, complete with a spear and shield. Noah loved them too, so we bought both of them as our first year anniversary present to ourselves. I knew exactly where they would sit; the warrior would go on the table behind the sofa and it would be the first thing you saw when you walked into the living room. The bear would go on a table in the sunroom, next to a carved bear lamp with a painted shade.

The next day, we bought a map of the area but decided to sightsee on our own rather than taking a tour. We had a Sonora style Mexican lunch with margaritas and handmade tortillas, and chips. After two drinks, I was ready to take a nap, but I wanted to stop by the stalls along the road back to the hotel. One jewelry maker especially caught my eye, and I ended up buying three leather and silver beaded bracelets for one wrist, plus a silver cuff bracelet with a scorpion imbedded in Lucite for the other.

"I want to stop and have my fortune read," I said.

"You don't believe in all that stuff, do you?" Noah asked.

"Not really, but we're here where all the healing power is, so why not?"

A few stalls down, an Indian woman wearing a beautiful beaded shawl sat and motioned me in.

"Beautiful bracelets," she said.

"Thanks."

"Sit, and I'll give you a glimpse into your spirit."

I didn't say anything, as she brought out a stack of tarot looking cards, but the illustrations were of Indian images and symbols. She laid them out on a table covered with a woven feather-patterned cloth and nodded her head slightly as she studied them for what seemed like several minutes.

"Come with me," she said, standing and motioning me to follow her outside. "Stand here, and face the sun. I want to see your shadow."

"Can I keep my sunglasses on?"

"Yes."

It wasn't an especially warm afternoon, but after a few minutes of the sun beating down on me, I could feel my skin heat up and soon beads of perspiration formed on my face.

"Ach..." she said as I reached to wipe my face.

She moved around me several times, and then a few minutes later said, "We can go back inside now."

With my hands, I wiped my face and followed her.

Once inside, she sat opposite me again, and looked at the cards. It might have been my eyes adjusting to the inside of the tent, but I sensed a change in her expression. When I blinked, it was gone.

"I see you are a very strong woman," she began. "You've done well for yourself."

She looked outside where Noah stood waiting, and said, "Is that your man?"

I turned to see him watching us. "Yes, it is."

"He's the perfect man for you. I can tell he supports you in all your endeavors."

I shrugged.

The woman looked at the cards, then up at me in thought. I wasn't sure how to read her face, and I instinctively tilted my head slightly.

"You'll have a good life together," she finally said. "A loving one, now that you've worked through your loss."

I couldn't stop myself from frowning as I wondered how she might know about the baby. That's what she must have been referring to.

"But I see there will be more," she said, gently touching my arm.

What did that mean? And why would she say something like that? Didn't fortune tellers stay away from negative predictions like that?

"But you are strong, and you'll find your way," she said, her smile brightening.

I hadn't realized I'd broken out in a sweat again, until I felt a bead of perspiration run down my back, and I stood quickly, making myself feel slightly dizzy. I quickly reached for the back of my chair to steady myself.

"Are you all right?" the woman asked.

"Yes, I just stood too fast. I'm fine," I said, although I was frantic to leave.

"You'll be fine," the woman called after me.

"Are you all right?" Noah asked when he saw me. "You look like you've seen a ghost."

"I'm okay," I stammered. "I was just getting overheated."

For the rest of the day, I didn't let him out of my sight. Was *he* the loss I'd experience? My heart was sick. Part of me didn't believe in prophecy, but another part of me couldn't help but wonder if the woman actually saw something.

Noah had asked the hotel for a good restaurant recommendation and they called and made a reservation for us at a steakhouse. I barely touched my food, and when Noah asked me if I was all right, I told him I thought I'd had too much sun for the day. When he wanted to make love afterward, I feigned the same illness and told him I just wanted to take a shower and get some sleep. I knew he was disappointed, but I just couldn't get that woman's prediction out of my mind.

What loss would I suffer?

We'd told my parents we were coming to Sedona, so we took another route home and stopped to see them. They both looked healthy, and I couldn't help but wonder if losing one of them might be what the woman was referring to. I repeatedly asked them if they were all right, and at one point, my mother asked if I was becoming a worry wart in my old age.

We had dinner at the Palace, where we'd eaten the first time I'd brought Noah to meet them, and again, he and my father walked around the restaurant and looked at all the relics from the old days. We spent the rest of the evening just getting caught up, and while their small community was so peaceful, I was eager to get home.

After lunch, my mother loaded us up with snacks and water, and we headed back. As we pulled out of their park, Noah took my hand.

"You're still a little distant," he said.

"I think the sun really affected me. But I'm fine. I'm just anxious to get back home."

"I had a great time, didn't you?" he asked, tilting his head as he had a way of doing—his infectious grin made me smile. Noah hadn't shaved while we were gone, and in the sunlight I caught the glint of stubble on his face.

"I really did," I said truthfully. That was until that woman gave me her dire prediction.

The long drive back through the desert made me sleepy, and as much as I tried, I couldn't stay awake. When I woke, we were back in familiar territory, and I felt my spirits lifting. I breathed deeply all the way up the mountain and pictured myself sweeping all the negative thoughts from my mind. By the time we pulled up to Noah's cabin, I was back to being myself.

The next day, Sarah and I had lunch, and she told me she and Josh had been talking about getting married.

"That's wonderful news. When?" I asked.

"Next year some time. I was wondering if you'd have a problem if we got married at the cabin? Where you and Noah had your wedding?"

I'd always thought it a perfect place for a small wedding, and I was flattered Sarah would want to get married there too.

"It won't take much to get it ready, so just let me know when you decide on a time," I said.

When Sarah originally decided to stay up in the mountains, I couldn't have been happier. Having her back in my life had meant more to me than she'd ever know. She could have gone anywhere and done anything, but she chose to stay up here.

"We'd be honored," I added.

CHAPTER FIVE

Spring turned into summer, and then when summer ended, leaves began to fall and all but the pine trees were bare. Winter that year was mild, and before we knew it, it was spring again, and Sarah and Josh were planning their wedding. We cleared the cobblestones in front of Noah's cabin, and I ordered fresh flowers to cover the iron gazebo. We planted flowers again in the beds lining the circular driveway, and filled in where the vincas bloomed around the boat in the roundabout.

Sarah's sisters came up and Sam and Ginny were there. Josh's parents were also there; his mother with a new younger boyfriend, and his father with his younger wife. Everyone stayed in the cabins. Sarah didn't want a fancy reception, so as our gift, we asked Ginny to prepare a buffet with barbecued pork, beans, potato salad, and dessert. She said she'd set it all up in the back of the coffee shop where we usually had meals when there was a group of us.

"I'm pregnant," Sarah whispered as we found a place to sit.

Although I'd noticed subtle changes in her, like fuller cheeks and frequent trips to the restroom, I was unprepared for her news. I'd thought taking care of her three sisters while she was growing up would have cured her of any thoughts of motherhood. I quickly realized that I was being cynical and I would never have said anything to her, even in jest.

"Are you okay?" she asked after seeing the surprise on my face.

My stomach knotted, but wanting her to know I loved her and wanted her to be happy, I gave her a warm and loving hug. I knew I wasn't the only woman who'd lost a baby, and I understood everyone else's life would go on, just as it already had. I'd been determined I wouldn't let other people's happiness get in the way of mine and until today, I'd hardly thought about it. Jealousy and resentment were too strong of words for what I was feeling, but I would have been lying if I said I wasn't feeling something mixed with happiness for her. I also knew with time, I'd feel differently. I tucked my feelings away, behind that wall I'd erected when we lost our baby; the one I pretended was never there, but one that even Noah couldn't penetrate.

And of all the people I knew, Sarah deserved some happiness in her life.

"I'm delighted," I said sincerely. "I just wasn't prepared for the news. You'll make a wonderful mother." I stepped back to look at her. "I'm genuinely happy for you both," I said again. "And just think, I'll be an auntie."

I hugged her again.

"I have another surprise," she said. She tried to keep her heartwarming smile to just the two of us, but she was radiant. "We've managed to save enough money to buy a cabin of our own, so we can finally leave you two to yourselves."

"Well, you're just full of surprises—you've been a busy girl," I said, and then I toasted her. "Here's to everything! I'll miss you!"

After we ate, I asked, "Have you started looking around yet?"

"We have and I'd love it if you could come with us to go back to one. I have some ideas about what we could do with it, but you have such a good eye."

"Anytime. Just let me know. At least you know someone who could work on it," I said for fun.

Josh and Noah started working on the cabin as soon as the escrow closed, installing a new multi-paned front window and French-style doors in the mudroom. They refinished the hardwood floors and painted the cabin inside and out. By the time they were finished, there was no budget to replace the washer, dryer and refrigerator, so we loaned them the ones from the laundry room/workshop below their old apartment. We had no plans to have new tenants move in, so we didn't need them.

The baby's room was a pale green with green and yellow accents, and Sarah painted one wall with a bear, fox, squirrel and a mouse sitting under a tree having a picnic and reading. She drew the same scene to use later as the baby's announcement.

I found some wonderful green plaid fabric and had our drapery workroom make curtains for the windows, and my upholsterer recovered a rocking chair Sarah found at the secondhand store.

In the early fall, Sarah and Josh moved into their new cabin.

When the baby was born, they named her Claire. She was absolutely beautiful, and when I held her for the first time, I kissed her sweet forehead, and for a split second, wondered what it would have felt like to have my own baby girl.

"She's perfect," I said, instantly falling in love. Suddenly, tears blurred my vision, and I said to Claire, "You're so perfect, I could eat you up."

By the first of December, the business and store were busy, Noah and Josh had more work coming in than they could handle, and the cabins were fully booked almost every weekend until the end of the year. Sometimes I felt like a hamster on its wheel. Work and life overlapped, and more often than not, I couldn't find the beginning or the ending. We were constantly doing something, and it seemed the days quickly turned into weeks, and the weeks into months.

Often I'd catch myself looking more closely into the mirror, and finding new lines around my eyes and creases in my forehead. On Noah, they looked distinguished, but on me, I only saw time slipping by.

Noah put it off as long as possible, but Daisy, the dog he rescued when his next-door neighbor died, along with Josh's dog Shep, both needed to be put down within weeks of each other. Heartbroken, they both moped around until they went down to the animal shelter, and they each came back with two new dogs. Noah's logic was that his dog Rufus was going to have to be put down soon, and he was planning

Dear Noah

ahead. Rufus continued to be the king of the bed, with his spot between us, and our new dogs, Duke and Jackson, slept by our feet.

It seemed overnight Sam was slowing down. He was mentally alert, but arthritis had set in and I could feel his pain as he lumbered around when it got cold out. We brought in one of Noah's young men, Billie, when we needed to do anything around the cabins.

"Just tell me what you need," we'd remind Sam.

"I can do it," he'd say, stubbornly.

More than once, he'd call in the middle of something, like raking the leaves, to ask if Billie could come out and finish the job. Instead of admitting the leaves were getting the better of him, he said, "Probably Billie would like to earn a little money."

"We'll have him stop by on his way home," Noah would say.

Noah would make sure there was birdseed in the bin by the front door, so Sam could still scoop it out and fill the bird feeders without having to lift the heavy bags. He still loved to water the flower beds and even if we didn't have any guests, he'd check the cabins every night before he called it a day. If the cabins weren't rented, he'd stay with Ginny and have breakfast with her at the coffee shop in the morning before coming back home. And if we did have bookings, Ginny would stay with him in his cabin, and they'd take their own cars back in to town and have breakfast. Either way, he was well fed.

Three years later, we lost Sam. The morning after a heavy snowstorm, he had a heart attack while shoveling snow at the cabins. Noah found him lying on the ground when he went by to see how he was doing. Even though we hired a man to clear the berms on the driveway when it snowed, Sam insisted he could do his part to clear the snow so people could drive in.

"It gives me something to do," he'd say.

They rushed him to the mountain hospital, and then helicoptered him down to Loma Linda Hospital. Noah drove me and Ginny down, and when we got to the emergency room, Sam was still lying there; he'd already been pronounced dead.

"I should have come by earlier," Noah said, helplessly.

"Sam was so headstrong, he wouldn't quit," I said. "And you can't blame yourself for this. He wouldn't listen."

We watched helplessly as Ginny went to his side. She took his left hand in hers and brought it to her lips.

"Oh, my Sam," she said, trying to hold back her tears. "You were always so stubborn and now look where it got you."

She touched his cheek, and said, "Oh dear. You haven't shaved in days."

Then, more to herself than to us, she said, "He's already cold."

My world shattered, but not as profoundly as it did for Noah and Ginny. Sam was Ginny's love, and she was so lost, I worried she wouldn't be far behind him. Noah tried to be strong for us all, but grief overwhelmed him and I wished I could take away some of his pain. I knew it felt like losing his parents all over again. When I asked him about the funeral arrangements, he thought for a few minutes and then asked me if I'd take care of them.

"I can't deal with it right now," he said, his voice breaking.

My heart ached for him. Ginny wasn't much help either, and kept repeating, "I just can't believe it."

So I took care of everything. I chose a simple casket with dark green lining—it reminded me of the pine trees in the woods. I wasn't sure if Sam would have wanted an open casket, but I decided to keep it closed. I'd only seen one person lying in state, and I realized no matter how good of a job the mortician did, it was impossible to fool the living into thinking their loved one was still alive.

We had the requisite celebration of life afterwards and although she could barely function, Ginny insisted her staff could help her pull it off at the coffee shop. Sarah made up three story boards with photos depicting his life; one when he was a boy on the family farm, one when he and Trudy were married and lived in San Diego, and the third, showing his life up in the mountains, including photos of him with Ginny. It seemed like half the town came by to pay their respects to Sam, and as comforting as the day was, Ginny and Noah were exhausted and I ended up with a terrible headache.

Ginny was determined to go home by herself. I wanted to stop in to the store to see how everything was going, but when Noah frowned at me, I knew I needed to go home with them. He'd become quiet and withdrawn, and I was worried about him.

"It'll all be there tomorrow," he said, not unkindly.

And the next day, although Ginny wasn't her perky self, she was back at work when we came in to have breakfast.

"What am I supposed to do?" she asked. Then she turned to Noah and asked, "How are you doing?"

He mustered a smile for her benefit.

A week later, Sam's attorney called and asked if Noah, Ginny, and I could stop by his office. Ginny was already there, seated in one of the chairs in front of his desk, and when she looked up, she looked like she'd aged ten years. It had only been a few days since I'd seen her, and yet her appearance unnerved me. Her once bright eyes and bubbly mannerisms had been replaced with a bleakness that shocked me. It was obvious she looked at us without seeing, and I rushed to her side.

"Oh, Ginny," I whispered. "Everything will be okay." I knew it was a lie, but what else could I say?

Eventually, Noah and I sat, and the attorney opened a manila folder.

"The cabins are yours," he said to me.

"What?"

I leaned in slightly, as if I hadn't heard correctly.

"Sam's will. He stated that when he died, the cabins would go to you. Free and clear. No more payments."

My head jerked back in surprise; I didn't know what I was expecting, but it certainly wasn't that. I looked at Noah and frowned.

"To Ginny, Sam has left you ten thousand dollars."

Ginny just closed her eyes.

"His checking account, the balance of his savings account, tools and his truck go to Noah."

I looked at Noah again, who was just as surprised as I was. He scratched his beard in thought.

"Thank you?" I said, more to myself than anyone.

"Give me about a week and I'll have all the paperwork taken care of."

Not long after that, Ginny put the coffee shop up for sale.

"I've plumb given up," she said one morning when we went in. "Hopefully, someone else will have the dream of owning a restaurant and take it over."

About a month later, she slipped and fell in the kitchen and fractured her hip. Her cook called 911. I was already in the store and when I heard the siren and saw the ambulance, I rushed down to see what was happening.

As soon as the ambulance left, I rushed back to the store to leave a note for Sarah and the girls to let them know I'd gone to the hospital, and to tell them that if Noah called, to tell him what had happened. Ginny went into emergency surgery and I impatiently waited in the hallway until the doctor came out and told me she'd done well and was in recovery. As soon as she was in a room, I went in to see for myself how she was doing.

"I'm fine," she whispered hoarsely.

I could tell she was in immense pain no matter how much she denied it. The color had drained from her face, and she barely kept her eyes open.

"You don't need to stay with me," she said.

"I need to make sure you're all right," I said, holding her hand much like she'd done when she saw Sam. "You'll be fine," I said, but I knew in my heart I was just trying to make both of us feel better. "Noah should be here soon."

Her face and arms had turned a pale shade of gray, and even though I knew it was from the trauma of it all, I had a difficult time rationalizing that.

I tried to push the images away, but when I looked at her, I saw death.

I visited her twice a day, and I brought her muffins and coffee from the coffee shop. She went into a convalescent home and I continued to make my trek there every day. The changes in her were dramatic; her skin color never returned to healthy and pink, and I could tell the physical therapy was grueling.

Ginny was transferred to a nursing home down the hill, which made my visits less frequent and more time-consuming, and I didn't see her for a few days. Within that first week, though, I noticed it was difficult for her to breathe, and she looked worse than she did right after her surgery. I waited for a nurse to return to her station outside the room so I could ask about Ginny's condition.

She quickly read Ginny's chart.

"She's developed pneumonia," the nurse said. "She's on antibiotics, and when the doctor comes in this afternoon, I'm going to mention I don't think they're doing much good. Plus, she has an infection at her surgery site."

It was difficult for Ginny to keep her eyes open, and while it broke my heart to leave her, I didn't know what else I could do.

"You need your rest," I said as I got ready to go. "I'll call you tonight."

When I passed the nurse, I said, "Please keep an eye on her. She doesn't look good."

I didn't even make it to the exit door before I started crying. I didn't know how I was going to tell Noah I was sure we were going to lose Ginny next.

That night, I called Ginny's room, but there was no answer. I thought possibly she was out for a breathing treatment, but when I tried back almost an hour later, there was still no answer. I called the main number of the facility and finally found someone who would talk to me.

"Let's see," the nurse said. "Oh, dear. It looks like the patient tried to get out of bed by herself, and she fell. Let me read the notes. Okay, she's been transferred back to the hospital."

It took forever for me to find someone at the hospital who could bring me up to date on Ginny's condition, but eventually I spoke with the on-duty doctor.

"The x-rays show she's re-fractured her hip. Unfortunately, osteoporosis has left her with brittle bones, and while it's speculation, she might have already fractured her hip, causing the original fall. She's in surgery, and we'll know more when she's out."

Noah and I stayed to be by her side when she recovered.

For Noah's sake, I tried to disguise the panic I felt when I saw her, but I wasn't very successful.

"Dear god," he said.

I could tell her lungs were still congested, and the morbid side of me wondered how, with pneumonia, they could have kept her alive during surgery. Her skin was bluish and her hands were cool to the touch.

I found an unused desk with a phone on it and called the skilled nursing facility at the hospital in Lake Arrowhead. I wanted to bring Ginny back up, even though I suspected it would only be for a short time. The woman I spoke with said she'd start the paperwork to get her transferred, and she promised to get back to me the next day.

Now all we could do was wait.

Two days later, she was transported back up the hill, and once she was in a room, we came by to check on her. We only saw her one more time before she died, but at least she was back home in the mountains.

Noah found the key she kept hidden under a pot on her porch, and when we unlocked her front door, I made Noah go in first. I hadn't been in Ginny's house in years, and I was taken aback by the musty smell of stale air. Like so many older cabins, the wood floors creaked, and I said aloud, "A burglar would have a hard time breaking in here and not being discovered."

Noah just looked at me like I was brainless, and I instantly felt that way.

"We need to find her phone book. I thought she'd mentioned having a niece somewhere," he said.

He found it in the small writing desk drawer, and while he sat at the dining table and thumbed through it, I found trash bags and began cleaning out the refrigerator.

"There are only two names here I don't recognize," Noah said. "I'll just have to call them both and see what we find."

The first number he called was disconnected. And the second number had an answering machine.

"This is Sandy. Leave a message."

"I think this is her."

Noah left his number, and after helping me bring the trash bags outside, we went home.

It felt like every time my heart healed, there was more death.

Sandy was indeed Ginny's niece, and she told Noah it would take her a couple of days to fly out. He told her we'd go ahead and make funeral arrangements if she wanted us to, and Sandy was grateful. Two days later, Noah picked her up at the San Bernardino airport and they stopped at the mortuary before coming by the store.

Again, half the town came by the coffee shop to pay their respects, and Sandy thanked everyone for coming. She'd started going through Ginny's things, and it didn't take her long to pack up the few things she wanted to bring home; mostly it was old photos, although she told me she didn't recognize most of the people in them.

"I'll have more time to sort through them when I get back." "If there's anything you'd like to keep, take it," she said to us.

I found a few things I wanted to keep—an old framed needlepoint that looked like it was from a hundred years ago and some white milk glass flower vases. Noah wanted Sam's pocket watch and bowie knife.

"I can arrange for someone to pick everything else up," I offered.

"I'd be really grateful if you could, Annie," Sandy said.

She left the next day, and we locked up the house again until Noah or I could make arrangements for the thrift shop to meet us back there.

The cafe sat empty for another year before someone stepped up to buy it.

Was this what the Indian woman in Sedona was trying to tell me? That I'd lose two people I cared deeply for?

CHAPTER SIX

Since 1932, Sky Forest Mutual Water had been providing water to the small unincorporated community of Sky Forest where we lived. It differed from public utilities; when you purchased your property, water rights came with it and you became a shareholder. Typically, residents paid a set fee for water, and a separate fee for maintaining the operations.

Noah met Todd Clark when he saw him reading our water meter one morning. After he took an early retirement from teaching down in Anaheim, Todd and his wife Toni bought two acres in a secluded area and built their dream house. They'd had a contractor build the house to the drywall, and Todd did all the finish work; the flooring, paneling, tile counters, and painting.

He'd become friends with one of the original Sky Forest families, and when their son was looking to retire from the water district, Todd had finished their house and was afraid he'd get bored; that's how he became their new general manager.

Todd was a one-man band. Part of his job was overseeing the office and keeping track of the water that was pumped in, and the other part was checking the individual meters every other month to keep track of the water usage. Unless there was an emergency, like frozen pipes, or pipes breaking, you wouldn't hear much from him. I met him when our water bill jumped to over a thousand dollars, from the typical hundred dollars.

"You have a pipe leak," he told Noah. "There's no way you would have known it since the water went back down into the ground."

"Holy cow," Noah said. "What do we do now?"

"I'll take care of the leak, *and* the bill," Todd said, "and I'll let you know when we need to shut the water off to do the repairs."

From then on, whenever they saw each other, they'd catch up on what was going on around town. A couple of times, they ran into each while having lunch at The Cedar Glen Inn and they began sharing a table.

Eventually, we ran into them one Saturday while having breakfast and they joined us. That's how I met his wife, Toni.

"I know who you are," she said, when I introduced myself.

I hadn't realized it, but she worked for the accounting firm in Lake Arrowhead that did our payroll.

From our breakfasts, I learned a lot about what was going on in the community.

"Not many people know it, but there's a ton of water under the highway—a reservoir, actually, where our water comes from. Our wells are on the south side of Highway 18, and that's where the action is too. I've caught copper thieves stripping out the electrical lines down there, and once there was an illegal marijuana grove that we took out."

"I didn't know that," Noah said, surprised.

"Because it's the sunny side of the mountain, I've also seen bears and mountain lions and I've dealt with my share of rattlesnakes."

"Yikes. I've never seen snakes," I said, cringing.

"Your property has a lot of shaded areas, and the snakes like to come out and warm up."

"Thank god," I said.

"A few years back, I came up against one. I moved a huge rock, and there he was. I made him angry when I threw some rocks at him, and he came at me so fast, I barely got out of his way. I hit him with a metal pipe I was carrying and stunned him; when he came to, he just looked at me and took off in the other direction. Since then I've worn snake gaiters, or guards, from the shoe up the leg, whenever I'm out in the field. If I was down the mountainside, one bite would do me in. I'd never make it to the hospital."

Toni winced.

"That and I keep a shotgun with me at all times."

I'd told Noah Todd reminded me of a younger Sam, both in height and lean build. They had the same gentle temperament, and the moment I met him, I could tell he had Sam's kind soul. They both spoke calmly and laughed often. I thought about Sam now, as Todd and Noah laughed.

From Todd and Toni, I learned about the old Santa's Village in Sky Forest, which was now vacant. We'd gone there when we had the Lake House in the 60s.

"It originally opened just before Disneyland did, and it was considered one of California's biggest tourist attractions before it closed down," Todd said.

"One fire up here burned a lot of the property," Toni added. "It's sat empty until a couple of years ago when a group of investors purchased the property, and they've been fighting with the county to get it opened again. For us old timers, we'll always think of it as Santa's Village, but they're going to call it Sky Park at Santa's Village since it'll be a year-round adventure park."

I said, "I'm glad to see it's being redeveloped."

"We'll have to check it out when it opens," Noah said.

"I'll let you know when it's getting closer, and maybe we can go with you," Todd said.

After that, Toni became a regular at At The Cabin, and one day she told me she'd love to work in the store in a few months when she retired from the accounting firm.

"I'd love to have you," I said. "You're hired."

A few months later, true to her word, the week after Toni retired, she started work. She knew most of our customers, which was a positive addition. Although she teased me for constantly buying so much merchandise, she was a natural at displaying it in the store. I hadn't known she was a quilter, and when I saw her handiwork, I asked her if she'd make things we could sell. We had a hard time keeping her handcrafted seasonal decorations in stock.

We were lost without breakfast at Ginny's, and when the sports bar across the street began serving breakfast, it became our new go-to spot. Toni, Sarah and I would often have lunch there too, and one afternoon, when it was just Toni and me in conversation, she asked how Noah and I first met. I shared the quick version of my marriage and coming up to the mountains to start over. I then asked her how she and Todd met.

"We were high school sweethearts. He saw me in *Oklahoma*, a school play he'd reluctantly gone to with a girl he hadn't wanted to go out with. He told me the minute I came on stage, he knew he was in love. Isn't that sweet?

"He came backstage after the play," she continued, "and that poor girl just stood there while Todd made a fool out of himself. I was a sophomore then, and he was a senior."

"You two make such a cute couple," I said. "It's so obvious Todd loves you to the moon."

"Yeah, I'm lucky there. But I love *him* too."

"Tell me about your family."

"Well, we have two boys; one's an attorney and the other is an orthopedic surgeon. I don't know where they got their smarts! They put themselves through college and they're married and have kids of their own. I have a brother. He moved to Tennessee years ago when he had a job transfer, so we don't get to see him very often. When my sister-in-law died, he fell apart, so his daughter came to live with us. Everyone's all grown now, and she has her own family too. She still calls us Mom and Dad. Todd has a brother in Idaho and a sister in Michigan. We're all over the place."

I told her about my sister Loni dying. "It was really hard on my parents," I said.

"I guess it would have been. I can't even begin to imagine losing a child. I'm sorry," she said thoughtfully.

For some reason, I felt comfortable sharing more about my relationship with my sister Loni.

"I hate to say I'm closer to my brother than Todd is to his," Toni said. "Families love each other, but they don't always have things in common."

I sighed.

"On a much lighter note," I said, changing the subject, "I don't think I've told you how glad I am you came to work with us. You're always so cheerful, and I've really seen an uptick in business. Plus, you've become a good friend."

"You've been a good friend to me, too," she said.

In October, the town hosted its yearly scarecrow contest. We normally filled the large wagon outside with seasonal artificial flowers, and Toni suggested we add hay and straw people.

"We can put straw children in the back with their parents seated in the wagon's seat."

Somehow, we found an old life-size unicorn with a broken-off alicorn, which was perfect for the wagon, and we repainted him brown. I found some old horse's reins, and we attached those to the horse and to the dad's hands.

"I know we'll win first place," Toni said, sweeping up all the straw once we'd finished.

"If we do, we'll have a hard time out-doing ourselves next year," I said.

I didn't want to gloat prematurely, but by the reaction from customers, and even the other stores, I was pretty sure we'd win. We became a popular stop for visitors, too; when I noticed people lined up to take their pictures with the display, I hired a student to take the photos so the entire group could be in them.

We won the trophy, but our glory was short-lived.

That same week, thousands of residents were required to evacuate their homes because of a quickly spreading fire a few miles out. Our entire town closed down and I grabbed our store cat, Dahlia, and headed for home. I'd never experienced such fear, even when lightning struck one of our cabins a few years back. Noah and I quickly packed up two suitcases with clothing, a few pieces of my favorite jewelry, and some personal items. I grabbed jackets, blankets, pillows and some bottles of water and set them all by the front door.

"We need to get going," Noah said.

"Is there anything else we need to take?" I asked.

I'd never lived in a community that experienced potential evacuation, so I hadn't ever given much thought to what else I would try to save in the event of an emergency. We could try to take our photos, but everything else I loved was too large to take; our grandfather clock, the canoe hanging from the ceiling in the living room, and the bronze statues.

"If the house burns down, everything can be replaced," Noah said, trying to coax the cat into the carrier.

When he said that, I froze. I couldn't imagine replacing everything we'd collected, and my heart pounded.

Noah turned to me and said, "Annie!"

I turned my attention to the task at hand.

"Get the leashes on the dogs. I'll start loading up the cars."

I somehow managed to leash the dogs, and I let them run outside. They were excited, thinking they were going for a ride, but little did they know they might not have a place to come home to if the fire reached the house.

I offered to take the store cat Dahlia with me, knowing she'd be unhappy with the drive and her crying would drive Noah crazy. Highway 18 was so backed up, I wondered if we'd ever get down. Noah was in front of me, and I stayed close enough to him to keep anyone from cutting in front of me—just seeing his car made me feel a little safer. The cat yowled the whole time, adding to my anxiety. Panicky drivers honked their horns, as if that was going to make traffic go faster.

We finally found a hotel in San Bernardino that allowed pets, and after we unloaded the car, we sat outside with the rest of their guests, wondering what was happening up the hill.

Not knowing was the worst. Almost everyone at the hotel was in the same boat; all of us had no idea how we would fare in the end. Some long-time residents recounted stories from previous evacuations, both good and bad, and tried to reassure us, but those like me, who'd never experienced the panic and uncertainty of it all, were frightened and nervous.

In our rush to leave, I'd forgotten to grab cat and dog food or a cat box, so I stayed with the animals while Noah looked for a pet store. On the way back, he stopped at an ATM and a grocery store where he bought muffins, orange juice, paper plates and napkins.

That first night, we tried to follow the news on the TV, but it was impossible to tell exactly where the fire had spread. Eventually, when the news just repeated itself, we tried to get some sleep. Dahlia stayed under our bed, and the dogs felt perfectly comfortable sleeping between us, like they always did. Neither Noah nor I slept much, and in the early morning, we were awakened by guests who'd gathered outside to get caught up on the news.

We stayed in that hotel for three terribly long and weary days until the evacuation orders were lifted and we were told we could go home. Once we packed everything and everyone up, with mounting fear and trepidation, we joined hundreds of others back up the mountain highway. We'd had no news about our properties and I tried to suppress tears as we turned off the highway and pulled up to the cabin to see there'd been any damage.

"Oh, Noah," I cried out as I jumped out of my Jeep. "It's all here. We have to check the stores."

We let the dogs loose until we could get them back into the dog yard, and then I transferred Dahlia into Noah's truck. Cars with returning residents packed the streets in town, making the drive in unbearably slow, but I could tell there was no damage to any of the buildings.

"What a miracle," Noah sighed, echoing my thoughts.

The next morning, however, we heard from a sobbing Toni—they hadn't been as lucky. Their cabin had burned to the ground! When we drove up to their house, they were there, sorting through the charred remains of their once-beautiful home. The acrid smell of burned wood still filled the air. The only thing left was the concrete foundation and the fireplaces; no furniture, just a blackened bathtub, a distorted washer and dryer, and the remnants of their kitchen sink and appliances. Metal bar stool bases protruded through burned timbers, and trees that were burned down were scorched stubs; those that still stood were blackened and bare of any foliage.

Every home in their neighborhood was gone. Miraculously, to the west, some trees were unscathed in the singed forest, but most were burned, so there was no hope for their recovery. The landscape was black and gray.

"The firemen left this on our driveway," Toni whispered. She held up a statue of a young boy gazing at a butterfly that had landed on his finger. "It was the only thing that survived the fire."

"You found some of your mother's china," Todd said, hugging her.

"Yes, we did." She shrugged in resignation.

We stood there, speechless, for what was there to say to lessen her pain? The silence in the air was deafening.

"We have room for you at the cabins," I said. "You can stay there until you decide what you're going to do. I'll have my old cabin ready for you, so just let me know when you'll be by. And I'm sure you can't think of it now, but if there's anything we can do for you, all you have to do is let us know."

I pulled her to me, and we both started crying.

Only a week passed when Toni said she wanted to come back to work. I knew they had a lot of decisions to make and they'd met with their insurance adjuster, who asked them to make a list of everything they'd lost. Even if they would have previously photographed everything in the house, the task would have been overwhelming. I suggested they start in one room, close their eyes, and visualize everything they could. There were no records left, so they had to place an arbitrary value on everything.

We invited Todd and Toni to have Thanksgiving dinner with us at the Saddleback Inn, but they went back down the hill to be with their children. Even though the town looked normal, most residents were in melancholy moods, and I worried about our holiday season. Once December hit though, tourists came up to see the damage the fires had done, and bookings at the cabins increased. We kept cabin one open for Todd and Toni, and another family who'd lost their cabin stayed in number three.

Over the last few years, we'd had people ask about renting the apartment above the garages at Noah's cabin, but we'd preferred our privacy. When another couple we knew decided to rebuild, they asked us if they could rent it until construction was completed over the next year. After a quick cleaning inside, we welcomed them and their two dogs.

The week before Christmas, Toni came to me before the store opened and let me know they'd decided not to rebuild.

"I don't think I can go through it," she said. "It'll take forever to clear the land, and then we'll need an architect, and Todd just isn't up to doing all that work again. We're getting too old, and the kids want us to move back down closer to them."

Disappointed I'd lose her, but appreciating their decision, I said, "I understand how you feel, and I don't know what I'd do if it were me."

"Plus, we still have grandkids," she said. "We've missed out on most of their lives while living up here."

My heart went out to her as images of the devastation they faced froze in my mind. As much as I tried to put myself in her shoes, there was no way I could truly feel the heartbreak of losing everything I had. I'd felt ashamed to admit I was so grateful we'd narrowly escaped the same fate. There was no way I could take any of her heartbreak away, except to be a good friend.

"As much as I'll hate not having you up here, I think you're making the best decision," I said. "You can stay with us as long as you want to, and you have your job until you're ready to leave."

They spent Christmas and New Year with their family and then Toni called me and said they'd made a decision about where they were going to live. They'd been looking around, and they were going to buy two mobile homes; one in Orange County near their kids, and another one just outside Prescott, Arizona.

"It reminds us of the mountains," she said.

"That's where my parents settled. They're in a park that reminds me of the mountains, too."

"I think we looked there. Since our boys are still in Orange County, we want to be near them, but still have a place we can get away to."

CHAPTER SEVEN

In 1992, my father died from a brain aneurysm. I'd just turned forty-five and my parents had come up to celebrate my birthday. The weekend had been relatively uneventful; they drove up on Friday, and we had a light dinner Friday night. On Saturday, we had prime rib at the Cedar Glen Inn and Sarah and Josh joined us. On Sunday, we slept in, had a late breakfast, and then we went out in the boat.

Noah convinced my mother to take a turn at driving around the lake, and I could tell she got a kick out of it. It reminded me of when we were all so young, and she was so proud of herself for trying our boat out. Just as she'd done then, she floored it, causing waves to splash on us all. She laughed at the way the wind blew in her hair, and she looked just like she had so many years ago.

They drove home on Monday and my mother called to let me know they'd made it back safely. On Tuesday, my mother went grocery shopping and when she came home, she opened the front door to call for my father to help her unload the groceries. When he didn't answer, she went back to the car and grabbed a couple of bags and brought them inside. That's when she found him slumped over in his reading chair.

She called 911, and then she called me.

I caught the first flight out to Prescott and stayed with her for a week. I hated that I felt like I'd become somewhat of a pro when over the years we'd made so many funeral arrangements, and while she put on a brave face, I knew she was grief stricken. The first few days, her face was so swollen from crying and her nose was so red she didn't want to leave the house. She made a list for me and I did the grocery shopping. Neither of us felt like cooking, and my mother barely ate, but I still grilled hamburger patties and made salads.

I offered to help her go through my father's things, but she said she didn't feel up to it yet. "I'll do it when I'm ready," she said, so I found a shelter in town and I wrote down their phone number and left it by the phone. She could deal with it when she was in a better place.

My parents had been planning on taking a trip back east to see the fall colors; they'd postponed it when my father fell from a ladder and broke his leg years back. I had her give me all the paperwork, but I wanted to wait until I returned home to cancel their travel plans. I didn't want to contact them while she was in the house, to take the chance she might overhear me. It was like another way to make my father's death more final.

I called Toni and Todd. They'd met my parents when they came up to the mountains and I wanted them to know I was in town. Fortunately, they were too, and Toni brought over some banana nut bread and a Mexican casserole. Even under the circumstances, it was good to see her. She and Todd came to the service, and she helped the ladies in the mobile home park set up for the post-funeral gathering at the clubhouse.

Noah drove out for the burial and spent the weekend. He asked my mother to make a list of things she wanted done around the house, so he could keep busy, but she couldn't think of anything. On his own, he went to the hardware store and bought new filters for the heater and air conditioner, and enough trash bags to last her for months. He changed the filters, checked the water heater for leaks, and made sure the caulking around the windows was tight.

I told her new neighbor we were leaving and gave him my phone number in case he needed me. He promised he'd look after the place and then I told my mother to let him know if she needed his help.

"I feel guilty leaving her," I said as we pulled out of the park.

"She'll be all right. Your mother's a strong woman—I know where you get it. You can come out to see her and we'll bring her up a couple times a year; it'll do you both some good," he said.

Noah always knew the right things to say to make me feel better.

I began checking in with my mother in the evenings, before we settled in to watch television or read. I asked how her day went, although I knew she'd never tell me how she really felt. I always tried to have something interesting to tell her about my day, and Noah would call out "Hi" in the background.

It was funny how I began missing my mother more, now that my father was gone, and I was certain it was because I knew she was alone and heavy-hearted. I made time on my calendar to visit her more frequently and we planned to bring her up to the mountains for a few weeks when it got warmer. I knew she loved our dogs, and I even thought about getting her a companion from the Prescott shelter, but she said she really didn't want the responsibility.

I understood.

When she came to stay with us, she'd come with me to the store and then keep herself busy cleaning and rearranging store displays. Or if she didn't feel like "working" as she called it, she'd bring a book and sit in a comfortable chair and read while I worked.

Customers loved it when I introduced them to her and they'd say things to her like "I just love your daughter's store" or "I love working with Annie."

My mother's face beamed when they said things like that, and when one customer reminded me how fortunate I was to still have my mother, I had to agree.

Our dogs were getting older and had a hard time making it up the stairs to her bedroom, but they made sure they scampered up to find a comfortable spot in her bed to help them all keep warm when it cooled off at night.

"I can't believe I'm letting a dog sleep in my bed," she said one morning as she gave the dogs treats. "Your father would have a fit."

"The dogs love you, Mother," I said, then suddenly added, "Have you considered moving up here to be near us?"

My question surprised her.

"Here, hand me your coffee cup," I said, to give her a minute to think.

I'd thought about it before, and I wasn't sure why I brought it up just then. Maybe it was because I worried about her being all alone. I constantly watched her now, how she moved just a little bit slower, or how she had to think a moment sometimes to remember what she was doing. I knew it was a shot in the dark, but I waited for her answer.

"I've thought about it, just like I've thought about everything since your father's been gone. I'm happy where I am, and I can't see myself packing everything up and moving."

She tilted her head slightly, like Noah tended to do, and smiled at me.

"You've made yourself a wonderful life up here with Noah and your businesses," she said. "Your father and I used to talk about you, and how proud we were of you."

I put her cup in the sink and then leaned against the kitchen counter. After Loni died, I was the only one they had left to feel proud of. I didn't read anything in to it other than how I must have given them something positive to think about when they missed her.

"I've certainly had my moments," I said, "but I'm really happy. I have a good life."

"That's all a parent wants, you know," she said, petting the dog and giving her another treat.

"You're spoiling her."

"That's what grandmas do."

For our tenth anniversary, Noah suggested we invite my mother to join us for a four-day cruise to Catalina and Ensenada, and at first she was reluctant to say yes.

"I don't want to spoil your trip by tagging along," she said.

"I talked to the travel agent, and they have a special going on for mothers-in-law," Noah said jokingly. "I've already made arrangements," he said before she could say no again.

She flew into San Bernardino, and we picked her up there before heading to the Port of Los Angeles where we'd be departing. I'd forgotten how many cars there were on the freeways, even when it wasn't peak traffic time. Noah dropped us off with our luggage and I got us checked in. After finding our life drill station, we found our rooms and had a quick lunch before we unpacked.

The first morning, a tender pulled up alongside the ship and it took us to the island, where we were greeted by the tour guide who would take us up into the interior. On a rough and bumpy ride, we climbed the hills and saw bison roaming the land and learned that bald eagles still nested in Catalina. I also hadn't known that the bison weren't indigenous to Catalina, but someone originally brought them to the island in the twenties for a movie and left them there.

After another night at sea, we docked in Mexico, and we boarded a bus that took us to a wonderful winery where we had lunch and sampled their wines. It was a beautiful property with a hotel and there were plans to build casitas that guests could rent long term. We saw a falconer with his hawk and he told us all about how he'd trained it. I was disappointed we didn't get to see it fly, and when I asked why, he explained the birds were let loose only in the morning and evening, when they were hungry enough to help keep the property rodent-free. Everyone lined up to have their photos taken with the bird and I was surprised it was so tame.

Once we were back on the tour bus, I said, "Even though I understand, I still wish we could have seen the bird in action."

"Would you really have wanted to see the bird catch and kill its prey?" Noah asked.

After I thought about it, I said, "Not really."

After dinner, we watched a musical revue with ice skaters, and I could tell my mother was really enjoying herself. I was glad she'd agreed to come along, and I knew she was too.

"I'm pooped," she said as we got back to the airport. "It'll be good to get back home."

"I'm glad you decided to join us," I said. "We had a great time."

After making sure her flight was on time, we headed back up the hill. I put my hand on Noah's thigh, as I often did when he drove, and he patted my hand.

"We had a good time, didn't we? But I agree with my mother, it always feels good to be back home, doesn't it?"

"I have to admit it does," he said.

After that, it seemed like the seasons changed in double-time, and the years passed even more quickly.

The people who'd bought Ginny's sold it not long after it reopened. The new buyer changed the name to Walt's, but kept most of the same menu with updated prices. We still ate there, but mostly for lunch. Every time I went in, I expected to see Ginny with her curly ponytail bouncing as she walked. I missed her laugh, and it just wasn't the same.

No one ever expected it, but somehow a McDonald's opened up down the street from the stores and they seemed to stay busy enough. I don't know how they did it since there were rules against any fast-food chains coming up to the mountains.

A new realtor took over the space where Mr. Weatherby's old general store was, which created unwanted competition for the older established agents, and a health food store moved into an empty space across the street.

New owners took over the Village and rents went up, so some old standby stores closed their doors. Ruth's bookshop was still hanging in there, but whenever I went in, she was never there. I never knew her full story, but I knew she'd come up to the mountains to begin a new life, and I always felt some kind of connection to her. She's the one who sold the cabins to Sam. Her girl in the store said she stayed mostly in Big Bear now, which made sense since her second husband retired from the boat repair shop years back.

Noah bought an old truck from the young man who ran the boat shop now; it turned out it originally belonged to Ruth's first husband back in the 70s. I made Noah promise if he was going to work on it, he'd keep it in the garage and not parked outside.

It seemed one right after another we lost our two dogs. Noah and I had talked about the inevitable; would we replace them when the time came? He buried them next to the other dogs, along the path out in to the forest and, as with the other graves, he made piles of stones as markers. And each time he buried one, he'd come back into the house, with his shoulders slumped and his head hanging down. He resembled an exhausted old man with his hat pushed back on his head, wiping the sweat off his forehead with his forearm. It broke my heart to see him so miserable.

I'd loved our dogs, but Noah had loved them even more. I cleaned and packed away their feeding and water bowls like I'd done for the cats over the years, so neither of us would have to see them in the kitchen, but for the longest time, we both looked for any signs of them when we came home at night. And it surprised both of us how hard it was to sleep at night without them as our companions.

As the weeks went by, we talked about them less, but every now and then, I'd catch one of us looking to where they would lie, or we'd comment on how we missed them greeting us at the door when we came home at night. In a way, thinking less of them made me feel somewhat guilty. When I shared my mixed emotions with Noah, he admitted he'd been feeling the same way.

In the end, we decided against having more pets for now.

Noah had been saving extra job materials in the garden shed, so when he and Josh had some downtime in between jobs, they repaired old shelters and built new enclosures for the animals at Wildhaven Ranch, the wild animal sanctuary in Cedar Glen. We donated rolls of fencing material and had them delivered up to the ranch to have on hand. They got a grant to build a structure large enough for tours and fundraising galas, and Noah, Josh, and the men donated time to help the general contractor get it built.

As if they didn't already have enough projects, Noah and Josh began buying and selling Jeeps. It started as a dare, when Noah found a Jeep he thought he could resell after doing a few minor repairs. Josh told him he couldn't make any money on it, and Noah proved him wrong. Once he sold it, they pooled their money and bought a second one that needed some work, and when they sold that one, I had Sarah make up a business card for them. She found a cartoon image of a red Jeep, and we started calling them 'The Jeep Brothers'. It became a common sight to see a Jeep for sale parked alongside our building.

Constantly on the lookout for a deal, Noah came across a truck with a snowplow attached to the front end, and he traded one of the Jeeps for it. When the weather was too bad for them to work, he and Josh alternated helping neighbors clear their property of snow, and to move the berms the county vehicles created when plowing the roads. When some of the local businesses asked if he'd help clear their parking spaces, he and Josh realized it was an opportunity to add a little side income.

For someone who'd often reacted with skepticism to some of my spontaneous ideas in the past, Noah hadn't had a problem coming up with his own money-making ideas. Sometimes I'd raise an eyebrow, but I never said a word.

CHAPTER EIGHT

Late snow and cool weather seemed to push the early spring out, and April rains drenched the mountain. It was impossible to escape the constant dampness; it was in the leaves and pine needles covering the grounds and even on the roads. Rain water seeped in around the fireplace at Noah's and even though we constantly wiped it up, I worried the moisture would damage the hardwood floor and cause it to buckle.

Eventually, the rain stopped and although neither the cabins nor the apartment above the garages showed any signs of water stains, Noah caulked around all the fireplaces for good measure.

Spring was generally a busy time for the design store, but the cloudy, wet weather seemed to throw our customers off balance, and for the first time that I could remember, we didn't have any new clients. Rather than let it get me down, I found I had some free time, so when Noah suggested we go somewhere for our anniversary, I was game.

"Why don't we go back to Sedona?" I suggested. I couldn't think of anywhere else I'd rather go.

Noah's smile broadened, and even after fifteen years with him, I still had a soft spot for him and that smile; while I hated the fine lines around my eyes, I realized that his made him even more handsome. My heart soared just looking at him.

We stopped again in Oatman, and it looked like tourism had remained a mainstay, for the burros were still there casually roaming the streets vying for food from all the day trippers. There were more gift shops and a few more places to stop for something to eat or drink. There was now an official stand where tourists could buy burro food, and I stood in line to get a brown paper bag of approved treats. When I turned to find Noah, I saw a foal clustered within a group of what I assumed were four females. He rushed ahead to get out of the pack and one of the adults followed him and cut him off by nipping his rear end. Startled, he turned and once he figured out what she was doing, he hung his young head, almost in defeat, as he made his way back in to the fold.

Before we left, we stopped at the Oatman Hotel for a soda, and we signed our names on a dollar bill and tacked it up on a wall full of them. Back on the highway, we saw several clusters of wild burros along the road and I couldn't resist asking Noah to stop. I'd brought some apples and reached in to the back seat of the Jeep as Noah rolled his window down.

"Hey girl," he said as one of the burros came up to the car.

"Here," I said, handing him an apple.

He put it in his hand and she came even closer. Soon her head was almost inside the car.

"Whoa," Noah said as she gently reached for the apple.

"I can't believe how tame they are," I said.

Several other cars had pulled over to the side of the road and the burros began milling around them, looking for food.

"I hope they're not feeding them junk," I said. "Here are a few more apples."

He began feeding another burro, and then we both saw a younger white one standing off in the brush. I tried to call out to it, thinking it might follow the others, but it only turned to look at us for a few seconds before it went off in the opposite direction.

"They're actually quite cute," I said. "I would have loved to see the white one up close."

Once the apples were gone, I crumpled up the plastic bag and added it to our trash bag up front. Noah's right hand was resting on the console gear shift knob, and I reached out and stroked his arm. I'd never stopped loving his muscular arms.

From our last trip to Sedona, I'd forgotten how winding the roads were through the mountains, and after we passed abandoned copper mines, we saw a still functioning mine off to the left. We drove through a green wooded area of the highway, still twisting and turning, then roadside mailboxes and campgrounds came into view. Eventually we came to a turnout on the highway, where a cluster of a few men, but mostly Native American women, sat at their tables filled with jewelry. In a way, it reminded me of the pop-up tents we saw coming in to Sedona so many years ago, and my heart skipped. Was the old woman who foretold my future still going to be there?

 I counted fifteen vendors selling similar merchandise, and it amazed me how they could survive competing against each other like that. Although I wasn't searching for anything specific, I stopped at every stall and while there were some amazing turquoise and silver pieces, there wasn't anything I would wear. I was disappointed to find nothing that suited me. It was just as well, for I'd discovered that even with a jewelry box full of bracelets and earrings, I always ended up wearing the same one or two things every day.

We stayed in a hotel called Little America in Flagstaff. Set on over five hundred acres of pine forested land at the base of the San Francisco Peaks, each room had a view of the forest. After we unpacked, we walked the grounds, and eventually made our way to the hotel restaurant where we had a late lunch. We hadn't thought to bring bathing suits, so Noah and I found something in the hotel gift shop so we could go out to the pool and sit in the Jacuzzi.

 Once we got back to our room, there was a soft knock at our door, and room service delivered two miniature bottles of champagne, some chocolates, and a vase of red roses.

 "Happy fifteenth," Noah said, touching his glass to mine.

 "And happy fifteenth to you," I said.

Afterward, we made love like an old married couple; with comfort and familiarity. The passion and urgency we'd experienced over the years had taken on a different level; more one of a deeper connection and every day closeness.

"You really are the best husband," I said, when we cuddled. We'd left the sliding door slightly ajar, and we welcomed the warm afternoon breeze as it touched our skin.

Noah's even breathing soon turned into gentle snoring, and I knew he was out for the next few hours. I took a quick shower and then found where I'd left off in my latest book and spent the rest of the early evening reading. Later, neither of us was starving, so we ordered a club sandwich to split and sodas from room service.

After breakfast at the hotel the next morning, we got gas and headed towards Sedona.

My heart raced as we drove into town and I recalled the Indian woman's predictions from so long ago. Apprehension turned to relief and a little disappointment, for the stands along the road were all gone now, replaced with clay or dark taupe colored buildings; gas stations, restaurants, banks, hotels, and even a place where you could rent all-terrain vehicles to drive the roads.

"I can't believe how everything's changed," I said in amazement.

In some ways, I was surprised, but in others, I was impressed with the progress the town had made.

"According to my directions, we need to turn right at the next street, then left, then right," I said, reading my notes. "It doesn't look like there's a hotel out here."

We drove through what was most definitely a high end residential area with homes in the same hues as downtown, dark clay or taupe, until we made the last turn in to the resort.

"This looks like a guardhouse," Noah said. "Not exactly what I expected."

A gentleman dressed all in khaki came to Noah's side of the Jeep. Noah gave him our name, and he checked his clipboard to see if our name was on the guest list. "Here you are. I'll just get your license number from the back."

He carried himself with such formality that it seemed like we were being stopped for a traffic violation. He came back to Noah's side and gave us a map.

"Head to the left and you can check in there. Enjoy your stay," he said, finally smiling.

The barrier arm lifted and Noah started off to the right before he realized he was going in the wrong direction. He backed up and turned left. We crossed over several speed bumps, although we couldn't have been going more than ten miles per hour.

"That was kind of creepy," I said. "I can't quite put my finger on it, but I almost feel like we're entering a compound."

"That's because we are," Noah said.

We passed a twelve miles per hour speed limit sign, which I thought was unusual, until I saw two deer comfortably grazing on what looked like several acres of green grounds to our right.

"Look!" I cried out as I pointed. "I wish we saw deer more at home."

"I see more than you do, but these guys are so tame."

Trees and bushes partially hid the guest casitas on our left, and then we came to the sign pointing to the hotel check in. We pulled up to a welcoming area, where we were greeted by more khaki clad attendants, who directed us where to go after we parked. We followed the cobblestones under a porte cochere, then entered the check-in area on the left.

"I know what it is," I said.

"What? What are you talking about?"

"The feeling I had. It's like the song, checking in to the Hotel California, but this place is beautiful."

Once inside, I got us signed in, and we got another map showing us where our casita was. We pulled into our parking space and I stood and looked out at the red cliffs as Noah took our luggage out of the Jeep.

"This really reminds me of the mountains, except that it's red," I said.

"It's quite spectacular, isn't it?" Noah asked, turning to see what I was seeing.

Our casita was incredible—it had a full size living room, dining area and kitchen, complete with dishes and utensils. One bedroom and bath was off to the right, four steps down, and what could have been a second bedroom was to the left and up four steps. It had been designed to be either a one or two-bedroom suite.

"This is amazing," Noah said, plopping himself down on the bed and stretching out.

And I had to agree with him. I hadn't told him how much it was costing us to stay there. Noah unzipped our suitcase, and I unpacked and hung our clothes. I checked my watch and said, "We should probably head over to the Jeep tour."

I knew Noah would love the late morning off roading adventure. When we got there, several groups were ahead of us in line, and as we were signing in, the gal at the counter told us that if we were pregnant or had had any back or hip injuries or surgery, they'd advise us against going on the tour. We'd had neither, so we signed the waiver, and then went to the loading area.

Our guide mentioned there would be a lot of bumps and rough riding ahead, and that it would be two hours before we'd be back to use the bathrooms. Rough riding was no exaggeration. We bumped around in the custom Jeep, sometimes climbing up inclines or going down banks so steep I wondered what the probability of us flipping over might be.

We stopped a few times to take a much needed break and to photograph the incredible scenery. The volcanic mountains and cliffs dotted with evergreens were amazing. Our guide pointed out rock formations that looked like a mermaid, a bell, a cathedral, and the Madonna.

"I can't see them," someone said.

I could. But then, I had a tendency to see faces in clouds and other inanimate objects. I always thought it was my creative nature that let me see things until I looked it up and discovered it's not so uncommon a trait and just part of normal human experience. The technical word for it is pareidolia and was once considered a symptom of psychosis. I'd often wondered if I was a little *off* when I saw faces, and only when it was so obvious, like faces or animals in the clouds in the sky, did I even point it out to people.

"Keep your eye out for our famous javelinas," the guide said. "They show up just about everywhere around here. They look like feral hogs, or pigs, but they're actually peccaries, which are medium-sized mammals with hooves."

"I've never heard that term," the woman standing next to me said.

I hadn't either.

The guide said, "Well, then, you'll be surprised to learn that horses, cattle, sheep and deer are peccaries. Javelinas somehow migrated here from Central and South America. They're considered wild game, and it's against the law to injure or kill game animals. Don't feed or approach them."

I wasn't the only one who turned to see if there were any wild animals around me.

"What do you do if they charge you?" someone asked.

"If you see one, you're best off if you go in the other direction. Make noise, wave your arms and throw something at them. People who live here keep a spray bottle of ammonia and water and spray them if they get near."

I was curious to see one, but only from inside the vehicle, not in person.

The irresistible urge to make a pit stop was growing stronger the closer we got to the end of the tour, and while I had to admit it was an exhilarating adventure, I was glad it eventually ended.

"Whew," I said as I stood and made sure all my body parts worked.

"That was great!" Noah said as he jumped out and stretched.

He'd rolled up his shirt sleeves, and I could see that the sun had begun its work. I'd always loved the way the hair on his suntanned forearms arms caught the sunlight. He took his baseball cap off and I could smell the sun in his hair as he ran his fingers through it before putting it back on.

"I'm hungry," he said.

We grabbed a quick lunch at a Sonoran Mexican restaurant down the street, and then I said, "I'm ready for a nap."

We went back to the hotel and after taking quick showers, the minute my head hit the pillow, I was out.

That night, I didn't think I'd be hungry enough to eat again, but I'd made a reservation at a steakhouse at the airport and I didn't want to cancel it. We shared a glass of merlot and took turns toasting each other.

"Happy anniversary," we both said.

Eventually, we made our way back to our casita and took showers to wash off the dust from the day's adventures. I'd forgotten to bring a clock to sit on my side of the bed, so a few times after I woke to see what time it was, I finally pulled the drapes back a little so I'd be able to tell when the sun came out enough to get up. We had no time constraints, but I always liked to wake naturally to the morning light.

We had a leisurely breakfast on the hotel restaurant patio, and just absorbed the surroundings. The mix of green trees growing in the orange cliffs against a clear blue sky was almost magical.

"I can see why so many people love coming here," I said.

I overheard the young couple at the table next to us discussing the tasting they had scheduled for later today. They were planning their wedding at the hotel. I couldn't help but think that if their guests were paying to stay at the hotel, they wouldn't have much money left over for a wedding gift. Unless, of course, they had wealthy friends.

Our waitress was talking to them about their upcoming wedding and her six children, and was explaining that two were from her husband, three were hers, and they just had a daughter between them.

"That must be quite the houseful," the bride to be said.

"Oh, it is," our waitress said. "For the most part, everyone gets along."

I looked at Noah out of the corner of my eye, and I could tell he'd heard the entire conversation. We just looked at each other.

"Well, what's on the agenda today?" he asked, finishing off his bagel.

"Not much. I'd like to go to Tlaquepaque. They had so many things to see the last time we were here. We can grab a quick lunch there when we're done."

Noah looked at me funny, and even I couldn't figure out why I'd be thinking about food after just finishing breakfast.

"Well, you never know when we'll be hungry again," I said, and gave him my silly grin.

We pulled in to the parking lot just as someone was pulling out, and I said, "Well, this is a sign of good luck." We strolled through the art galleries and custom clothing stores, and we came to a store with the most beautiful woven rugs.

"I wish we had a place for one," I said.

"They *are* pretty incredible," Noah said. "I don't know what we'd have to get rid of to bring one home."

"Okay, then, buy me an ice cream and I won't pester you about bringing home something new."

I *did* find a wonderful painting of a red fox in the forest that would fit perfectly in our downstairs bedroom, and I didn't have to twist Noah's arm much to buy it. At one of the jewelry stores, I found a black leather braided bracelet with a silver clasp that looked handsome on Noah's wrist, and he promised me he'd wear it only when he wasn't working so he wouldn't lose it.

It seemed that all we did was eat, and that night, we had dinner at the same Italian restaurant we ate at for our tenth anniversary. The evening was warm and perfect for sitting outside on the patio. We shared a glass of wine and then, after dinner, we had Maritozzo, which was a small bun filled with custard. I reminded Noah that in the olden days, men would give their fiancé one with a ring or piece of jewelry inside.

"Should I be careful while I eat it?" I teased.

"Oh, darn it, I forgot to ask the waiter to put it in there," he said. "But I *do* have something I can give you later."

"I'd rather have the jewelry," I teased.

That night when we got back to the hotel, I checked in with my mother and told her we'd head for Prescott after we backtracked to stop at Bearizona, a wildlife preserve in Williams. It would make a long day, but Noah had read about it in the resort magazine and we both wanted to see the animals.

"Keep your hands inside the vehicle," the ticket seller at the gate said as we drove up. "And if the bears get close, roll up your windows, and no stopping."

Of course, we followed most of his directions, but I couldn't help asking Noah to stop so I could take photos of a mother goat who'd just given birth. Noah found bears everywhere, and once he pointed them out, we stopped to take photos. I was worried cars behind us would honk at us, but when I turned to look around, they were doing the same thing.

"I think we're seeing more bear and deer here than I've ever seen in the mountains," I said. "Look, they even have their own hospital," I said, pointing to a series of buildings on our left. "I've read over half the animals here are rescues."

Driving into my mother's park always made me feel like we'd just entered a private forest, and that day was no different. A few homeowners were out tending to their gardens, and I noticed some temporary motor homes were parked in the designated visitor parking where I'd seen them before. One visitor must have been planning on staying a while, for there were lit patio lights strung between the trees, and potted flowers brightened up the table they'd set up for meals.

We parked just outside my mother's mobile and the moment I opened the car door to get out and stretch, the aroma of something delicious wafted through the air. It was coming from the kitchen window.

My mother was a wonderful cook, but over the years, she'd done less of it, especially now that it was just her.

"Is this what I think it is?" I called as we came in.

"I made a roast," she said, wiping her hands on her apron.

"Well, it smells delicious," I said, rolling our suitcase in to the extra bedroom.

"We'll have a nice anniversary dinner," I could hear her saying to Noah.

"I hope no one kicks you out if we stay," he said, kissing her on the cheek.

"I'll lie and tell them you aged fifteen years since they last saw you," she said. "It's a dumb rule anyway, but I can see why they don't want a lot of young people taking over the park."

"Is there anything I can do?"

I peeked under the lid of a pot filled with mashed potatoes.

"Yum," I said. "Although I can't believe I'm actually hungry. I think that's all we've done is eat."

"Let's sit for a minute and you can tell me all about your trip."

My mother poured us all a glass of iced tea, and we talked about the Jeep ride and the animal preserve. She brought us up to date on another neighbor who'd moved out, and the new neighbor who moved in.

"Doris is a single lady, and we've gone to the clubhouse to play cards a couple of times. She's teaching me Canasta. Her husband died years ago, and she doesn't have children. That's too bad, isn't it? Well, enough chitchat, let's eat," she said.

"This is right up my alley," Noah said, rubbing his hands together.

I'd set the table and my mother brought the serving dishes out.

"You've gone all out, using your china," I said, teasing her.

"Well, why not? I can't remember when the last time was I used it. Here—start."

After dinner, we walked around the park to let the food settle. Her new neighbor was out and my mother introduced us. Another neighbor walking his dog greeted us with a wave.

"I'm glad you have this place," I said, giving my mother a shoulder hug.

"We all watch out for each other," she said.

The next morning, we loaded the car and took my mother to a new little restaurant she'd wanted to try. Breakfast was delicious, and she knew half the customers in the place. It reminded me of being up in the mountains when we all greeted each other.

"When do you want to come up again?" I asked.

Dear Noah

"Soon. I'll let you know."
"I love you, mom," I said, hugging her goodbye.
"I love you too, honey. Call me when you get home."

CHAPTER NINE

I was looking for something new to read, so after an appointment one afternoon, I stopped in at Ruth McCallum's Books & Co. in the Village. It was one of the few remaining old stores left, and I always tried to do my business with the locals. A young woman I didn't recognize was working the store, and she cheerfully greeted me as I came in.

"Welcome," she said. "I'm Catherine, if you need any help."

"Thanks," I said, stopping first at the table where the new books were displayed.

Catherine went about her business, dusting shelves and rearranging books at the back of the store.

"I haven't been in for a while," I said.

"Julie, the older lady who worked here, finally retired, and I'm afraid Ruth is right behind her. They've raised our rent again, and Ruth doesn't get in much anymore."

"Oh," I said. Catherine had answered my question before I even asked it.

"Ruth's been looking for a buyer for a while, but so far, no one has stepped up. You know her husband, Jacob, died a few months ago. He was a few years older than her."

I paused and said, "Oh, I'm sorry to hear that."

I didn't know much about Ruth McCallum, other than that's who Sam and his wife bought the cabins from a long time ago. Sam told me she'd lost her first husband, and then met Jacob, and when they decided to get married, she sold everything but the bookstore and moved to Big Bear and opened a second store there. I wondered if she still had that store, too.

As if reading my mind, Catherine volunteered, "She's sold the Big Bear store. She has terrible arthritis, you know. And it gets so cold up here, it's always acting up. Her kids don't want bookstores. Ruth says they're busy with their own careers."

"That happens, sometimes. Children don't always want to follow in their parent's footsteps."

I set one book down and picked up another. I hadn't intended to buy a used book, but I found myself wandering over to that part of the store. The mustiness made me think of what it would be like to be down in a cellar. Not a terrible smell, just a stale or airless one. It was always something I found curious enough that on my way back to my stores once, I stopped at the library to see if they could tell me how to remove the smell."

"The odor, which some people love," the librarian explained, "comes from the organic materials in books, like the cellulose and lignin. When these begin to disintegrate, they can give books an earthy or musty smell.

Past the used paperbacks, I stopped at the leather bound hardcover editions. I loved old books, and whenever I found covers I liked, it didn't matter much what the book was about; I'd buy it for the décor. I found three books that would fit perfectly on the shelves around the living room in our cabin and brought them up to the counter. I also picked up the latest John Grisham novel, *The Partner*, and added it to my stack.

"Don't you have a store in town?" Catherine asked.

"I do. It's interior design and home décor," I said.

"I saw that a new furniture store moved in across the street. I went in there with my mom."

"Yes," I said, letting out a disheartened breath.

"What are you going to do?"

"I'm not sure yet. We *do* sell different things, but it would be like a used book store opening up here in the Village. It would certainly make life a little more complicated for the store."

"I've heard that's it's a good one," Catherine said.

She'd obviously already checked it out, and her comment brought me down a few more notches.

After she rang me up, she said, "Enjoy the books, and I'm sure you'll think of what to do about the store across the street." As an afterthought, she added, "Your stores are wonderful."

I appreciated her vote of confidence. The truth was, the new store was a worry for me. I knew a larger store could not offer the level of service we did, and although I hadn't been in there yet, I knew they'd have a lot of furniture and accessories geared for people who wanted to decorate their homes up here. I'd already mentioned the store to Noah, but we hadn't talked about it in any detail.

I knew if I thought about it enough, I could come up with something, so the next morning, I went into the new store and introduced myself and welcomed them to the community. I quickly realized they would appeal to someone who wanted to furnish an entire home and make their purchases off the floor. It didn't appear they did custom décor like we did. While I stood there talking with Rebecca Summers, the owner, I had the crazy idea of telling her that if any of her customers needed flooring or window coverings to send them my way. But then, for once, I didn't let my impulsiveness take over, and I kept my thoughts to myself.

That night, I told Noah I'd gone into the store to welcome them, and after looking at me like I was insane, I told him about my idea of sharing.

"You're nuts, you know that?" He shook his head at me.

"I'm serious. And I thought you'd be glad to hear me tell you what I'm thinking about doing before I just jump in there and do it for a change."

"Well, I'm happy about that, at least." He gave me that look again, and then said, "You're going to do it, anyway. Might as well do it sooner than later."

The next morning, I called to see if Rebecca was going to be in later, and told her I'd like to come back in and talk to her. I could tell she was a little skeptical, but she agreed, and that afternoon, I went back in.

"I have an idea," I started. "We both have a client base we want to serve, so why not work together if we can?"

Her eyebrows narrowed and I could tell she thought the same thing about my idea as Noah did, but I continued.

"If I have clients who need to work with an interior designer, but don't want to wait for custom furniture, I could do their floor plans and then refer them to you. And on the other hand, if you have customers who need floor coverings or window treatments, you can refer them to me. We could either work it out on a referral basis, where we each earn a commission of our respective sales, or we can keep it simple and just refer our customers. I play fair in the sandbox, and I'd assume you would too."

"What if our services overlap?" Rebecca asked, hesitantly.

"Then you and I talk about it, and there are no hard feelings. It's ultimately what the client wants, so as long as we don't try to sway them, then I don't see any issues."

She shrugged and then looked at me like she was sizing me up. When I saw the beginning of a nod, I knew we had a deal.

"Give me some of your cards," I said. "And here are some of mine." I extended my hand, and we shook.

I was gloating all the way back across the street when I decided to stop in at the sports bar and get an iced tea. From the rack outside, I grabbed the latest issues of the homes for sale magazines and tucked them under my arm. When I came inside the design store, Sarah greeted me.

"How'd it go?" she asked, handing me a new note.

"We have a deal," I said, full of myself.

"Constance Fisher wants to re-do her office."

"Okay. I'll give her a call."

I went into my office and set everything down on my desk. I'd drawn in a breath as I took a sip of my tea, and I somehow snorted it back out through my nose. On the cover of one of the magazines was the image of a house I'd never forget. It was Grayson Underwood's home!

"Are you okay?" Sarah asked, rushing to my doorway.

I coughed and then reached for a tissue to blow my nose.

"What is it?"

I shoved the magazine towards her, but she tilted her head, trying to comprehend what I was showing her. Of course, she'd never seen Grayson's home!

"It's his home," I said.

"It's whose home?"

"Grayson Underwood. The man I had the—*indiscretion*—with. When Noah took off."

Her eyes widened, and all she said was, "Oh."

Although she didn't say anything more, her face spoke for her.

"Oh," she said again. Then she added, "What now?"

"What now, nothing."

Instantly, images of him flooded my mind; like the first time I met him at his house on the lake, and how when I introduced myself to him and called him Mr. Underwood, he said 'Call me Grayson'.

He'd looked so much like Robert Redford with that thick reddish hair and charming smile, and I hadn't wanted to admit it then, but it disarmed me. For years afterward, I'd looked back at the ways he'd insinuated himself on me by his seemingly innocent but intimate comments and quick gentle touches to my hands and arms. My stomach turned as images of us having sex clouded my mind.

"Are you all right?" Sarah asked. "You're white as a ghost."

I'd never shared the details with her and I'd all but forgotten him and my bad choices until the photo of his home stared me in the face.

The living room in the photo was just as I'd left it. He hadn't changed a thing.

"I wonder if he's died," I said softly. "He'd be in his late seventies now."

"Or maybe he just doesn't come up here anymore. Are you sure you're okay?"

"Not really, but I'll be fine."

I could tell the color had returned to my face, for I was now having a major hot flash. I was anxious for Sarah to leave me alone so I could wallow in my regret in private.

"Did he ever contact you again?"

"No. And I wonder if he ever found happiness. I don't know what that would have meant to someone like him."

The rest of my day was wasted on thoughts about my life and things I never should have done. Mostly, I thought about those things I could never fix. Like Grayson.

When Noah came home late that afternoon, hearing the sounds of his truck crunching the gravel in our drive didn't bring me the normal sense of peace of mind it usually did. I was certain he'd see my face and read the guilt I carried with me; I would have preferred having more time to myself.

I couldn't stop the replay in my mind—about Grayson coming up to the cabins after I'd told him I'd made a mistake letting our relationship go so far, and picturing Sam standing there cocking his shotgun, hoping it would convince him to leave. And when Noah showed up, it was almost as though I was throwing my infidelity in his face; how in a way I blamed him, because it never would have happened if he hadn't left me when I needed him.

The back of my throat burned, and then I rushed outside, hoping the fresh air would keep me from being sick.

"Hey, are you all right?" Noah asked, rushing to me.

"It must have been something I had for lunch," I said.

"Well, come inside. It's chilly out."

"I'll take a few more minutes out here. I feel better already," I lied.

I no longer felt sick, but I couldn't face Noah, either.

That night, I picked at my dinner and said I was exhausted; and later that night when Noah reached for me in bed, I think it was the first time I feigned not feeling well to avoid making love with him. I rolled over and pretended to drift off, but sleep evaded me.

I woke with a headache, and when we stopped for breakfast, as we did most every day, I took some more Tylenol.

"It looks like you still don't feel up to par," Noah said, reaching for my hand.

"I think I'm just tired. And it could be the weather change." I was grasping at straws.

I tossed the home magazine in the trash once I got to the store, but not before I punished myself by taking one last look at it.

"Go away," I said to myself.

Then I called Constance Fisher.

CHAPTER TEN

On a Thursday that next spring, my manager at the cabins, Johnnie Spencer and his fiancé, Louise Tate, were anxiously waiting for me at the cabins when I pulled into the drive.

"Sorry I'm late," I said, grabbing my suitcase from the back of the car.

"We don't have to be there for another hour, but we were getting nervous," Johnnie said.

He and Louise were going to be married by the justice of the peace up here, and I was filling in for them for a few days while they had a quick honeymoon. Johnnie had been my manager for almost three years, and I knew I'd created some unnecessary stress for them by losing track of time.

He was only about twenty-five now, but years ago, during a heavy snowfall, he fell off a snow plow and his foot was crushed under the blade. Wasting away and growing tired of disability, he'd come to me asking for a job. Cliff, my manager at the time, had been offered a good job with the county, and needed to move back down the hill. So the timing was right and Johnnie assured me his bad foot wouldn't keep him from taking care of the property. He was a friendly young man, and for the last three years, he had become invaluable to me and Noah.

Now, he was ready to get married, and both he and Louise thought the cabin was a comfortable place to start a family.

"I changed the sheets for you," Louise said, her face turning pink with embarrassment.

"I'll do the same when you come back," I said playfully. "What do we have going on?"

"Nothing for a couple of days, but then two couples are coming in on Friday. But we should be back Friday night and can take over."

I gave them an envelope with a hundred dollars in it, and then we hugged before they took off.

"Have a great time," I called out, as we waved.

We'd all gotten cell phones earlier in the year, and even though I'd arranged to have any incoming calls for the cabins forwarded to my phone, I still had the answering service on standby in case I didn't have my phone with me. We'd also installed our first fax machine, and I had to admit that learning all the technology was a little overwhelming for me.

Since we had no guests, after I got settled, I went in to the store to get caught up with never-ending paperwork. We were busy, and no matter how hard I tried, I always seemed to have something left to do.

"Is it just me, or is there more to do lately?" Sarah asked when she came in.

"It's not just you. But today, I'm going to go home with a clean desk."

"Seriously?"

"Well, I'll settle for an organized one, then."

"Good luck," she said.

Noah was going to stay with me in the cabin, so we met for dinner before driving over there. I'd never actually slept in the office cabin, and it felt strange to think about staying there; it had been almost twenty years since I was there in my own cabin. It felt like we were in someone else's home, and actually, we were. First it was Sam's and now it was Johnnie's. And soon, Louise would add a female touch to the place. Thankfully, I'd remembered to bring a book and while Noah watched television, I sat and read.

"I don't like sleeping in someone else's bed," I said. "I'm having a hard time getting comfortable, and for some reason, I miss the dogs."

"The sheets are clean and they smell good, so just think about it like staying in one of the cabins, or a hotel."

Noah was always so practical. I punched him and then turned on to my side.

The next morning, I thought it was odd when Thalia Alvarado from the market called to see if we had any cabins available for a few weeks. I didn't want her to think we were desperate for lodgers, so I said, "Let me look and see what we have," before I told her we had plenty of room. I knew her from Stater Bros. market up here where she was a checker, and I didn't want to pry by asking her why she needed a place to stay. Maybe she'd had damage to her cabin and needed to be out of it while the workmen were there. I hung up, figuring I'd find out soon enough. I told her I'd leave her a key under the bird feeder outside cabin two.

"And call me if you have any issues," I said.

That night when I got back to the cabins, I found Thalia sitting by a crackling fire in the fire pit. I left my things in the car and walked down to join her.

"It's a beautiful evening, isn't it?" I said.

"Sit," she said.

I took a deep breath and closed my eyes.

"Sometimes I can never get enough of the mountain air to suit me," I said.

"I feel the same way and I've been up her over twenty-five years."

"So, what's going on with you? I haven't seen you in the market lately."

"Well, I have the craziest story to tell you."

She leaned forward in the Adirondack chair, and for a moment I thought she was going to get up. But she sat back and sighed.

"My nephew was found dead a couple of months ago."

She pressed her lips together in thought.

"They thought he was run over by a car. Well, he was, but that wasn't what killed him. He was a little on the slow side and found a great job at a mortuary down the hill. He'd worked there for a couple of years.

One night, about two in the morning, someone found him under the car, between the front and back tires, and indeed he'd been run over."

She pulled out a pack of cigarettes and said, "Do you mind if I smoke?"

"No," I said. "Go ahead."

"I've tried to stop, but all this mess got me to start again. So I went down to be with my sister, and I had this harebrained idea to rent my cabin out for a few months to make a little extra money instead of just letting it sit there. I hired a realtor in town to take care of it. That's why I need a place to stay."

She lit her cigarette and exhaled a huge cloud of smoke.

"It turns out that wasn't such a great idea. Sure, I made a few bucks, but now I'm back and the people staying there don't have to leave for a couple more weeks. So now I'm going to have to spend money to stay somewhere."

She brought the cigarette to her lips, inhaled, and then blew a smoke ring as she exhaled.

"Anyway, it seems the car was stolen, so they took it to the impound lot. They brought my nephew to the mortuary where he worked. My sister said they didn't need to do an autopsy since they knew what killed him. They had his burial and just when everything seemed to be calming down, a detective went to the impound and checked out the car. There was no damage to the front end where my nephew would have been hit before he was run over, so they did a more thorough test of the interior and found his blood inside."

"Good god," I said, shocked.

"Yeah. So now they're figuring something fishy is going on. Well, it turns out the mortuary took out a life insurance policy on my nephew."

"What?"

"Well, someone at the mortuary went in and took out a policy, claiming he was my nephew, and took a physical and everything. Funny that he added accidental death benefits, and the mortuary was listed as the beneficiary."

"Thalia," I said, speechless. "I don't know what to say."

"I know. And of course, the life insurance policy is bogus, which would have been a godsend to my sister."

Thalia lit another cigarette.

"This makes me want to light up myself and I don't even smoke," I said, still amazed. "This is almost as crazy as a plot for a movie."

"Right, huh?"

"I'm so sorry your sister had to go through this. And you too."

"I don't think she'll ever get over this. It makes me glad I never had kids."

We sat in silence for a few more minutes, and then I shrugged myself out of my chair. For some reason, her story reminded me of the other random tragedies I'd known about; the murder of the little girl when we first got our lake house cabin up here, the young man who'd wandered from the rehab facility and been found dead on the mountain side, and of course, John Murphy who'd committed suicide in cabin five so many years ago.

Individually and collectively, these were tragedies most likely no one had thought about in years.

"I'll bring over a counter top hot plate so you can at least make something to eat while you're here. I'll have Noah find it when he gets home."

"That'd be great, Annie. Thanks."

"And I can give you a good rate on the cabin, if you'll do your own housekeeping. When you change your bed, you can use the washer and dryer in the office."

"I appreciate that. I'll give it a good cleaning when I leave, too."

I was bursting to tell Noah all about Thalia when he got home, but he was so impatient to show me what he'd been up to, I didn't want to take the wind out of his sails.

"I think we should make a bucket list," he said. "I've been thinking about it and if we don't make a list of all the things we want to do, we'll never get around to doing them."

"What brought this on?" I asked.

"Well, I had to go down the hill for some materials, and I passed by this travel agent. I was curious. So I went in and found this cruise to Alaska."

I started to interrupt him.

"Now before you say anything, what if we went on it for our twentieth? It's not that far away and it would give us plenty of time to plan."

"Is this something on your list?"

"Well, I only thought about it when I was looking at all the travel brochures. But yes, it would be."

I hadn't given a bucket list or traveling much thought, but Alaska sounded great.

"I'd definitely be interested," I said.

"Good, then. Let's start thinking about things we'd like to do before we get decrepit."

I waited until we went to dinner to tell him about Thalia.

A few months later, a young man stopped by the store. I was busy with a customer, so I told him I'd be right with him.

"Johnnie at the cabins said I could reach you here," he said, handing me his card.

"William Barlowe," I said aloud, reading it.

"That's me. But you can call me Will. And it's Barlowe with an 'e'."

"I see. Okay, Will Barlowe with an "e", how can I help you?"

"As you'll see from my card, I'm a location scout and Universal is planning on doing a film set up here in the mountains. I need a setting with cabins, and your name is on the list to check out," he said with a quick smile.

"And how exactly does that work?" I asked.

"Well, I have certain parameters I need to work with based on the story. I like to say I look for real places for fictional locations."

"And what's the story about?"

"After a breakup, a woman returns to her family's cabins, and a Hollywood actor comes up to prepare for an upcoming role."

"Ha!" I blurted. "It sounds like my life!" I said, finding it impossible to keep a straight face. "Can I star in it?"

"Well, um," Will hesitated.

"I'm just kidding."

"Oh, I can see that."

"So you need a set of cabins?"

"Yes."

"And how long would the filming take?"

"Probably three weeks."

My next question was going to be, 'And what would I be paid,' but instead I said, "How does the studio pay for that?"

"It would be approximately ten thousand per week," Will said.

"And what about any damages? I've heard stories about how things can get damaged during filming."

"The studio would take care of any repairs and pay for any changes they might want on the set."

"Hmm," I said. "Do you want me to meet you at the cabins?"

"That would be great if you have time. I stopped by, so that was the first step."

"Ok, what works for you? I can meet you in about an hour."

"That would be fine. I'll see you there."

My interior alarm went off, and I thought about calling Noah, but I wasn't sure anything would come of my meeting, so I got busy finishing up some paperwork so I could meet Will.

He was walking around the cabins, his camera dangling around his neck, and making notes on his clipboard when I pulled in. He nodded his head, acknowledging me.

I waved. "I'll be in the office," I called out.

About twenty minutes later, he came in and asked if he could see inside some of the cabins.

"Not that there will be many inside shots, but I'd like to take some photos of the layout if I can."

I started with cabin number one, and we chatted as he looked around.

"You know, a movie studio built these cabins in the late 1920s," I said.

"*Really?*" Will asked, surprised. "Which one?"

"I don't remember. I'll look it up in my guest book if you'd like. I still have all the records from back then."

"That'd be interesting to note. Who decorated the cabins?"

"I did. I'm an interior designer."

"They're super looking," he said. "They feel like the quintessential old cabin. You did a great job." Will paused as if in thought and then took more photos.

"Thanks. It's what I love to do," I said. "When will you decide where to shoot the movie?"

"In a couple of months. I have a few more places to check out, and then I'll send everything in to production. But I like your place."

"Thanks. It would be kind of exciting to be a part of something like that."

"Have you ever watched a movie being filmed?"

"No."

"It's very labor intensive, and it takes forever to get one shot done right."

"It doesn't seem that way when you watch a finished film."

"That means we did our job."

Will gathered all his paraphernalia, and I walked him to his car.

"Thanks for your time," he said, shaking my hand.

"You're welcome. Thanks for looking me up. Hopefully, something will come of it."

"Oh, you were going to look up the studio."

"I forgot. Come in to the office and I'll find it for you."

Will looked around the lobby and took more photos while I found the old guest registers. I kept them handy in one of the file cabinets, and a few minutes later, I found what I was looking for.

"It was Cecil B. DeMille," I said.

"Wow. I'll use that detail."

I watched Will's car drive off, and I suddenly had a premonition I would regret not telling Noah about my meeting. While I wasn't certain the studio would choose the cabins, I couldn't help but think there was a good chance of it, and then I'd find myself in my old role of making decisions without talking to him about it first. Meeting Will triggered memories of the times I'd created complications in our early relationship—like buying the design store and later expanding it to the next space without talking to him about it before I made the commitments. While Noah never made me feel like I had to ask permission, I knew if I would have run my ideas by him to get his opinion first, it would have caused less tension between us. Had I opened a door he may not have wanted to go through?

I knew it'd be worse if the film company said they were interested later and I had said nothing about it, so when he came home, I grinned sheepishly, bit the bullet, and said, "Oh, I forgot to tell you…"

Johnnie and Louise were due back on from their honeymoon later the next day, so in the morning before I left to go into the store, I had Noah help me give the place a thorough cleaning. I'd bought new pillows for the sofa in the office and a large evergreen tree for one corner. Recalling how I always kept bowls of scented pinecones throughout our family lake house, I collected, then cleaned and scented a bowl of them, and set them on the coffee table. I'd already ordered a personalized name sign for them with the letter 'S' on it, and Noah helped me hang it above their bed.

Once we'd changed the bed, I put some chocolates on their pillow, and then did a load of laundry before we locked everything up.

There was something magical about getting married; it was a time to plan your new lives together. You're hopeful for a happy life, and you can't imagine anything happening that would change it all. I wished them many happy years together.

I hoped they had a wonderful honeymoon, and I also hoped they'd be happy in the cabins for a long time to come.

CHAPTER ELEVEN

The next year passed so quickly, it reminded me of watching a movie where the pages of a calendar fly off into thin air, and it suddenly becomes a new year.

In March, Ginny's changed hands again, and I was hoping it wasn't a bad sign. I couldn't help but wonder if she'd roll over in her grave. No one knew if it was because they couldn't make it, or if someone came in and offered them enough money to make it worth their while. I would have loved to get my hands on the remodeling project, but the new owners tore everything out before anyone was aware they were going to make any changes.

"Well, at least now we know what it's going to be," Sarah said one morning. "They've put a sign in the window that says Coming Soon! Joe's Diner."

"Leave your card and ask if they need any graphic design help with the menu," I said dryly.

Within the month, Joe's opened and, as with any new business, it seemed people lined up to get inside and check it out. Joe, the new owner, had done an impressive job redecorating and when Sarah and I went in for lunch, I hated to admit anyone could do as good a job as I could.

"My pride is wounded," I said.

"Are you pouting?" she asked, trying to suppress a smile.

"Don't pick on me."

Joe had kept the newly installed ceramic flooring and old buckets that had been retrofitted into light fixtures, but he recovered the old sagging booths and replaced the tables and chairs. He put new blinds along the back wall which and added a woodsy pattern fabric valance. I didn't want to admit whoever helped him had a good eye, and I actually looked for things I would have done differently. Finally, I figured it out.

"I would have done different artwork."

"Are you kidding me? You're being a brat."

"Well, I would have."

After we finished, I went to the restroom, and they'd taken out the two cramped stalls and made it a single large bathroom with new flooring and walls.

"Now I hate it for sure," I said, picking up my purse. "I admit I'm a little bitter they didn't hire us."

"I can see that, but you'll get over it," Sarah said, nudging me as we walked back to the store.

Where was Sarah's pity when I needed it?

The air was cool and still one morning in April when the loud siren and flashing lights of our town fire truck brought everyone out to watch as it raced up the street to the movie theater. Bright, angry flames shot into the air, and even from a block away, I could tell there would be extensive damage. Only a month ago, the owner closed it down for remodeling, and what might have started out as a simple project looked like it could now become a total loss.

It always annoyed me when lookie-loos showed up at an accident or emergency scene, and sure enough, within minutes, people gathered around and watched as firemen battled the flames, and an ambulance took someone away. I knew we'd eventually hear the details, and sure enough, within the hour, Louise Huxley came into the store to fill us in. She'd been one of those people who wanted to know firsthand what was going on.

"I overheard them say someone most likely started the fire," she said, breathless from her walk back down the street. "And one of the workers was taken away with smoke inhalation."

The theater was fortunately built within a natural windbreak area so the fire didn't spread to surrounding trees and buildings, but it took all afternoon to extinguish the fire. Once it was under control, all but a few firemen remained to ensure there were no hot spots left. They sifted through debris and sprayed down any areas that could possibly reignite.

The grocery store down the street sent over cases of bottled water and sandwiches for those who could take a break and eat. And when Noah came by the store, he checked in with the men to see if there was anything he could do to help.

The air was still, but the smell of smoke and sulfur wafted through town. It was the same smell I smelled when we went to Todd and Toni's burned down house, and I couldn't help but think about them.

Guards were posted throughout the night, and in the morning, emergency fencing was put up. Within a few days, crews were cleaning up the site and hauling away debris. One minute the theater was there, and the next all remnants of it were gone.

For our nineteenth anniversary, we celebrated by spending Saturday night down at the world famous Mission Inn in Riverside. When I made our room reservation, I also made a reservation for the Sunday brunch, which was always an extra treat. It was a miracle we got a table at a wonderful Italian restaurant across the street, called Mario's Place.

"This was one of the best Italian dinners we've had in a long time," Noah said, sitting back in his chair and patting his stomach.

I'd had something new for me; shredded zucchini called zoodles. It was delicious, with a fraction of the calories of traditional noodles, and Noah had lasagna.

We'd eaten early enough that the stores were still open, so we walked around the promenade and window shopped. We went into the antique store and I found a bronze dog statue, some old pipes in holders and a few old leather-bound books. Noah found a large wicker fishing creel and several reels that we could hang on the wall next to a vintage fishing pole and taxidermied fish he'd found a few years ago. I'd sworn there wasn't room for one more item in the cabin, but somehow we managed to keep adding things to our collections.

That night, I told Noah to take his shower first, and then, after my turn, I slipped into the new negligee I'd bought and stood in the doorway.

"Ta da," I said, leaning against the doorway to our room.

My eyes were drawn to Noah, and my breath caught. He was lying in bed with the sheet partially covering his legs and abdomen, and I was transported back in time almost twenty years ago, before we started our relationship. He joined me at the San Francisco furniture market when I was making all the decorating selections for the restoration of the cabins. To save on expenses, I'd only booked one room with a sofa bed, and he was relaxing on the bed waiting for me to come up to go to dinner. It was a warm summer afternoon, and he'd unbuttoned his shirt to cool off. I startled him when I opened the door, and he'd jumped up and fumbled with this shirt, but not before I took in his muscular upper body with a hairline that traveled from his belly button to below where his jeans started.

I remember my breath caught then, and it did so again now. It was like it was yesterday. In all our years together, I never grew tired of his handsome face and his masculine body.

I felt myself grow warm, and Noah shot me an approving but mischievous smile.

"You remind me of San Francisco," I said.

"I remember," he said, "and not making love to you that night was one of the hardest things I've ever done. I couldn't be in the same room with you without thinking about being together. But then you know that. You know I wanted you the minute I met you, when you were checking into the cabins."

"And now you have me. It's been nineteen years, and I can't believe it," I said. "Where did the time go?"

"Well, if you want to finish what you came out here to do to me, I'll show you how time flies."

Noah pulled the sheet back and there was no doubt he was waiting to show me how he felt. I teased him by my taking my time removing my negligee and letting it drop to the floor. I knew this was going to be a night just like when we first fell in love. When his caresses brought me to such heights, I later cried because I had someone so kind and gentle who loved me.

In the morning, we waited for the sunlight to shine through our windows to wake us. Even then, we were both lazy, but eventually we got up and showered. We almost missed our reservations for brunch downstairs. We made several trips through the buffet, filling our plates first with fruit and sweet rolls, and then going back for prime rib, eggs, bacon, and waffles. When we were finished, I couldn't believe I'd eaten so much.

"We had to restore the calories we burned last night," Noah said when I told him I was stuffed.

We went back to our room and packed our bag. I did the cursory last look around to make sure we had everything, and then I called for the valet to bring our car around. We had a few minutes to spare, so we went downstairs. I loved looking around the hotel lobby and admiring the mix of Spanish, Moorish and Mediterranean architecture, along with the meticulously landscaped outdoors. The hotel took up an entire square block, and it was a fascinating destination. So many famous people had stayed there over the years, and they did an excellent job of maintaining the property.

"We should come back for the holiday when everything is lit up," I suggested. We'd thought about it over the years, but had never taken the time to come down. I'd heard it was almost like going to Disneyland with all the lights and crowds.

There were three things I remember most about that July.

Although the mountain was known for its sometimes fluctuating weather, what I was most surprised by was the fog. We'd had the expected May Gray and June Gloom, but when the town woke to July days of morning fog rolling in, it was perplexing. After starting out on the cool side, the days turned warm. While I normally tried to stay out of the sun, by the time the sun came out, I found myself taking a break and letting the warmth soak into my skin.

The second thing I recall was seeing a large For Sale sign go up on the fence around the movie theater. We wouldn't find out until later that old Mr. Langley had gotten in over his head when he started his remodeling project; he tore out some walls and found extensive termite damage and dry rot. The project had already run over budget, and he figured the only way he was going to come out ahead was if a major fire destroyed the building, he could use the insurance money to finish restoring the place. Speculation was that when he started the fire, he hadn't planned on the building burning to the ground.

And the third was, sadly, Mr. Langley ended up losing the property and going to jail for insurance fraud. Even sadder, the property would sit cleaned up but vacant for over a year before a new investor stepped in to build a new theater.

In the fall, rumors spread that our historic ice skating rink was going to close. Built in 1988, it was the training center for Olympian skaters and had become world famous when Michelle Kwan trained there. In all the years I'd been up in Lake Arrowhead, I'd never been to the rink, as it was primarily touted as a training facility for beginners and skaters from around the world. It was always sad to watch as businesses ended up closing their doors, and I hated to see the closing make the headlines of the local paper.

After a heavy snowstorm that winter, the roof caved in, and when no one stepped up to buy the building, it was demolished.

For months, I'd driven by a piece of property along the highway and every time I did, I was more intrigued by it. The For Sale sign out front had a phone number on it, and I was tempted to write it down. It looked like there was a small diner with a bar attached, several retail stores (two of them vacant), and four cabins. Surrounded by tall pine trees, it reminded me of a small western town, with a combination of log exteriors and worn redwood plank siding. It was actually quite charming.

Oh a whim, I pulled over one day and got out and walked around. While there were two entrances, one for the bar and one for the diner, when I walked in to the diner side, I saw it was just one large room. Two men who were sitting at the bar drinking beer turned in my direction.

It smelled like a mixture of bacon and old cigarettes, but it wasn't unpleasant.

"Hey there," the bartender said. "Can I get you something?"

"I'd just like an iced tea," I said, finding a booth on the diner side.

The bartender brought me my tea and then checked on the couple a few tables over, just finishing their lunch.

"Here you go," he said as he gave the man the check.

"See you later," the husband said as they got up.

"See you, John," the bartender said, picking up the cash.

After about ten minutes, I got up, paid my bill, and walked outside. I peeked into the yarn shop that was open; over in a corner, two women were knitting, and two others looked like they were trying to decide on yarns. Someone was at the cash register, and it appeared the store was holding its own. I then looked in the windows of the stores that were empty; since it was a route I didn't ordinarily take, I didn't recall what they'd been before. There was no old signage in the windows and nothing inside gave me any clues.

The cabins looked inhabited; one was large enough to be a house, and the remaining three cabins were larger than mine, so I thought they could be at least one bedrooms. A For Rent sign was taped to one of the windows.

"Can I help you?" a woman asked as she came out of the largest cabin.

"I was just looking at the property," I said. "Is the owner around?"

"No. She used to live here in the big house, but she's moved down the hill. I hate to see her sell it, knowing the rent's going to go up when she does."

I nodded.

"If you're interested, you can call the number on the sign. Her name's Margaret Campbell, but she goes by Maggie."

"Thanks, I will. Have you been here long?"

"About six months. I moved in when she went down to live with her daughter in Fontana. Are you from up here?"

"Yes," I said. "My name is Annie."

"I'm Amy. Nice to meet you."

She reached out her hand, and I shook it.

"Thanks for the info. I'll give Maggie a call," I said, taking one last look around.

When I got back to the store, I called Maggie and when she didn't answer, I left her a message. That night, I told Noah about the property, and it surprised me he actually acted intrigued. Maybe we'd been together long enough that my wild ideas no longer threw him for a loop.

"I've seen the property," he said.

"What if we could buy it?"

Now he made a face, and yet I could tell he could be interested.

"I left the owner a message," I said.

He looked at me noncommittally and then said, "See what she says."

His reaction amused me, and when he looked at me, he said, "What?"

The next morning, Maggie called, and we talked for almost thirty minutes. She told me she'd originally lived in Twin Peaks, and then when her husband died, she sold their cabin and moved into the one on the property.

"I wanted to be around other people," she said. "Now, though, my daughter wants me to be down by her, and although I hate leaving the mountain, it makes sense. I can't see keeping the property if I'm not up there, so that's why it's for sale. I'd like to sell it by owner, if I can. My attorney says if I find the right buyer, he can draw up the paperwork. I know it needs some work, but you sound young. That's the kind of person who needs to buy it. Someone who'll work on it."

My head was spinning when we hung up. With Noah and me restoring the property, we could bring back all its character. Then I had the craziest idea of all; what if we went into partners with Sarah and Josh?

It would be a wonderful opportunity for them, and it would be less of a financial burden for us. I had no doubt we could turn it around, and by having partners, the restoration and management could be shared. After being friends for so many years, I felt confident we wouldn't have any issues; no matter what we did with them, they always carried their own weight. I would talk to Noah about it when he got home.

Two weeks later, the four of us sat down and signed all the paperwork. We went in as equal partners, and we set up a separate checking account to manage the finances. Noah and Josh were the perfect ones to work on the restoration, and Sarah and I worked on ideas to bring the exterior back to life. The guys replaced any damaged wood on the buildings, then they stained it a rich brown. We wanted to add red shutters, and Sarah drew an outline of stocky pine trees and I asked Noah if he could cut these out of wood.

He scrunched his face in thought, and then said, "I don't see why not. I'll cut the front out of one side and the back out of the other."

They turned out amazing. Once we saw what he could do, we came up with images of a bear and a deer and when they were finished, we hung them outside the cabin windows. We filled galvanized metal water troughs with flowers and set them under all the windows, and then laid out gravel walkways around the cabins and edged them in rocks like those at our cabins.

By the end of October, we had a used book and knickknack store in one of the spaces, and a tenant for one of the vacant cabins. Sarah and I had talked about making the cabins weekend rentals, but permanent tenants would make the management easier, and we wouldn't have to have someone on site to oversee the property. In November, the last store was rented and two new tenants signed rental agreements for the stores.

CHAPTER TWELVE

Usually people didn't want to think about projects during the holidays, so I was surprised when a few design jobs came in during November. Both clients didn't live up here full time, and they wanted to get started before the snow came. The design store itself was slow, so I had Sarah go with me on both jobs so we could split our time.

The At The Cabin store was busy with both fall and Christmas sales, and we did a mailer encouraging our customers to bring in the card to receive a discount just to promote sales for a weekend. When so many people came in, I wondered if it had been such a good idea to do that, fearing we'd run low on merchandise, but we ended up selling more than double what we'd expected.

We filled our outside wagon with a synthetic pine tree and surrounded it with red and white artificial poinsettias. We'd left our scarecrow family intact from the fall scarecrow contest and while they were getting a little weather-beaten, we spruced them up by adding red and green plaid hats and scarves.

Christmas was on a Sunday that year, and even though business usually slowed down on Christmas Eve, I kept the store open so I could finish bringing out any back stock for the after-holiday sale starting Monday.

Noah took the day off and came by the store around one, and then we headed over to Sarah and Josh's for hamburgers and hotdogs for

Christmas Eve dinner. Since Ginny and Sam were gone, Sarah had become our go to place for Christmas dinner. Their children were older now, but they still wanted to open something before they went to bed, so I gave them what all aunties like me did: money. Somehow, I'd started a tradition of taping dollar bills end to end, and finding new ways to set them up so they would come out of a package. It was obviously no surprise, but the kids loved it, and we all got a kick out of watching them count their money.

On Christmas day, we all exchanged gifts; Sarah had gone back to doing watercolors, so I got her a personalized leather art journal, and I gave Noah and Josh storage clipboards they could use out in the field. The kids were the hardest to buy for, so I got them gift certificates for the new mall that opened in San Bernardino. It meant Sarah would have to take them down, but I figured that way, they could get whatever they wanted.

The day after the New Year was the official close of our after-Christmas sale, and Sarah's son and daughter came in to help us pack up and inventory what was left of our Christmas merchandise. Over the years, we'd learned to set the store up by category; for example, bears had their own displays, as did birds and mountain décor, so we each tackled a section and clearly marked the boxes as we taped them closed. I was grateful the weather had cooperated so far, and we were able to use the area outside to the left of the store to stack everything so that either Noah or Josh could pack it up in one of their trucks, and store it accordingly in the warehouse for the next year. That way, when we were ready to set everything up again, we could have them bring it over in stages.

Even though our Christmas sale was officially over, customers still trickled in to see what we had left. During the sale, we brought out the Bingo spinner and filled it with ping-pong balls marked with different discounts. That was the first thing that got packed away, and if customers came in and found something they wanted, we gave them fifty percent off whatever we hadn't already packed up.

Once I could see light at the end of the tunnel and knew they'd be all right without me, I worked in the design store, making new file folders and packing up last year's business receipts. But movement in the front window caught my eyes, and when I looked up, a woman who appeared to be in her late sixties was shielding her eyes with one hand so she could look into the store. In her other hand was an adorable black and tan dog with an orange bandana tied around her neck.

She saw me and waved.

I motioned with my hand to come in while I made my way to the front door.

"Are you open?" she called, slightly pushing the door in. "I see all the boxes outside."

"Ah. We're just packing up holiday merchandise, and we've made quite a mess, but we're definitely open. Come in."

With a handful of files, I made my way to the front of the store and I stepped aside so she could come all the way in.

"I'm Annie," I said, introducing myself. "Come in and look around. I'm just trying to organize myself for the new year."

"I've seen your ad in the newspaper and have been meaning to stop in. We had company over the holidays and this was the first chance I've had to get out. I need to work on my house." She kissed her dog on the top of its head. "Look at all this, Thelma."

She looked around for a moment. "I'm Maria Harmon," she said, reaching her hand out to shake mine. "Maria Theresa, actually. My mother had a Spanish girlfriend, hence the Spanish influence. But I just go by Maria."

She was striking yet relaxed, with her pure white simply styled hair and red lipstick, and she wore a black turtleneck sweater, black pants, and an emerald green linen blazer.

"Where's your home?" I asked.

"I live in Crestline."

The San Bernardino mountains' major artery is Highway 18, and if you travel far enough, it'll take you to any one of the collections of small towns up here. Starting with Crestline and Valley of

Enchantment, beyond that, there's Rim Forest, Twin Peaks, Agua Fria, Blue Jay, Lake Arrowhead, Sky Forest, Running Springs, Green Valley and finally Big Bear.

Over the years, I'd had clients from most of our little towns, and I recalled two I'd recently had from Crestline. One was a woman who wanted to decorate her home to turn it into a rental when her family wasn't using it. She wanted each room to be different, and it brought back memories of restoring my cabins years ago. The other customer was a company who bought an old rundown hotel and turned it into a mini corporate retreat.

"What are you thinking of doing?" I asked.

"Well, my husband and I just retired. He was the phone company's top salesman for the Yellow Pages and I was an x-ray technologist in Los Angeles. My father lived up here until he had to go into a home, and when he passed away, Joel and I decided to move up here. The house is a mess, what with a bachelor living there all by himself for so many years. I think the place needs just about one of everything. I hate to get rid of the old look, but it definitely needs help."

She spent a few minutes looking at some hanging fabric samples, and then she moved over to the area rug display.

"We don't have a large budget," she said.

"That's fine. You don't need one if we help you. I just need to know what you'd like to do if it was a perfect world. Then we can come up with some happy mediums. I like to work with what someone has first, and then come up with a plan."

"What do you think, Thelma?" she asked her dog. She was rewarded with a kiss.

On the morning of our appointment, I found Maria's home on a quiet, tree-lined street that hid most of the surrounding houses. Most of the homes had wood carved name and address plaques nailed onto the tree nearest their driveway, which was the only way someone could find the right address. When I saw their sign, I pulled in, and when I got out of my car, I immediately breathed in the earthy, woodsy scents of the deep forest.

Even before I knocked, Thelma barked to announce my arrival. With a pipe in his mouth, Joel opened the door, but not before he reached down and picked Thelma up.

"She gets excited and runs off if we don't keep an eye on her," he said. "Come on in."

She squirmed in his arms and as I stepped in to the entry, her tail was wagging and her tongue was licking her lips, ready to either bite me or give me kisses.

"This lady doesn't want you slobbering all over her," he said, finally putting her down.

Today, Thelma was wearing a red floral neck scarf to match Maria's red top and black pants. I reached to let her smell my hand, and she enthusiastically licked it before she jumped to lick my face.

"Thelma!" Maria scolded. "You know better than that."

"She's really cute," I said. "We've always had dogs, and I miss having them around. What is she?"

I dropped my purse as I petted her, and Thelma quickly had something new to investigate.

"We rescued her and we know she's a Schnauzer mix, with a lot of terrier. Well, come on in," Maria said, leading me further into the living room. "See what I mean? There's stuff everywhere, and we're staying here, but we can't move in until we clear it all out."

I got out my notebook and said, "We don't have to do everything all at once, like I mentioned in the store, but tell me what you'd like to see? What do you like about the room? What would you like to keep, and how would you like to see it when we're finished?"

We went room by room and I made notes.

"Can I take a few photos?" I asked.

"Oh, dear. It's all quite a mess."

"We'll get through it, but it's a way for me to remember details about the rooms. It's a lovely home," I said truthfully. "And it's larger than it looks from the outside. I can see why you love it."

The house was built with my favorite materials; log on the outside, with a mixture of log and knotty pine on the inside. The three bedrooms just needed deep cleaning and decluttering, and the bathrooms could stand to be updated. The showers and toilets were old.

When we made our way back to the kitchen, Maria said, "I really like the old kitchen, but I hate the counter tops. What can we do?"

I told her about what I did with Carrie Davis's kitchen, how we left the old cabinets intact, but put on a new live edge wood counter. I noticed the laundry room was more of a shed outside along the kitchen wall, and after taking a look at it, I suggested we cut an opening through the wall and weatherproof the room so she wouldn't have to make the trek outside every time she wanted to do laundry.

"I like that. What do you think, Joel?"

"Whatever you say, love," Joel said, tapping his pipe into an ashtray. "Me and Thelma are just here to keep you company."

"Joel is such a dear. We've been married almost thirty years now," Maria said. "He's actually my third husband," she whispered conspirationally. "Both husbands one and two were bums, so I tossed them out. They say the third time is a charm." She winked.

She tried to contain herself, but let out a stifled laugh. It surprised me she was so open and honest.

"Yeah, well, Noah and I have been married almost nineteen years. I was married before," I said. "He's a keeper too."

"Well, good for you, honey," Maria said, patting my arm. She then nodded slightly and said, "I wouldn't mind replacing the living room furniture." She wrinkled her face. "But I don't want to bust the budget. We did well selling our house down the hill, and I want to keep some of that money in the bank."

I knew just the place to take her. Once I worked out a floor plan, we'd stop in the furniture store across the street from the design store and see what she could purchase from the floor.

"Where do you want to start? I was thinking the master bedroom, and then the living room?"

"That's what I was thinking too," Maria said. "I want to get moved in, so we might as well. What should I do first?"

I gave her my ideas for the bedroom first. I made a list of things she could do herself, starting with the obvious; cleaning out the closet, dressers, and shelves and separating things she wanted to keep versus throw away or donate.

"Are you going to hire someone to oil the walls and clean the wood flooring?" I asked. "I have someone I can recommend. You'll have to stay somewhere while they do it, but if you're not going to officially move in yet, it might make sense to finish the sorting and have it done all at one time. It's up to you, though. That way, when you get your new bedroom furniture, you can move in."

"I like the way you think," she said, nodding.

When I got back to the store, I worked on Maria's floor plans, and then I called Rebecca from the furniture store across the street and talked with her about bringing Maria in. So far, our business relationship had worked out even better than I thought it would. I'd already brought in a few clients, suggesting furniture pieces they could use, like I was going to do with Maria, and a few of their customers had come in to the store, letting me know they'd been referred to us.

In the meantime, Noah said he'd be available the next day to look at the countertop in the kitchen.

"We can grab a bit for lunch, before," I said to Noah.

CHAPTER THIRTEEN

After our meeting with Maria, Noah and I met at a place Noah knew about called The Stockade.

"I haven't been there in ages, but it always had great food. I think it just changed hands, so I wouldn't mind checking it out."

I knew I'd found the right place when I saw the weathered wood front that looked like a saloon in an old western movie. An oversized American flag mounted on top of the front billowed in the cool breeze, and bunting flags were anchored to the exterior wood panels of the porch. Three souped-up motorcycles with leather saddlebags were parked to the left, but I found a place to park just past them. I had a horrible thought about someone accidentally knocking them down like dominoes! I wondered if they'd think it was funny if I went in there and told them I'd done that.

I stopped to read the old weather-beaten wood sign that announced vittles, whisky, daily specials and Sunday brunch. At the bottom, in bold letters, it said FRONT DOOR with an arrow pointing to the right, and underneath that it said, Back Door Is In The Back.

I went inside and passed two middle-aged men paying pool. A third stood to the side, and when I saw leather jackets hanging on a hook, I wondered if they were the bikers. When I saw how rough they all looked, I decided to keep my humor to myself.

The barman asked, "One?"

Dear Noah

"No, two," I said.

"Anywhere you want to sit," he said as he wiped down the countertop.

The main room was dark, but my eyes quickly adjusted and I found a table over in a corner where Noah would be able to find me. I ordered us both something to drink.

Signed dollar bills were stapled everywhere on the ceiling beams and the walls just like the place we stopped at in Oatman, Arizona. There were taxidermied deer heads, pictures of John Wayne, and even a buffalo head mixed in between them. Something smelled good, and my stomach grumbled.

A few minutes later, Noah came in and found me.

"What a place, huh?" he said, looking around.

Noah ordered spaghetti with chili, and I opted for my standby, a club sandwich.

Just as we were finishing, a man who looked to be in his late thirties came in and gave the barman a fist bump.

"Hey Chip," the barman said.

"I'm assuming that's the new owner," Noah said.

In a knitted cap, a wool checked Pendleton shirt jacket, jeans and boots, he reminded me of how Noah and his men dressed when they were working outside. He pulled his cap off and hung it on a hook by the bar. He ran his hand through his light brown hair and then made his way around the tables.

"You two doing okay?" he asked us.

"Great. Are you the new owner?" Noah asked.

"That's me. What do you think of the place?"

"The food's delicious," I said. "And I love the décor. Have you ever counted how many dollars you have hanging up there?"

"We have. It's over five hundred. Crazy, huh? If you want to leave a dollar, I'll make sure we find a place for it."

"Sounds good. We will," Noah said.

"Where you guys from?"

"Sky Forest," Noah said. "Right off Kuffel Canyon."

"You're kidding. I just bought and remodeled the commercial property on the corner. The stores and the sandwich shop."

"Where the hair salon and bottle shop are?" I asked.

"Yeah, and I'm trying to get the old Hungry Bear Sandwich Shop turned into a BBQ, but the county has been dragging me on for forever, so I'm thinking of making it a coffeehouse."

"It's a perfect location for one. We wish you luck," Noah said.

"Well, it's really a small world, isn't it?" Chip said.

"It is. And again, you've done a great job here," Noah said, taking out his wallet.

"No, here, let me get that. We're neighbors."

Chip picked up our bill and headed back off towards the bar.

We left a sizeable tip.

Noah took off, and I stayed in town.

I'd only been in the Goodwin's Oak Trunk store in town a few times, and I wanted to see what was new. I strolled through the aisles of scrapbooking paper supplies and other craft materials and then looked at fabric that might make cute valances for over Maria's kitchen sink. I couldn't resist the candy counter, and when I saw dark chocolate-covered almonds, I had to buy some. Hopefully, they'd make it home without me eating them all. I checked out the ice cream choices and broke down and had a scoop of mint chocolate chip in a cup. There was an antique store I hadn't been to for a while, so before I headed back home, I went inside. I found some old leather-bound books and a bronze chipmunk statue I couldn't resist.

It was almost three o'clock when I checked my watch, and I considered not going back to the store, but I still had some paperwork on my desk, so I made myself turn onto the road into town. I was glad I did, for when I got there, I had a message from Noah that he and Josh were going to work late and we could go grab a bite when he got home.

The next morning, I met Maria at the store to show her the floor plans before we headed across the street to the furniture store. I wanted her to have an idea of what I was thinking before we went in there so she could decide which pieces were most important to her. Rebecca let us wander through the store, and when we finally made some decisions, we showed her the pieces we wanted. She wrote up the order, and she and Maria made arrangements for delivery. A distinct advantage to using the store was that everything could be purchased from the floor and we didn't have to wait weeks like we would have to if I'd special ordered it.

"Do you feel like lunch?" Maria asked. "I'd like to treat."

I was always hungry, so we went to Joe's Diner. Maria hadn't been there, and commented on how nicely it was decorated.

"Did you do this?" she asked.

I wanted to tell her I could have done a better job decorating, but that would be lying, so I just said the new owner did it himself.

"So tell me about yourself," Maria said.

I was always careful about sharing too much about my private life when clients asked. A client once told me about an affair she'd had with her husband's best friend, and once someone has shared something like that with me, it was impossible to unhear it. Every time I saw her after that, it was like she was wearing a placard, and I was glad when she eventually moved off the mountain.

I told her about buying the cabins and restoring them, then about starting my design business up here. I told her Noah and I had been married nineteen years, and that I loved being in the mountains.

Maria said, "I'm originally from Memphis, but we eventually ended up in Albany, New York, then California. I met Joel at the supermarket of all places. We kept running into each other and he finally asked me if I'd like to go to the movies."

She paused, as if thinking. "For forty-five years, I was an X-ray technologist doing CTs and MRIs in Los Angeles," she said.

"Wow," I said, surprised at the length of time she'd spent in her career. "Tell me about that," I said. "Did you have any interesting cases?"

"Well, for years I was in the Trauma Center in the ER. That's where we got all the extreme cases. The stress of being on call was sometimes overwhelming, and I remember one night, I was called in seventeen times to scan patients. Most patients went from ER to me, then to the operating room. I felt I was a key factor in saving almost ninety percent of those admitted."

I hadn't expected such a profound story, and I truly wanted to know more.

"I've never met anyone who had that type of job. I don't know if I could do that."

"Well, I didn't start out thinking I was going to do that sort of thing. I thought it would just be taking someone's X-ray."

Her face softened, and she smiled. "One of my favorite patients was a young man in his thirties. He had testicular cancer, and had just started his treatment. He was told he'd never have children. Can you imagine hearing that if you wanted to have a family? Well, when he was thirty-two, he came in for his scan, and in his arms was the most beautiful baby I'd ever seen. I was supposed to be professional, you know, but I couldn't help crying."

She reached for my hand, and her brown eyes were full of warmth.

"You know," she continued, "I had a bout with lady cancer, so I never had children of my own. But I had plenty of nieces and nephews to spoil. And our new neighbor up here has the cutest little girl. I'll have someone else to dote on."

This was one time I wanted to share with someone about my miscarriages, but my professionalism kicked in, and my pride was right behind it.

"You're lucky," I said. "I don't have children either, but my best friend does, so I've had her children to love. "

Lunch came, and for a few minutes, we ate in silence. I was still curious about Maria and her job, so I continued. "Did you retire from the trauma center?"

"Oh no, I eventually went to Cedars-Sinai in L.A., where I got to meet a lot of famous, and not so famous, actors. I learned they were all just people, though, when they came in. They were just like us. I can't divulge any names, but I met one of my favorite actors, and he was so nice. He said, 'I love it when you tell me what to do,' when I was telling him when to hold his breath."

She chuckled.

I shook my head in admiration for her.

"I don't know if I could do what you did," I said again.

"Well, I'm sure you've had some interesting clients. What can you share about them? I'd think you know a lot of secrets that you can't tell, like me."

"Let me see," I started. "This one's a doozy. It's not about a client, but I didn't find out until after I bought the cabins that a man committed suicide in one. Number five, to be exact."

Maria's hand involuntarily went up to her mouth.

"Actually," I winced, "He killed a family from Crestline."

Now Maria's eyes widened.

"I know the story you're talking about," she said. "Normally I don't keep secrets from Joel, but I just found out that the family didn't live very far from us. I haven't decided yet whether or not to tell him. I'm afraid he'll freak out. What do you know about it?"

Maria leaned in.

"His daughter, the one whose father killed the family, actually told me the story. She came up while we were restoring the cabins and wanted to see where her father had hung himself. She'd called around and figured he'd stayed in a cabin up here. Years ago, when he died, her mother told her it was from a heart attack. Alyce was her name, and when her mother went into a home, she found newspaper clippings in her mother's belongings."

Maria's face had paled.

"Have I upset you?" Now it was my turn to seek out her hand. "I know I have." I gave it a squeeze and paused to let it all sink in.

"Do you want me to continue?"

"Absolutely. It just took me by surprise."

"Well, I checked the guest register, and a John Smith had stayed in cabin five around that time. The previous owner had used it as storage for over twenty years. Of course, there was nothing there for her to see. While she was helping me clear it out so we could use it, she told me what had happened; her father killed his best friend and business partner, and the *whole* family. She was obviously really disappointed she didn't leave with any answers, except that he'd indeed been there. But a few weeks later, I found the note he'd left. He'd tucked it inside an old mantel clock. Sam found it when he was cleaning it up to use it."

"What did he say?"

"Not much. I don't remember it exactly, but he said something like, *I've destroyed one family and now I'm destroying mine. I'm a monster.* I thought about not telling her I'd found the note, but Sam, who I bought the cabins from, and Noah told me I should send it to her. I did, but I never heard from her again."

"That's terrible."

Maria's mood had turned pensive, and I was to blame. One day, I would hopefully realize there are some things that are better left unsaid.

"I'm sorry if I've put a damper on our lunch," I said.

She gave me a weak smile, and then said, "No, you haven't, really. It's just such a terrible story. I don't think I'll tell Joel. He's so sensitive lately." Then she brightened and whispered, "I think it's his age."

"I have a more humorous story I can tell."

"Please."

"I had another client in Crestline. His name was Joe Baker, but he wanted people to call him Tex. And, yes, he was from Texas. He was an old rodeo rider, and he wore the largest belt buckle I'd ever seen. Noah had done odd jobs for him on and off over the years, and he invited him to one of our Memorial Day Festivals. He was demonstrating his roping techniques, and would give kids a dollar if he couldn't catch them with his lariat. Now, he was so good at it, he caught everyone who dared him, but he gave them a dollar, anyway.

"He eventually came in to the store and said, 'Noah tells me you're pretty good with organizing things. Tells me you keep him in line.'

"'I don't know about that,' I replied, 'but I do make him pick up after himself. You're very good, by the way. And I'm curious. Did you win that buckle?"

"'I sure did ,' he said, 'and I have plenty more at home. That's one thing I wanted to talk to you about. I promised my wife I'd get my collection organized, but I've never gotten around to it. I figured now was a good a time as any.'

"'Is your wife excited you're finally going to do it?' I asked.

"He said, 'Oh, she died years ago, about ten years after we moved up here. I didn't want to rush into it.'"

"It was all I could do to keep a straight face. I asked him when he wanted to get started, and he said any time I was ready. We set up a date, and although Noah told me how much there was to work with, I wasn't prepared for what all there was."

I counted on my fingers as I tried to recall everything he had.

"There were deer heads, mounted steer horns, a bleached out cow head, roping trophies, rifles, a bow with arrows, a bearskin rug, Indian blankets and rugs, paintings of deer and bear, and framed photos of him on the bulls. To make a very long story short, I asked him to take down anything he didn't want to keep hanging on the walls, and to sort through the stacks of books and collections he had sitting around on the floor.

"When we had our next meeting, I expected to see a nearly empty house, but I was in for a surprise; he'd only taken down a few things, and the stacks of books hadn't shrunk; they were just moved in to different stacks."

"Oh, dear," Maria said, stifling a laugh.

"That's what *I* said. I reminded myself it was my job to make this work. I asked him if he trusted me, and he raised his eyebrow and twisted his mouth in thought. 'I guess,' he finally said. I told him he'd need to leave while I did my handiwork. I had one of Noah's men help me take everything down, but Joe sneaked back in to the living room and said 'I guess you're takin' the bull by the horns here'. Then he turned around to leave.

"I told him to take a deep breath, because everything was going to be fine, and he'd love what I'd done when it was finished. We regrouped and rehung everything, and what I didn't use, I hung somewhere else, like down the hallway or in other rooms. I found his two display cases of belt buckles and buck knives and organized them. I took it upon myself to go through the books in his bookcases and I was able to eliminate some I thought weren't important and found homes for most of what was on the floor. In amongst it all, I found a framed photo of Joe and his wife and hung it in his bedroom.

"When he saw it, he mused on some private memories, and then said 'That there was one cowgirl I couldn't tame.'

"I should have written down some of the funny things he'd say, like 'I chewed more gravel than I care to remember,' meaning he'd been thrown from many a horse, or 'lickety split'. When I hung one of his handguns, he called it his shootin' iron. I never could call him Tex," I said.

I pushed my plate away, which was my way of telling myself to stop eating, then said, "So, there you have it."

When the waitress brought our check, Maria reached for it.

"It's I who should be buying *your* lunch. I'm so glad to have you as a client," I said.

"No, I told you the treat was on me."

We hugged before Maria got into her car.

"I've really enjoyed my day with you," she said.

"I'm really glad to have met you. You're a very special person, and the world needs more people like you."

I waved as she drove off.

That night, as I was telling Noah about my day, I tried to think of other things Joe used to say.

Noah said, "I remember him telling me 'you're barkin' at a knot' when he thought I wasn't going to be able to fix the leak around his fireplace. You know, he passed away a couple of years ago."

"I didn't know." I was sorry to hear that. "He was quite a character. I wonder what they did with all his things."

My next meeting with Maria was a week after her furniture had been delivered and set up. I knew they were happy with it, especially Joel, who had a new recliner.

"Are you a reader?" Maria asked when I saw her. "Do you like to read books?"

"Oh." She'd caught me by surprise. "I do, but not as often as I'd like to."

"Well, I've just started going to a local book club that meets on Wednesdays, and I'd love to invite you to one of our meetings. We take turns deciding which book to read, and then we talk about it at the next meeting. I think you'd like the ladies. There's about ten of us."

She started rattling off their names.

"Kathy used to work in a bank, and Leila—we call her our queen because she oversees the meetings—and then Liz manages to come, even though she has three kids."

"Leave Annie alone," Joel called from his new recliner. "If she decides to come to a meeting, she'll meet the women herself."

"Pfft," Maria said, waving him away with her hand. "I think Thelma needs a walk, Joel. Men. Anyway, consider yourself invited."

"It's almost impossible for me to get away during the week, but let me think about it." It *did* sound interesting. The problem was, I hadn't figured out how to find the time to read in years.

Noah replaced Maria's old countertop with a live edge wood one, and it updated the entire kitchen. When they oiled down the house, they did the kitchen cabinets as well, and it made a world of difference.

We spent the afternoon hanging pictures and arranging some accessories Maria had unpacked, and set out. I was a fan of setting aside everything we *didn't* use and storing it somewhere close so we could use it on another project. Maria was fine with that, and I helped her put the rest of the boxes in one of the guest bedrooms.

"They'll be fine in there. No one's planning on coming up that I know of," she said.

After we'd finished, Joel came back with Thelma and gave out a whistle.

"Well, you timed that right, didn't you?" Maria teased. "We did all the work. Do you like it?"

"I certainly do, my love," he said, giving me a wink.

CHAPTER FOURTEEN

It was the end of March by the time I realized I hadn't made arrangements for our anniversary trip to Alaska. Every time I thought about it, I got distracted. I didn't know how time had slipped by so quickly. One day, I was saying "I do" in the cobblestone area between the trees at Noah's cabin, and the next, almost twenty years had passed. Why I thought about David now, I wasn't sure, but where I'd once been a young girl thinking I'd be married to him until the end of time, I was now getting ready to celebrate twenty years of marriage to a completely different man.

While those years with Noah hadn't been perfect, they were close enough to it. If asked, I'd say we'd rank nine and a half out of ten. He'd tolerated all my whimsical—but good—ideas, and I was sure he was grateful I hadn't had many more brainstorms in these last few years that he wasn't onboard with. We were a good match; I was generally the idea man and doer, and he was definitely the doer.

I sometimes wondered if I should have slowed down and enjoyed the moments more, because they all seemed to fly by. Even more so as we've aged. Someone once said it was our perception of time that changed; we always had the same amount of minutes and hours in a day.

He was the wind beneath my wings.

What a wonderful thing to say to him when I bought his anniversary card.

Dear Noah

The other reason I'd mentally set our anniversary aside was I'd taken on a new client, who honestly had been running me ragged and it wasn't a great time to go anywhere. His name was Archie McIntosh, and while he and his wife Fiona had come to America for over fifty years, it was sometimes difficult for me to understand them, for they both spoke with a strong, lilting brr. With dark graying hair and pale eyes, Fiona was normally quiet and unassuming, and for the most part, went along with his imposing personality. While Archie was very definite about the majority of the decisions, every now and then, I'd catch him giving her a quick glance, and I wondered if, in private, she ruled the roost.

They were building a new home, including a boat dock in a wonderful gated community built around a cove called North Bay, and I always remembered the story Archie told me about buying the lot.

"The moment we drove through the gates, we knew this was where we wanted to build. We'd decided on a plot of land and the home plan we wanted. The estate agent, a modest little fellow, looked at his list of available properties and said, 'It doesn't look like that lot is available.' Well, that wasn't going to go over well with Fiona, so I took him aside and said, 'I'll bet you five thousand dollars, you can't fix that.' And he turned white as a sheet."

I'd been doing some furniture floor plans for them, and hadn't focused entirely on what he was saying, until he said five thousand dollars.

"So, once he got his color back, he went back to his plot plan and scratched his head. 'Well, Mr. McIntosh, it looks like I might have made a mistake.' He said. 'It doesn't look like there was a deposit on this one you're interested in, after all.'"

At this, Archie roared with laughter.

"And that's how we got that plot."

In an ideal world, when someone is building a new home, or even looking over plans an architect has drawn up, it's the perfect time for an interior designer to step in. Issues with electrical and plumbing can be avoided, and furniture placement can be recommended. At Fiona's insistence, I'd started working with them before they broke ground, and while Archie rarely confirmed it, when it was just Fiona and me, she pointed out how many potential issues I'd avoided by bringing something to their attention. As the building progressed, we needed to work more on the furniture placement, and I was surprised Archie eventually stepped back and let Fiona decide what she wanted to do.

"I think he's full of hot air," I once told Noah.

Archie owned a medical supply company, and in his words, he'd done quite well. He'd sold the company to his employees, and since their children were off and married, they were planning on moving up to the mountains full time once Archie's consultancy term ended. Until then, they came up to their small cabin on the weekends.

I finally confessed to Noah that I hadn't booked our trip and I was surprised he wasn't upset with me. He'd been busy getting ready to start a whole house re-do, and he agreed the time had gotten away from him, too.

"If we're going to do it, we need to do it now," he said.

I called our local travel agent, and after checking around, she told me miraculously there was still time to book a cabin. We only had two weeks to pack, and I felt stressed thinking about everything I still needed to do. It was almost impossible to sleep the night before our flight, for we had to get up at 3 a.m. to get to the airport in time to catch our flight to Vancouver, Canada, where the ship would sail.

I'd done something frivolous; I'd booked us first class, so even though the pancakes were as firm as frisbees, we still had breakfast. We stood in line after line and finally boarded the ship, then dropped our carry-on bags in our cabin and went down to the buffet. We were both tired and didn't feel like touring the ship, so we went back to our cabin and took a nap. The ship was leaving the harbor as we woke and got ready for dinner.

On our first day, we sailed all day and learned to navigate the ship. Our cabin was at one end and everything else was at the opposite end, but we were able to sleep in and then all we did for the rest of the day was eat. The next morning, our first stop was Icy Strait Point, where we saw charming red buildings built on pilings as we came to port; seeing them was like a picture postcard. The sky was completely gray, and there'd been a prediction of showers all day.

We originally had three tours booked for the day; one to see Alaskan native dancers perform, one to take an open air tramway up to the top of a hill, and the most promising one was to take a whale watching cruise. We were disappointed when we had to drop the dancers because the tour time was pushed up, making it impossible to do all three.

Rainy weather soaked our clothes the moment we disembarked, but we took it in stride. We knew the tram ride was doomed when we started up the hill and it was so foggy we couldn't see a thing. Like being in the mountains, the fog was beautiful, but it ruined the views of the valley below. We turned around without getting off and then made our way to the whale watching dock.

By then, the rain turned into a light drizzle and we were both surprised the sea cooperated with us and didn't make anyone on board seasick. For two hours we kept our eyes glued to the ocean waters and eventually we saw the moist air releasing from the blowholes of three whales before their tails quickly went back into the water. Everyone on board oohed and aahed as they alternated rushing from one side of the excursion boat to the other, and I didn't say anything, but I was disappointed we hadn't seen more. On the way back into port, we saw a school of dolphins swimming alongside us, almost as if they knew they were a source of entertainment to us.

We were starving by the time we made it back on to the ship, and the main dining room was packed. We waited over a half hour to be seated at our table, and Noah ordered a bottle of wine. I forgot to order my dinner with no gravy, and while I waited for our waiter to graciously have a new plate made up for me, I had a chance to study the other diners near us. Several young families sat with their children, and I was pleasantly surprised and grateful how well-behaved they were. When one child timidly waved at me, I waved back. His mother looked up and smiled.

"To our first day at sea," Noah said, toasting us. "We made it through the day."

"Yes, we did."

"Honestly, I was a little disappointed in the day. How can you come to Alaska and not see whales?" Noah said with a shrug and a grin.

"I was expecting to see whales propelling their bodies out of the water, like you'd see on National Geographic. I think I expected more after watching all the animals in the marine biologist's presentation last night."

It was still gloomy when we got to Skagway, but the rain stayed away. We took a vintage train ride, retracing the original route to the White Pass Summit, where thousands of fortune seekers made their way through this same trail into the area to get rich in the 1897 gold rush. Unfortunately, most of them either died from hypothermia, malnutrition or in avalanches or went back home, broke.

A mudslide on the road prevented us from taking a bus tour to British Columbia, so instead, we came back down the pass and went to our next stop—Liarsville. It was a tiny remote town named after journalists who came to the area during the Klondike Gold Rush, and printed tales of great wealth and prosperity. They treated us to a salmon bake, and since neither Noah nor I ate salmon, we filled our plates with baked beans, cornbread, scalloped potatoes, and cake. Local town folk entertained us with a silly singing skit before we got to pan for gold.

I couldn't help but feel bad for the older people who tried to navigate the ground with their canes and walkers. They tried to make the best of it, but the mud from the rains the previous day made the mud in some places impossible to get around.

"I promise I'll never get old," I whispered to Noah.

The highlight of the day was visiting the old brothel museum upstairs at the Red Onion Saloon. A young woman dressed in flashy historic attire and calling herself the madam gave the tour, which included climbing up a set of stairs. I saw those same people from Liarsville go back outside and wait for us there. When the tour ended, we all took photos of ourselves with her, and when someone gave her a tip, she tucked it into her bustier.

At dinner that night, our head waiter asked about our day, and we asked if he'd gotten the chance to leave the ship.

"I did," he sheepishly admitted. "I needed deodorant, and I was craving food from my homeland. On the ship, we get the same food every night," he whispered.

I surmised he was from the Philippines, as was a lot of the staff, but I asked him anyway.

"Do you have family back there?" I asked.

"Yes, I have my wife and children."

"When will you have a chance to see them?"

"Oh," he said, thinking, "In another two months. And then I'll have three months off." His face brightened.

"Now, don't go home and make another baby," I joked.

He laughed.

"Does your wife work?" I asked.

"Yes, she's a doctor."

"Oh," I said, a little surprised.

"She works in the operating room as an anesthesiologist, and her parents watch the children."

That night at dinner, along with an older couple near us, we celebrated our anniversary with a candle in our dessert and a serenade from our waiters. It was the first night we weren't both totally exhausted, and after quick showers, Noah and I made love.

Before we landed in Juneau, the ship sailed into the Endicott Arm and we saw Dawes Glacier. Some passengers actually got up at five in the morning to go out on to the ship's helipad in the freezing weather, but I was happy looking out our balcony door at six. At seven, we wrapped ourselves up in the thick bathrobes the ship provided, and we watched as the ship entered the fjord. While I'd expected to see great walls of ice on either side of us, there were only towering rock walls with a few icebergs floating in the water. As we got closer, though, I had to admit, seeing a glacier closely surrounded by shades of turquoise in the turquoise waters was an incredible sight. Small vessels, most likely carrying tourists, sailed close to the glacial mass, and I could only imagine seeing it up close where you could appreciate the magnitude of it. We heard the popping sound of a portion of ice crack and fall off into the water and then took photos of it floating in front of us.

The captain turned the ship three hundred sixty degrees around, so everyone on board had the same view. Over the loudspeaker, the cruise director reminded us this was home to a variety of wildlife, including humpback whales, harbor seals, bears and deer; unfortunately we didn't see any of those.

We docked in Juneau, and we saw the Mendenhall Glacier, and it was amazing to see how light reflected off the ice. Bald Eagles were everywhere, some soaring above or perched on trees. We sat for a while and just listened to the sounds of the waterfall, and I imagined they contained every frequency within the range of human hearing. Before we headed back to the ship, we made one last stop, and got a quick lesson on the life cycle of salmon at a hatchery.

Our final destination was Ketchikan, where we toured Potlatch Totem Park. Originally occupied by indigenous people, it is now privately owned. As promised in the tour's description, Totem poles welcomed us as we entered the grounds, and they were scattered throughout the path we took, letting us know visitors were welcome. The soles of our shoes were getting dirty from walking on the wet ground throughout the park, and we passed an older woman who had most likely lost her balance and fallen. Several people from her tour stood around her, signaling us to go on.

We wiped our feet at the entrance to the tribal house, a replica of the way people lived not so many years ago. I should have written down some of the stories he told about the totem poles and how they were used to convey legends, stories, and events. At one time, they were the only form of communication for the coastal Native Americans, as they had no written language of their own until the mid 1960s.

The tour ended with a trip through the building where they were carving a new pole, and it was interesting to learn about how they made the colors from natural pigments found in plants and ores (naturally occurring deposits of rock) and why they used them.

They used red, black, green, blue, and yellow, and each color had a specific meaning: red from red ochre clay material representing blood, war or valor; black from graphite or soot, for power; green for the earth, and blue for the skies, from copper ores; and yellow, from marigold blossoms or sunflower petals for sun, light, and happiness.

The bus ride back to the dock was unusually quiet, which made me think everyone on board was tired and probably dozing. Noah's head leaned against the window and I caught myself nodding off a few times myself.

We'd made dinner reservations at one of the specialty restaurants and while the food in the main dining room was good, this dinner was exceptional. We shared a filet mignon and a spaghetti Bolognese, and for dessert, Bananas Foster.

When we returned to our room, we were both full, and Noah patted his stomach.

"No one says we can't celebrate our anniversary twice in one week," he said as he seductively did a little dance.

"That's a move I haven't seen yet," I said.

I still loved looking at Noah, and when he asked me if I was happy, I could tell by the way he looked at me, he was a content man.

That night we had to pack our bags and leave them outside our rooms, and of course I waited until the last minute to realize I didn't have enough luggage tags. When I told our room attendant he panicked, and then once I looked farther into our disembarkation packet, I saw the extra tags I needed and called him. The next morning, along with half the other passengers on the ship, we grabbed a quick bite to eat in the buffet before we disembarked. A bus to the airport was waiting for us and the minute I got on board, the trip had ended for me and I started making notes, reminding myself of all that I had to do once we got back home.

As I'd felt a hundred times before, once we left San Bernardino, the winding road of Hwy 18 and the cool mountain air calmed me.

Chrysteen Braun

While the landscape of Alaska was beautiful and green, the trees in Lake Arrowhead welcomed me back home.

CHAPTER FIFTEEN

I saw Maria Harmon a few more times over the next couple of months when she would pop into the store to say hi. She brought me up to date about Joel's kidney stone and Thelma's trip to the groomer. She was ready to redo the guest bedrooms, and she told me over and over how much she loved living up here. And then I hadn't heard from her for almost a month, so I gave her a call but her answering machine picked up. One day, she showed up with a boot on her left foot. She'd fallen on their trip up to see Joel's sister in Oregon, and the store was her first outing.

"And Thelma needs a tooth pulled, so it feels like one thing after another."

Noah's project was turning into a job from hell, in his words. He was in constant conflict with the owner; the house was going up for sale once they finished, so the budget was tight, and often Noah would come home complaining that when he suggested something that really should have been addressed, the owner shot him down.

"All he wants to do is cut corners, and I don't like it," he'd said.

One Friday, I got a frantic call from Noah, who was at the hospital with one of his men.

"Is he going to be all right?" I asked.

"It's a dislocated shoulder and broken arm, and we all have a lot of bruises, but it could have been a lot worse."

When he got home later that night, he filled me in on the details. The house they were working on had two decks, and two of his men were trying to make repairs to the top one. Noah was on the bottom deck, going over the plans to rebuild it. They heard the spine-chilling, cracking sound as the termite-riddled wood of the top deck collapsed on top of him.

"Suddenly, I was under a mound of decking material and for a second, I was so disoriented, I thought I'd been crushed to death," Noah said. "Only slivers of daylight filtered through the dust, and the musty air almost choked me. The men were yelling, 'is anyone hurt?' and then I heard John cry out in pain. I could feel the weight of the two men who'd fallen with the top deck, and I pushed on some wood to let them know where I was."

"'I'm here,' John cried out again. 'Get me out!'"

Someone called an ambulance and by the time it got there, Noah was still coughing, but he patted his guys on the back and thanked them for acting so quickly. He rode in the ambulance with John to the hospital, all the while assuring him he'd be all right.

"We were all just lucky we didn't get killed," Noah said again that night in bed.

Even though the ER doctor gave him Valium, I could tell he was distressed.

"I love you," I said, cuddling next to him.

"Jesus, Annie, my eyes still burn from that dust," he said, rubbing his eyes.

I got up and found some eye drops, and after I dosed each eye, we lay there in bed. Eventually, I could tell from his slow, even breathing, that he'd drifted off to sleep. I relaxed, but just when I dozed off myself, I woke with a start. Suddenly, the image of that Indian woman in Sedona who read my fortune so many years ago came to me. She'd known I'd had loss in my life, and then told me I'd have more. I hadn't thought of her in years, and nothing had come of her prediction. But now, I wondered if Noah's accident was what she'd been talking about?

That night, we both tossed and turned, and each time one of us turned over, it woke us both. Noah cried out once, and the image of the Indian woman came back to me. When I finally got up, he rolled over, and I let him sleep. I was grateful he had the weekend to recuperate.

I went into the shop for a few hours on Saturday, and after calling Noah to check on him, I brought home something simple for dinner. His eyes were still a little red from all the dust, but I could tell he'd rested.

"How'd you do today?" I asked, setting our dinner out.

"Pretty good. I took another pill and then slept a while. It felt good."

I ruffled his hair like he was the little boy he looked like.

"Are you hungry?"

"Yeah, I am."

"You know I'm here for you if you need to talk about it," I said, sitting down at the kitchen table.

"I think I'm good. I talked to the guys, and John's doing okay, so that made me feel better."

"Good."

"But I've been thinking," Noah said, tapping his fork on his napkin.

I waited for him to continue.

"You know how we started our bucket lists?" he asked.

I nodded.

"Well, I'd like to add something to mine," he finally said. "I didn't say anything earlier, because I didn't want you getting riled up. But I want to go on a hunting trip."

He didn't give me a chance to talk before he added, "You know Bert at the Trading Post, well, his cousin has a pack station in Idaho. This is his last season, and he's getting ready to retire. He told Bert if he was ever going to make the trip up there, it had to be this year."

I didn't say anything.

"I've been looking in to it and Josh and I could go in the next two months and hunt black bear."

"Bear hunting?" I asked. "But you've never shot and killed anything. Why would you want to do that?"

"Well, even if I don't get one, we'd go out on horses, and with a guide, we wouldn't get lost."

"You sound like a ten-year-old right now," I said crossly. I couldn't believe he'd even want to do something like that. It was one thing having taxidermied deer and elk around us every day, but I couldn't imagine what he'd even want with a bear.

"And if you *do* catch something, besides a cold, what on earth would you do with it?"

I could see that not only had I questioned his ability to hunt, but I assumed when the time came, if he saw something, he wouldn't be able to shoot it. Without meaning to, I'd belittled him; I'd hurt his feelings and I could see it in his face. I'd talked down to him and I heard the words the second they crossed my lips.

It was the first time I'd seen a muscle quiver in his jaw. I'd hit a nerve. He put his fork down and then his brittle smile softened slightly.

"If I did, I'd have either a bearskin rug or a bear's head."

"Oh my god, Noah," I started, and I couldn't stop. With both my hands, I pushed the hair back off my forehead. "You were almost killed, and now you're thinking about going off hunting in the mountains somewhere where I'm sure there's no phone?" I laughed to cover my annoyance.

I said no more, and we both sat there in silence.

Noah's entire demeanor spiraled as he gave me a resigned shrug. He'd been trying to think of something he could do to get away and try something new, and I'd been focusing on nearly losing him in a freak accident. There was no reason why he couldn't go hunting, if that's what he really wanted to do. And even if they shot nothing—which I secretly hoped they wouldn't—it would be a wonderful opportunity for him and Josh to go do something exciting and daring.

I got up from the table and went over to where he was still sitting.

"I'm so sorry," I said, standing. I pulled his head to my stomach and hugged him. "I didn't mean to be so mean to you. I just couldn't believe you'd actually be interested in doing something like that, especially a day after what just happened."

Noah was silent for a few moments, and then he turned and hugged me back.

I heard it in the thinness of his voice when he said, "It does sort of sound like I'm trying to be a daredevil. It just sounded exciting when Bert talked about it."

"Dear Noah. You've always been there for me when I've had my crazy ideas, although I have to say they never involved hunting or killing. And I understand why you'd want to do something like that. It's a once in a lifetime experience."

He stood now, and we hugged. His soft lips found mine, and he kissed me slowly and thoughtfully.

"You're right," he said, as though he had no energy to argue.

After a few heavy sighs, he began to bounce back.

"I *have* been there for your harebrained ideas, and I've never held you back."

"You're right, and for that, I love you even more than I should!" I punched him.

That night, we made love. At first, Noah's kisses were almost punishing and angry, but then they turned surprisingly gentle as he touched me in ways that only he knew how to. Afterward, we lay there, and I told him I loved him.

But I couldn't get the Indian woman out of my mind.

CHAPTER SIXTEEN

If you lived in the mountains long enough, you got used to the random fog that drifted in unannounced, but everyone I talked to that May commented on how unusual it was to *begin* the month with gray foggy mornings. It reminded me of years ago, when I was in the boat with my mother one foggy day and she commented how beautiful it was to look at the mist surrounding the trees, turning them from green to dark gray. I always thought of that when the fog started rolling in, making everything look mysterious.

Each morning, by around eleven, the fog would begin dissipating, and the sky would turn a vivid blue. The days warmed up, and customers came out.

We were at a point we needed another salesperson in the design store, and at Sarah's suggestion, we hired a young girl named Addie. She was a friend of her son's and after meeting her, I agreed she'd be a pleasant addition for both stores. Despite her young age, she was likeable and confident, and she handled herself with surprising maturity.

I'd long ago figured out Lake Arrowhead was a perfect place for a fresh start, and once Sarah told me Addie's story, I knew that while she hadn't come up here on her own, she had embraced the opportunity to challenge the unknown. She was one of four children, three girls and a boy. When she was ten, her parents divorced. She and her older brother came to live with their father up in the mountains, and two years later, after they arrested her mother for doing drugs, the two younger sisters moved up too.

"The father smokes, and is a bit of a boozer," Sarah said. "Once Addie let it slip, she worried he'd one day burn the house down. Until a few years ago, he had his share of women friends, and then met a gal named Sally at the Stockade. She's a long-time resident of Twin Peaks, and ever since she moved in a year ago, her father's turned over a new leaf."

"Is Addie planning on staying up here?" I asked.

Most of the time, the minute kids graduated from high school, they headed off to college somewhere or moved down the hill for more job opportunities.

"There aren't a lot of options for young people up here, especially if they want to continue their education."

I hated the thought of training someone who wasn't planning to stay with us.

"Her boyfriend works at the lumberyard, and he wants to stay up here."

"Well, she seems like she'll fit in, so if you like her, and she can help you out, let's go ahead and hire her," I said.

Not long after that, a customer with two rambunctious little girls came in, and from the minute they entered the store, they were hitting each other and yelling. I looked at the mother, who just looked the other way, I was sure, hoping the girls would just disappear so she could shop in silence. I hoped for the same, but once I looked their way again, I couldn't help but remember the times Loni and I argued. Albeit, if we ever acted this way, my mother would have grabbed us by our shirts and dragged us out of the store.

I remember being so angry at Loni once for grabbing my stuffed cat by the leg and swinging it back and forth above my head until the body tore free, and it flew across the yard. While my eyes widened in horror, Loni looked at the cat's leg in her hand, saw the humor of it all and burst out in laughter. Suddenly, her laughter stopped, and she looked at the cat's leg again.

"I'll sew it for you," she said, taking on a more serious tone.

"I hate you," I said.

The weight of my words still echoed in my mind.

I went to the young girls and asked if they'd like to help me hang some fabric samples, hoping they'd quiet down. I saw their mother roll her eyes as they quickly followed me to where a stack of fabrics sat.

"We need to clip them with the hanger, and then hang them by color. Can you do that?" I asked, showing them how it was done.

The older girl pushed her sister aside and grabbed the first fabric; then while she was hanging it, her sister tentatively took the next fabric and followed suit.

"Thank you," their mother said. "We just bought our cabin, and I want to redecorate it."

"You've come to the right place," Sarah said.

That next Friday night, Sarah and Josh joined Noah and me for dinner at the Cowboy Bar. We hadn't been there in what seemed like ages, and after bringing our drinks to the table, Noah reached for my hand. On the dance floor, he pulled me to him and we comfortably swayed to the music. He started humming in my ear, just like he'd done a hundred years ago when he first held me in his arms on this dance floor. He still wore English Leather cologne, and I slowly breathed him in.

"Umm," I said. "You smell irresistible."

Noah kept his mouth near my ear and said, "Good."

When we returned to the table, our dinner had been served, and the guys talked about everything they wanted to bring on their hunting trip. Living up in the mountains meant they had most everything they'd need, but they made a list and Josh read it off.

"The pack station is providing everything we need, like tents, blankets and cots. All we need are canteens, flashlights and batteries, heavy boots, sleeping bags and jackets. Oh, and beanie hats and underwear."

They both laughed at that.

"I'm thinking about splurging on a new pair of boots," Noah said.

"Man, new boots would not only alert our prey, but they'd be so bright, we wouldn't even need our lanterns at night," Josh said, pushing Noah the way they still often did. "Not to mention, everyone would know you're a newbie."

"Yeah, I guess you're right," Noah said, obviously disappointed.

"What about thick socks?" I asked.

They both looked at each other like the thought had never crossed their minds.

"Can I at least get some new underwear?" Josh teased. "Better yet, buy some new ones and keep them here. We can bury our old stuff up there."

"You guys are a million laughs," I said, shaking my head.

That night, the minute I climbed into bed, Noah reached for me.

"I love you, babe," he said as he kissed my neck.

"I love you too, Noah."

I knew he'd been waiting for me, for when he slid next to me, I could feel his hardness against my leg. But he took his time and within a few minutes, he was where he wanted to be; on me, and inside me, and I breathed the smell of him, and tears came to my eyes. I knew that in a moment he'd have left his mark. I was the woman he loved, and I knew it.

Two days later, Noah's rolled up sleeping bag was standing in the sunroom next to his duffle bag. Neatly rolled inside it, were his old underwear and socks. I'd already seen their replacements in his drawer. Even though they were going to be gone for a week, he was only bringing one extra pair of jeans.

"They'll be able to stand up by themselves when the trip is over," I said.

"That's all part of roughing it," he said proudly.

It was almost as if he wanted to spend every waking minute with me, for everywhere I turned, Noah was there. On Saturday night, we had dinner—just the two of us—although I'd thought we'd join Sarah and Josh for steaks to celebrate. After cleaning up the kitchen, I jumped into the shower. I knew Noah would want to make love, and I wanted to wear his favorite perfume. He joined me as he sometimes did, and I could tell by the way he kissed me, he was needy. We made love twice that night. Something we hadn't done since we were younger, but I didn't turn him away.

On Sunday, they left.

I knew they were flying into Lewiston, Idaho, where they'd drive to another small airport before flying into the meadow where they'd pack their horses and ride out. I thought about him all day, picturing him getting up on a horse and riding for hours to the camp. Several times I caught myself smiling, wondering if he was going to have a sore butt from being on a horse for so long a time. But it served him right wanting to go.

The first night they were gone, Sarah and I went to the Cowboy Bar, but somehow it wasn't the same without the guys. I could tell she felt it, too; we were both kind of quiet. I was never spooked when I came home to a dark house, but as I pulled into our circular drive, the cabin sat there, just a shadow in the moonlight. I wished I'd at least turned the porch light on. I unlocked our door, and my hand reached for the light switch, and within seconds, the sunroom and living room were filled with light. We hadn't had dogs or cats for years, but I was half expecting someone to greet me. It felt odd.

I was restless, so I started a new book, *Girl with a Pearl Earring*, and ended up not putting it down until after midnight. I took a quick shower then climbed into bed, and I almost patted the space next to me, calling up any one of our old pets to lie on the bed with me. I hadn't thought of them for so long.

On Monday, William Barlowe, the movie scout, called.

"If you're still up for it, we'd love to make arrangements to film at your cabins," he said.

"When?" I asked

"In October."

"I'm sure Noah will be fine with that, but there won't be any snow yet," I said, thinking. I quickly calculated what our income would be if every cabin was rented and the studio would actually be paying us more.

"Okay. Let's plan it then," I said, hanging up.

I needed to start a list of things to tell Noah when he returned.

I told Sarah when she came in and she said, "That's exciting. I'd be interested in seeing how they film. Maybe the kids would like to see it too."

"We can make a night of it. They're filming during the day and night, so we should have plenty of time."

"Isn't it weird not having Noah around? I don't think Josh has been away for more than a night since we've been married. It's strange."

I agreed.

I always loved the fragrance of pine, and the next morning, when I noticed a low-lying branch from one of our trees, I decided to cut some smaller pieces and put them in a vase. Noah had rebuilt the lopsided shed to the right of the cabin years ago, and I unlocked the door to go in and get my shears. I searched first for any spiders that might be lying in wait for me, and when none were obvious, I went in. Not that I used my gardening tools often, but I had to move the building materials Noah stored in there to get near them. I finally found my shears and went back out to cut my branches. A quick breeze filled the air with the scent of the freshly cut pine, then I noticed several dandelion pods floating in the air. I still marveled at the fresh mountain air.

With pine boughs in my hand, I returned my shears to the shed and made myself a mental note to add re-organizing it to Noah's list. Inside, I filled one of my favorite vases with water and arranged the pine branches, then set it on the dining table in the kitchen. I leaned over to get one last smell before I finished getting ready for work. When I heard a scratching sound coming from outside the kitchen door, I turned to see a squirrel sitting there, looking in. I didn't want to startle him, so I slowly looked around the kitchen to see if there was anything I could feed him. There were some nuts in a bowl at one end of the counter, and even though I knew my movements would most likely startle him, I grabbed a handful. By the time I got to the door, of course, he was gone, but I still set them outside on the deck, hoping he would return. I thought of Noah, and how he always chided me when I fed our critters, but I couldn't help it.

I grabbed my bags and as I headed out the front door, I noticed our birdbath was dry and dirty. That would be tomorrow's project.

At the end of our street, I stopped while a school bus picked up children, and I saw Laurie from the post office waiting while her daughter got on the bus. When the bus drove off, I called out to her.

"Good morning."

"I hear Noah and Josh are off on a hunting trip," she said.

"Yes, and I hope they don't catch anything," I said, rolling my eyes. "The last thing we need is a bear's head or rug."

I hadn't picked up yesterday's mail yet, so I pulled into the post office parking area and waited for her to open up. There wasn't much of interest—the renewal notice for our social membership at the Lake Arrowhead Country Club, a bill from our homeowner's insurance and our DMV registration tags, (another chore for Noah)—and I tucked them all in my bag. I'd open them when I got home.

I was grateful for a somewhat quiet day, for I had a ton of things to do to get ready for the Memorial Day weekend festival. Noah and Josh would be back in time and we needed them again to manage the street traffic. We had a meeting scheduled that night with the other stores along the street, and it looked like everyone was going to join in. We'd raised the participation fee, and I was wondering how many grumbles there'd be. As in the past, if a store didn't take part—meaning paying something towards covering expenses—they wouldn't be on the list of donors. The first year of the festival, the used bookstore across the street didn't want to contribute and they weren't included in the advertising. After that, they were one of the first stores to give me their check. I'd asked everyone to bring in whatever they wanted to for the grand prize gift basket, and Sarah and Addie offered to make it up this year.

Before the meeting, Sarah and I went to lunch and talked about the guys, the festival, and just enjoyed each other's company.

"I'm glad we have the dogs," Sarah said. "At least they keep me company at night. They both wonder where Josh is, and Rex circles the blanket a few times before he finds a comfortable spot to lie down. He's funny."

I told her about missing our animals.

"It sounds funny, but I haven't changed Noah's pillow case. His smell relaxes me, and it's easier to imagine he's there," I said. "Wow. That was revealing."

I'd become somewhat embarrassed.

"I have a new staging to go to this afternoon," Sarah said, changing the subject. "At the rate we're going, we should probably have a couple more sofas and end tables."

"Pick out some things you like and order them," I said. "I need to get some bills paid today," I said absently.

By Tuesday, I thought I would have adjusted to not having Noah around, and when the sunlight peeked through our bedroom window, for a moment I forgot I was alone. Then I turned to see Noah wasn't there and for the rest of the day, I found I was also dwelling on how lonely it was to be by myself. I'd never given it much thought in the past; first because he never went anywhere for very long, and second, thoughts of living by myself hadn't entered my mind since Noah took some time away right after my miscarriage.

Without him, all the sounds in the house were magnified; I suddenly heard the ticking of the grandfather clock in the living room, and when the hour chimed, more than once, it startled me awake. Once I got my bearings, I tried to concentrate on the repetition of the ticking to put me back to sleep.

By Thursday, I'd begun to acclimate. I found I actually started embracing the tranquility of the silence. I didn't have to worry about waking Noah if I got up early. Or just the opposite; if I wanted to sleep a few more minutes, the sounds of him getting ready didn't keep me from falling back to sleep.

And when the squirrel scratched at the back door again, I didn't feel guilty for feeding him some nuts.

Thursday night, Sarah and I went to the Cowboy Bar again, and I found myself people watching. I looked at other men, some much older than Noah, and each one I saw seemed to glare with issues. Some were too heavy. Some were rail thin. And some of them looked like they had major health issues, and wouldn't make a fit candidate for a mate if I was looking for one. Some men were handsome, but then they laughed too loudly for my taste. Or they looked around the room as if they were looking for a new woman they could conquer.

I had to laugh at myself.

"Why are you smiling?" Sarah asked.

"Oh, just looking at all the people in here tonight. Just people watching. Thinking if I had to get to know them, it almost makes my skin crawl."

"*What?*"

On Friday morning, before I left for work, I put some nuts out for the squirrel, and I refilled the bird feeder. I stuck the list I'd made of things Noah could do when he got home to the refrigerator door and checked it out.

Clean the shed.

Put the new tags on my car.

Send the DMV registration in.

Climb up on the library ladder and dust all the knickknacks on the bookshelf.

I added, fix the cracked glass pane in the sunroom window.

I was sure there were more things, but I didn't want to overwhelm him the minute he walked through the door. He was supposed to call me Saturday to let me know they'd made it back to the small camp, and then Sunday they were flying back in to Ontario.

Dear Noah

When I got to work, Sarah was already there, laying out the poster for the Memorial Day festival, and I said a quick hello before I went into my office. A stack of new catalogs had been collecting on the corner of my desk, but I wanted to go through them before I put them in the bookcase. I'd code the price lists so there would be no mistakes with either a multiplier to mark up or down. And once I did that, I'd replace the old with the new.

I went down to Walt's to get us coffees before we opened at ten, and the newest edition of Homes for Sale magazines was out, so I grabbed a couple. With my hands full, I juggled to open the front door and tripped over my own feet, dropping them.

I literally felt my heart drop as I looked up at Sarah. Sheriff Brody was standing next to her, and she held on to his arm. All the color had drained from her face. It wasn't warm out—in fact, I'd noticed a slight breeze in the pine trees across the road when I came back to the store—but there was perspiration beading on his forehead. He'd taken off his hat and was nervously twisting it in his hands. Something was terribly wrong, and I felt what I could only describe as a fierce fluttering in my chest.

Then my mind raced. It was Josh. Something had happened to Josh.

"There was an accident," Sarah said, scarcely audible.

I dropped the coffees and rushed towards her.

"Sarah, I'm so sorry," I started.

"No, Annie. It's not Josh. It's Noah. He's dead."

Part Two

CHAPTER SEVENTEEN

Even now, all I can recall is that I heard muffled sounds as my mind closed down and I reached out for Sarah as I steadied myself. My ears rang and my head pounded; I felt like I was watching a movie where there was no sound, but you knew someone was being told the terrible news. Someone was dead.

"They're still in Idaho," Sheriff Brody said, his voice quivering.

Stunned and sickened, it felt like my brain was shutting down. I was mindless. Everything was happening in slow motion; Sheriff Brody still twisting his hat, and Sarah reaching out to steady me. My entire body turned icy, like my blood had quit flowing. I'll never forget the look on her face as I fell to the floor. My teeth began to chatter, and she quickly looked for something to cover me with. I let my head rest on a stack of fabric samples, and I closed my eyes.

I then felt a tear slipping from the corner of my eye.

I could hear Sarah asking questions.

"What happened?"

"I'm not sure."

"Where is he now?"

"They're in Lewiston," Sheriff Brody said.

"Is Josh with him?"

"Yes."

Somehow, I regained the strength to sit. I struggled to believe he was gone, and then my mind became suddenly clear.

"When will I be able to see him?" I asked.

Horrific visions of Noah's body tormented me. I wanted to see him, but then I didn't want that last image of him etched forever in my mind. Suddenly, I didn't know *what* I wanted beyond waking up from this horrible nightmare.

Sarah made arrangements for us to fly out that afternoon.

"I'll have Addie and the girls take care of the festival," Sarah said.

I hadn't even thought about that.

We stopped by her house first, then mine to grab a few changes of clothing, then we headed to the airport. One moment I was strong and lucid, and then, like a snap of a finger, I felt dead inside. Even though we got there late, the morgue accommodated us, and when we drove up, it felt like Sarah had to drag me in.

I saw Josh before I saw Noah. He hugged me first, then Sarah.

"We were riding back into camp and laughing about how sore we were. His horse stopped and suddenly it got quiet when we heard the rattling and hissing sounds of a snake. We couldn't tell where it was coming from, but Noah's horse reared and he fell off, hitting his head on a nearby boulder."

He and Sarah waited outside the room while I went in.

My beautiful Noah's cheeks were pallid and sunken, and the gray stubble of his beard made him look dreadful. Of course, I reasoned, he was dead. On the right side of his face, there was a swollen gash where he'd hit his head when he'd fallen from his horse, and bruising covered the rest.

I wanted to believe he looked like he was sleeping, but he didn't. When I finally found the courage to touch his hand, it was rigid. His face was cool and yet I kissed him. I didn't really want to, fearing he would smell like death, but I knew if I didn't, I'd always regret it.

The few times Noah and I talked about death, we agreed we both wanted to be buried at the cemetery in Lake Arrowhead. But now Noah would have to be cremated so I could bring him back sooner. Once again, I found myself at a mortuary, numbly trying to make decisions. Sarah came with me and I was grateful for her support. Later, when I could deal with it, I would decide where to spread his ashes.

My mother came to stay with me, but her presence didn't bring me much comfort. It only made me want to cry. I didn't want to talk about it, and I tried not to be rude. I wanted to be by myself, to wallow in self pity for my world as I'd known it, had abruptly ended. Was this how she felt when I stayed with her after my father died? Had she dreaded those same endless nights that finally turned into dawn?

I stayed in our room and I heard every noise my mother made on the wood floors. Even though I swore I wasn't really sleeping, every creak sounded like a lightning bolt and jolted me awake.

I decided the best way to begin the healing process was to pack up and donate Noah's clothing. My mother helped the best she could, but I found I was snippy with her when she held something up; I wanted to touch each piece by myself.

Once we were finished, Sarah came to pick everything up and take it all to the thrift store in town. I didn't want to deal with telling people there how I felt, although I knew they could take one look at me and know.

That first week, even though my mother encouraged me to, I couldn't bear to go in to work. Eventually, I'd have to show my face, but for the time being, I really just wanted to go somewhere and hide.

Sarah and my mother made the arrangements for Noah's service. I'd seriously thought about not having one; I think it was just another way for me to deny the truth. And the truth was, I thought if I didn't deal with his death head on, maybe it wouldn't be true.

I wanted Noah to be buried so I could join him when I died, so we split his ashes into three urns. In a private ceremony, I had one buried. For everyone else, Josh chose a spot in the forest he thought Noah would have liked. Even though the tall pines shaded us in the afternoon sun, it was warm. The air had turned humid, which no one expected, and everyone fanned their faces with the printed memorial Sarah had written.

Josh's parents were there; his father and wife, his mother with someone I didn't recognize. My chest tightened like someone was squeezing me and I tried to calm myself by taking deep breaths when I saw Maria and Joel Harmon, Hudson and Constance Fisher and Carrie Davis and Paul Larson standing to one side, waiting. There were also people I recognized, but their names eluded me. Sarah must have called them. My old hairdresser and friend Laura and her husband Jason were there, along with Bert from the trading post, and Johnny Spencer, who managed the cabins, and his wife Louise.

I waited in vain for the pain to fade, but it burned inside me.

My mother stood with Sarah, Josh, and their two children, Robert and Ava. Josh stood quietly, staring at his boots, his hands shoved in his pockets. Seeing him standing there like that reminded me of how Noah stood the same way, hands in his pockets, when I threw him one of my curveballs. I had my own pain to deal with, but I saw the darkness that passed over him. He sniffled and then ran a hand over his eyes.

"Oh Josh," was all I could muster.

Sarah gripped his arm and then draped her arm through his as she pulled him closer. My heart was breaking twice. But the people who also meant a lot to Noah, his parents and Sam and Ginny, were absent.

Someone's perfume hovered in the air, and I searched my mind for the memory. It reminded me of the first time Bunny Bryant came in to Ginny's to talk to Noah about doing her remodeling. I hated the intrusion at the time, and I resented it now.

Josh composed himself and spoke

"Thanks all of you for coming here today. I know Noah would have hated all the attention, but it means the world to Annie and us. My son

Robert and I built this bench for Noah. Son, make sure it's on stable ground," he said to his son. "We don't want anyone falling off if they decide to come up here to visit."

They'd built the bench with a live edge white pine top and cedar log legs. Robert found what looked like a good spot and set the bench down. For good measure, he dusted it off with his sleeve.

Just then, a great white owl screeched as it flew over us. Everyone looked up and I couldn't help but think maybe Noah was reminding us he was still out there watching over me.

It seemed everyone there turned to me. Was I going to say anything? The air around me was thick with awkwardness. I saw them all as a snapshot in time, and my chest tightened like someone was squeezing me. I tried to calm myself by taking deep breaths. I waited for the pain to fade and I wanted to be anywhere but there—and when I felt the only thing I could do was thank everyone for being there, I took another breath and did my best to force myself to smile. Even I could tell it was a glum one.

Before I said a word, though, I heard a woman I'd not yet seen, cry out in pain.

"Damn it!"

All eyes turned towards her, and she was sprawled on the ground, tangled in the roots of a large pine.

"Oh, dear God," I blurted.

Even after almost twenty years, it was impossible to not recognize Bunny Bryant.

My hands flew to my forehead, and it felt like my stomach folded in on itself. For a few seconds, I couldn't breathe. Sarah rushed over to me, and we just stood there watching as Bert from the trading post helped her up.

Bunny was still trim, and her platinum hair was pulled back in a ponytail. Even from over thirty feet away, I could see she had a rock on her left hand, no doubt from some poor sod she'd managed to latch on to.

"I'm so sorry, Annie," she cried. "I only wanted to pay my respects."

CHAPTER EIGHTEEN

The only good news about Bunny Bryant upstaging Noah's memorial was that once I recovered from her grand entrance, I started laughing.

"It was *her* perfume I smelled earlier," I said to Sarah, and I laughed even harder.

Everyone there turned to me, and I was sure they thought I'd become hysterical.

I wasn't far from it.

Thankfully, Bunny didn't get the message we were having a buffet at the Country Club. Charles, the chef, prepared a light lunch, and when I realized I couldn't avoid talking to the group, I stood. The room suddenly grew quiet, and all eyes were upon me. My mother, who was sitting next to me, patted my hand as if she was saying, 'There, there now. Everything will be all right.'

When my mother and I returned to the cabin, I thought a long hot bath would make me feel better; at least it would relieve some of my tension. I'd let the water run so hot it almost scalded me as I got in, but I immersed myself, and let the water cover my hair and face. I thought about drowning myself but I didn't know how to do it—plus I was a coward and I knew my death would only create more problems for everyone.

I drained the tub and then stood under the shower to wash my hair. In all honesty, I didn't feel any better.

We had a few bottles of wine in the rack above our refrigerator, and I poured myself a glass of merlot. My mother was in the living room mindlessly watching television, and I stuck my head in and offered her something before I came in to join her. My parents only drank socially before my sister Loni died, and afterward, they drank even less. I wasn't surprised when she declined.

I sat in one of our side chairs, my knees pulled up to my chest, and slowly felt the wine dull my anxiety, and I finally began relaxing. I let my head fall gently to the right and then to the left to stretch the tight muscles in my neck, and I hoped I'd be able to fall asleep.

"I'm headed for bed," I said after a while.

"Try to get a good night," my mother said.

Our bedroom smelled stuffy, so I cracked the window open to let the fresh evening air in. I stood there for a minute and felt the coolness wash over me. I sighed, then crawled into bed. The moment my head hit my pillow, the spicy smell of Noah filled the surrounding air. I mentally counted back the days since I'd last changed our sheets, and I realized I hadn't done so since before Noah left on this trip. It was one of the things I forgot to put on his list. To help me change the bed. It was a chore I hated doing by myself.

I always thought it melodramatic when, in a movie, someone raised the clothing of someone they'd lost to their nose to remind them of their smell, but I found myself reaching for Noah's pillow and exchanging it with mine. I thought of his hair pulled back into a small ponytail, of his beard, and how he constantly smoothed and stroked it when he was deep in thought.

"It makes me look cool and rational, especially in tense situations," he'd say when I asked him what it was about playing with his beard.

Maybe it was just my imagination, but the next morning when I woke and looked in my mirror, I felt like I looked more refreshed.

I would keep him near me for just a few more nights.

I encouraged my mother to go home; frankly I wanted to be by myself. It was impossible to relax completely with her constant worry about me, and yet I believe her presence compelled me to at least attempt to wear a happy expression and pretend that I was doing fine. I didn't go in to work that week, but instead, we tried to think of things we could do to break the monotony. One day, we drove to Big Bear for the day and walked around. We had hamburgers and ice cream, and we stopped in a used bookstore where my mother bought something to read. The next day, we went to the Village and walked out to the lake. When I bought food for the ducks, it reminded me of when I first met Noah, and we sat and watched them as they ate. We had brunch at the Belgian Waffle Works.

"I've always loved their waffles," my mother said when we were served. "A new breakfast place opened in Prescott, but it's not as good as this."

When we finished eating, my mother asked, "Are you going to be okay if I go home?"

I gave her a big hug.

"Yes, Mother. I'll be fine. I just need some time to get used to it all," I said. "I'll probably go back in to work after you leave. I need something to do besides sit around feeling sorry for myself."

"I think work will do you good," my mother said. "Busy hands and idle minds have knitted many a sweater, or something like that."

I smiled.

"Your father once told me something his father used to say when their business wasn't doing so well. 'When adversity comes, receive it favorably.' It means to take things as they come. You'll be fine. You're strong and you still have a lifetime ahead of you. I know it doesn't feel that way now, but you'll eventually see."

The next morning, before my mother left, I had her help me change my bed.

But I kept Noah's pillow aside.

I spent the rest of that day doing laundry and cleaning the cabin. I tried to not think about my life as it was now, but the harder I tried, it only made me think about it more. I'd forgotten we'd made lists of things we wanted to do before we were too old, and I had a glass of wine while I read through them.

My list included a visit to New York and the Statue of Liberty. I wanted to see Angel Island in San Francisco, where my father was processed when he came to America, and I wanted to travel somewhere by train, to visit a castle and to write a book. Noah's list was much longer; he wanted to take a trip to Africa, go on a hot-air balloon, sky dive, drive Route 66, see the Alamo, swim with sharks, ride a mechanical bull and get a tattoo.

I wondered if he'd had a premonition he would die young?

Suddenly, I thought about that Indian woman from Sedona.

"Are you happy now?" I asked.

That night I finished the bottle of merlot and fell asleep in my chair.

I thought a change of surroundings might help me snap out of my funk, so I called Johnnie at the cabins to see if my old cabin was available for the night. My call surprised him; I could hear it in his voice.

"We have someone coming in tonight, and I was going to put them there..." he said. "But I can just as easily put them somewhere else."

"Good. Then I'm going to be spending the night tonight."

I packed a change of clothes, had a quick late lunch, and then stopped by the grocery store to pick up another bottle of merlot and chips to help me get through the night. It wasn't the first time I'd half expected to see our old camp cats, Jezebel and Socks, welcome me as I drove in. I unpacked my bag and then sat outside by the fire pit where I used to find solace, but no matter what I did, it didn't change the fact that I was alone. All I heard was the silence ringing in my ears. The once calming wind whistling through the trees now became a distracting noise. And all it ended up doing was bringing up flashbacks of divorcing David, then meeting Noah and being unfaithful to him. How could I possibly think back to those times when my grieving was in the present? I hated it that my thoughts robbed me of my grieving for Noah.

I tried to comfort myself with happy memories, but instead of making me feel better, they dragged me down. I made myself spend the night, but I was restless, and I woke with a headache.

The next morning I moved back to our cabin, and in my mind, I constantly listened for Noah's truck on the gravel driveway or the stomping of his boots to rid them of mud before he opened the front door. When I did a load of laundry, I remembered how he'd sometimes come home and drop his clothes in the mudroom and in his underwear and socks, he'd gather them up and tiptoe to the laundry room. He must have thought it would avoid creating a trail of sawdust if he carried them that way. I used to get cranky with him if he tracked dirt in on the hardwood floor, but now I would have given anything for his messes.

Thoughts of him continually intruded into my day. I was achy and exhausted, but I couldn't sleep. I felt drained and lifeless.

The way I felt was short of being indescribable.

I walked our land, past the stream, and down into the clearing. There was a chill in the air, but I found a place in the sun to stop and close my eyes. That's when I laid down on a carpeted area of pine needles and cried. My throat ached and I let the tears roll down my face and neck. I saw no reason to seek help, because it wouldn't bring Noah back. I knew my life still had a purpose, but it didn't feel like it then.

The silence was making me crazy. The next day, I went back to work. Sarah had stepped up and run the stores, just like I knew she would, and it was almost as if I'd never left. Everything was still there. I'd asked her to remind everyone I didn't want any attention drawn to me being back. I didn't want anyone to talk to me unless I talked to them. I knew it was asking a lot of the people who cared about me, but I didn't think I could deal with their pity.

Then I went to the animal shelter and brought home two dogs and a kitten. I now had bedfellows.

Dear Noah

Little by little, my days became more bearable, and it was just the endless nighttime that haunted me. Having the dogs and the kitten brought me comfort. I could talk to them and say silly things that people say to their pets.

"Are my boys hungry?"

"Ready for breakfast?"

"Momma loves you."

The wag of their tails or a mew from the kitten gave me all the answers I needed.

CHAPTER NINETEEN

I knew time would take some of my pain away, and it did. I found it easier to talk to people about the accident—and had mixed emotions about it still being the talk of the town. I kept Noah's remaining urns on the fireplace mantel, like bookends, and to make light of it all, I started saying "good morning" and "goodnight" to him.

It surprised me how well I adapted to being on my own, but I'd still catch myself needing to touch the things that made me miss him. One thing I hadn't touched was the dining table in the kitchen. I hadn't sat there since my mother left weeks before, choosing to avoid the empty chair where Noah sat when we ate, or where he would pay bills and do the paperwork he always dreaded. Covering it with a blanket only made the chair stand out more, so I ended up moving it into the hall closet so it wouldn't glare at me.

But one day, I realized everything was unbalanced, so before I left for the store, I brought it out and set it back where it belonged.

On the weekends, Sara and Josh would sit with me on the cobblestone clearing, and sometimes we wouldn't utter a word. I knew I didn't want to talk about losing Noah, and I was sure they didn't want to talk about it either. Sometimes, just the silence and the dogs were all we needed.

I can't say that I eventually didn't think of Noah, but I found there were some days I could deal with his death. If I heard a favorite song, I'd still sometimes wonder what it would be like to dance with him again; to hear him hum in my ear, or feel his warm breath on my cheek and his strong arms holding me—

Sometimes when I met Josh and Sarah for an early dinner, I'd notice the skin on Josh's forearms had turned brown from working outside in the sun just like Noah's use to. I'd never noticed the way Josh shielded his eyes from the sun, the same way Noah did. After being friends for so many years, they had many of the same mannerisms.

One time, I wondered if when they made love, like us, they assumed there would always be time, and maybe we didn't treasure our time together the way we could have. I now knew it was because life had a way of taking that time and turning it into just another day.

Fall was coming, and I welcomed the change in seasons. Sarah and Addie worked on the annual scarecrow contest. I could see how Addie was eager to learn and be a part of the business, and normally Sarah loved teaching her new things. But even though Sarah and I went through the motions, something was missing. For me, decorating the store for the holidays had become more a chore for me.

On the morning of the scarecrow contest, I popped into the market for some cookies and sodas for the day, and where in the past I'd been able to duck in and out without her seeing me, Thalia's register was the only one open. I could feel my face redden as I approached her.

"Oh my god, Annie," she said brightly. "I've seen you in the store a few times, and I just wanted to tell you my heart goes out to you."

"Thanks," I said. "I'm hanging in there."

"I also wanted to tell you I talked my sister into coming up to stay with me. I told her the mountains were a great place to start over. She's been here for about a month, and so far we haven't had many catfights!"

Her warm smile echoed in her voice, and I felt doubly guilty about avoiding her for so long. Thalia was a sweet woman, and I could tell she only wanted to make me feel better.

We didn't win the contest that year, and I wondered if it was because our hearts just weren't it like in years past. I knew she was disappointed, but then I had to remind her how many times we'd won it in the past.

"Just think. We've given someone else the opportunity to win," I said, trying to sound cheerful.

When winter came, on the days the snow covered the ground, it felt like everything old had been covered with the future of what spring would bring. I was still amazed at how the snowflakes seemed to dance in the air. I walked the property with the dogs the way Noah and I used to, and the snow muffled my food steps. The dogs ran briskly and often jumped as though they were trying to keep from getting their paws wet.

In the past, the land had brought me so much comfort and pleasure, but lately, even the rustling of the wind in the trees didn't comfort me. And when I walked with the dogs, all I could think about was how, on that one walk, Noah and I had talked about getting married.

Most winter days, even though the air was cool, I'd opened at least one window or door to let the fresh air in. When gray clouds skittered across the sky, every now and then the sun would peek through, proving there was a ray of sunshine out there.

I didn't put up a tree that year. Everywhere I went, Christmas music played, and it was making me crazy. I took a week to drive out to Prescott to pick up my mother, and we'd be back in time for the two of us to celebrate Christmas Day at the country club.

"I have plenty of Christmas at the store, and a new kitten can wreak havoc with a tree," I told everyone.

I knew I wasn't fooling myself or anyone else, and then Sarah invited us over to spend the day with them.

"Only if we do Christmas for the kids, and no music," I said.

"I promise," Sarah said.

My mother and I went to the lodge for the Christmas Eve buffet, and it was nice to get out and not have to worry about entertaining anyone. Two days after Christmas, I drove her back home.

At the beginning of spring, even though the air was still cool, I started going down to the lake. I fed the ducks, and despite myself, I mustered a smile at their antics. They had no idea how life as a human being could be; all they cared about was eating and mating, and I wasn't even sure in which order.

It wasn't warm enough for a lot of people to be out in their boats, but one day, after breakfast at the Waffle Works, I fed the ducks as usual, then sat and watched as a lone boat sped across the lake, creating a wake behind it so close to the docks it made the ducks wobble back and forth. Some jerks shouldn't be allowed on the lake, I thought. It reminded me of the four of us out in the boat, that one Fourth of July when out-of-control revelers were escorted back to the landing. Tears suddenly blurred my vision, and I wiped my glasses on my blouse. I dried my eyes and then looked around to see if anyone was watching me. Why was I pretending I wasn't crying?

I brought the dogs to the lake with me one morning, and on the way home, I took a detour and drove out to a spot where we used to have picnics. I let the dogs out, and then sat at one of the picnic benches.

Back then, Ginny would have made fried chicken and potato salad, Sarah would have brought the deviled eggs, and I would have cut up fruit. One year, I brought sponge cake and strawberries for dessert, instead of cookies. Josh and Sara brought their dogs too, and the four of them had a field day. Sarah's son Robert found a bird's nest and brought to us. It had fallen from a tree and I, for one, was glad to hear he'd found no eggs or dead babies next to it. It was a miracle of nature, and I was always amazed how they collected materials and built their nest.

"It's like a blueprint," I said to him, "but birds instinctively know how to build them. If you want to keep it, dry it on low in the oven to kill any bacteria."

The three boys played tag football, and by the end of the day, Noah had a strained back and couldn't lift anything for a week. I stepped on a bee and even though we iced it, my left foot swelled up like an elephant's and I ate an extra helping of potato salad to make myself feel better. Robert was a feast for mosquitoes, although the rest of us survived unscathed. Ava sat in the shade and read, and tipped over when she fell asleep, and we all laughed at her.

I was sure it was spring then, when the weather could be unpredictable, and thunder rumbled off in the distance. But the sky was blue, and no one seemed to notice until rain drenched us all.

I smiled at the memory, and it felt good.

Now, I watched the dogs run and chase each other, until something deeper into the forest caught their attention and they bolted.

"Tucker! Cooper!" I called out.

I ran to where I'd last seen them, and called to them again, but all I could hear was a rustle in the bushes.

My heart raced, thinking they might be chasing after something that could hurt them, and I called out to them again. Within seconds, they chased each other back out into the clearing, and I didn't know whether to swat them or kiss them.

"Don't ever do that again," I scolded. "You come when I call you."

Like they knew what I was saying.

We hosted the Memorial Day festival again, although my heart wasn't in it. We'd organized it every year and I couldn't let the chamber or other businesses down. Josh and Robert worked the street, and Addie managed the sale table outside. I was going through the motions, and I greeted everyone with a smile. By the end of the day, the charade exhausted me.

And just when we all thought June's gloomy weather would never break, by the Fourth of July weekend, everyone complained about the heat. We welcomed any cool breezes that came our way. Summer eventually slipped into fall, and I watched the wind gust through the trees and that's how I felt—like my life was still being tousled about.

Dear Noah

By the time the air had turned cooler and the color in the leaves had begun to fade, I finally realized I'd run out of ways to feel like getting up in the morning. There was only so much more I could expand my business and, as it was, I was already working seven days a week. The harder I tried to ignore it, the truth of it persisted; I was the only one who could change my life. The mountains had provided me comfort when I most needed it, but now, being up here only reminded me of all those I'd lost.

CHAPTER TWENTY

When I first came up to the mountains, I wasn't intending to live here, so when I thought about where I'd go now, I couldn't think of anywhere else I'd want to be. I'd had many happy years here with Noah, more than a lot of marriages last today.

I wasn't sure where I'd end up. I'd never been to the islands in Washington state, but I'd always pictured them much like the mountains, beautiful, enchanting, plenty of green, and rainy, rainy, rainy. I didn't know anything about Utah, Colorado, Arizona, or Nevada, but none of them sounded interesting. I'd never lived on a ranch in Montana, although I quickly set that idea aside when I thought about Grayson Underwood.

I called my mother and asked if I could come to stay with her for a while. She reminded me about the strict 'no guests under fifty-five' policy at the mobile home park, so I booked a room at the Grand Highland Hotel. It actually worked out better for me, for I could spend my days with her, then after dinner, I had time by myself at night. Sarah said she'd watch the dogs and check in on the cat, and when I was ready, I took the dogs to her house and headed out.

We did touristy things we hadn't done in many years, like going to the antique shops, the bookstore, and having ice cream at the parlor across the street from the city hall. Sometimes, we just sat outside her mobile home where we watched the comings and goings of the park.

Most days, my mother and I went out for breakfast and dinner, and sometimes I'd sit with her and watch her favorite TV programs. At night, I'd either go back to my room, or sit on the hotel patio, have a glass of wine, and people-watch.

One day we drove out to the lake we'd gone to when I'd brought Noah here the first time I introduced him to my parents. He and my father had taken a short walk and my mother and I sat at one of the tables, turning our faces toward the sun to feel its warmth. I knew then I loved him, and I was pleased they instantly took to him.

That seemed like a lifetime ago.

We sat there now and set up a picnic lunch at that very table overlooking the lake. It was a lazy afternoon, and we watched a small boat with a trolling motor make its way slowly around the lake. Later on, we were entertained by a couple of older gentlemen on the dock who got their fishing lines tangled as they were trying to get set up. They eventually worked it out and decided fishing opposite each other was going to be the best way to avoid having that problem again. We ate our lunch in silence, and I appreciated the peacefulness.

After about a week of quiet time, I'd made a decision and was ready to head back home. I'd told my mother I was planning on relocating, but also that I hadn't made up my mind where that would be. I didn't say anything to her, but I now knew where I was going to end up. Staying with my mother always reminded me of the mountains—it was so clean and picturesque.

I'd decided.

I'd sell everything and move to Prescott.

When I shared my news with Sarah, she said, "I'm not surprised. It seems like a natural place to be, out there with your mother."

She offered to buy the design business and retail store. She'd worked with me side by side for almost twenty years, and she was the best one to keep them both going. I made her the same deal the previous owner, Liz, had made me so many years ago when she was ready to retire; Sarah could give me a small down payment and make reasonable monthly payments on the balance.

She and Josh had a strong marriage, and her children were grown, so she could put in the hours it would take to keep up with it all. Josh offered to buy Noah's construction business, but all I wanted was for it to continue.

"He would have wanted you to have it," I said. "You two were almost partners, anyway."

We agreed to keep the commercial property with the cabins, and Sarah said she'd manage it. When I penciled it all out, I didn't really need the income, but I could at least tuck it away for a rainy day.

I listed the B&B for sale and was surprised and a little brokenhearted when it sold so quickly. A young couple who wanted to get out of the city purchased it, and I filled a notebook with the finer points of operating the place. I shared the history of three of the cabins, and how I'd never pursued looking into the bag of money we found in cabin five after the fire. I struggled with telling them about John Murphy, who'd hung himself so long ago. In California, if the death happened over three years ago, you didn't have to disclose it, but in my mind, both Noah and Sam told me I should do it if I ever sold the place. Surprisingly, the couple was intrigued by it all.

When it came to selling Noah's cabin (as I still referred to it), my heart broke a little more. It was where we sat in front of the fireplace on chilly nights, and where we'd loved each other and our dogs. We'd spent many happy years there. No babies had been born, but we'd had each other.

Over the years, several friends had expressed interest in buying the cabin if it ever came up for sale, so I reached out to two of them. One stepped up and made me an offer. That's when it hit me full force; I was definitely moving away, and while it broke my heart to leave it, I knew keeping the cabin didn't make sense.

I had a realtor I knew help us with the paperwork, and then I made a trip back to Prescott to find a new house. I knew I wanted to buy something rather than rent, so I had one of the local realtors show me around. We spent two days looking at houses, and most of them were just that: houses. Nothing reminded me of the mountains; nothing called out to me. I could have lived in any of them, but I wanted to love where I lived.

Finally, the realtor said, "I think I have something you might be interested in. It's been on the market for a while, and needs some work."

My ears perked up, and the minute we drove up to the property, I knew it was perfect. The house sat on two acres, surrounded by mature pine, maple, and ash trees. It had a stone exterior with a cobblestone driveway and a covered porte cochere. Inside, the living room, family room and kitchen had gorgeous open beamed ceilings. All the wood, including the kitchen cabinets, needed to be oiled, and the hardwood flooring needed refinishing. There was older carpeting in the bedrooms, which could come out and be replaced with more hardwood. All that, and a coat of paint, would do the trick. I could picture everything from the mountain house fitting in, and there was so much space, I'd even need to find new treasures. It was exactly what I needed.

It was serendipitous, just like when I moved to the mountains and bought the B&B so many years ago.

I opened escrow and then made the trek back up to Lake Arrowhead. In between packing, Sarah, Josh and I drove my Jeep to where Noah and I used to go off roading, and once we found a good spot, we spread some of Noah's ashes. Next, we went out onto the lake and spread more. I kept a handful to spread at the cabin, and then I'd take the other urn with me to Prescott.

"Here you go, buddy," Josh said, doing the honors.

A gust of wind caught Noah's ashes and blew most of them out to the port side of the boat, and those that remained rested on top of the water. I don't know why I thought the ashes would automatically dissolve into the lake, and I was a little unnerved to watch them take so long to sink. I turned to look at Josh and Sarah, and they too seemed shaken. Unexpected tears filled my eyes, and Sarah took my hand.

I called Maria Harmon to tell her I was moving down, and she insisted we have lunch.

"It may be the last time I see you," she said.

"Well, that's a terrible thought."

When we hung up, I realized it was probably true.

We met at The Stockade in Crestline, and I told her how Noah and I had added a dollar bill somewhere to the wall, and Chip, the owner, had come by to see how we were doing.

I told Maria about spending time with my mother, and how Prescott reminded me so much of the mountains. And then I told her about the new house, and how I was looking forward to fixing it up.

"It's right up your alley," she said, putting her hand on mine. "I'll miss you, though," she said, and as they had a habit of doing, my eyes teared up.

"I'll miss you, and life up here," I said. "And I wanted you to know that I've always felt guilty about not joining your book club."

She laughed.

"You would have enjoyed it."

I'd drawn a floor plan of my new house so I would know where everything went when the movers came to unpack me, and I methodically packed everything in the cabin up into boxes labeled with the bedrooms, kitchen and so on. I packed several boxes marked Miscellaneous, for things I knew I wanted to keep, but wasn't sure where they would go.

I was a fan for getting rid of things I no longer needed, and yet it was surprising to see how many items I could donate. I'd gone through Noah's clothing some time ago, and I still kept a few of his heavy shirts and his coats. But I hadn't actually cleaned out his closet, so I spent an afternoon reminiscing and packing what I was going to take. I hadn't been sure what I'd do with his old work boots and boxes on the floor, so I pulled everything out and then brought in a few more trash bags.

As I'd done many times in the past, I went through a box of old photographs and newspaper clippings. There were articles about his parents' deaths, and he'd even kept those from Sam's and Ginny's memorials.

Dear Noah

What I didn't expect to see was a photo of Noah and the high school football team; the one his mother must have seen when she made him quit the team. I couldn't help but smile as I remembered him telling me the story. There were plenty of photos of him as a baby and young child, but not many of him as a young man. And then it made sense to me; he'd lost his parents in high school, so the family photos stopped.

Instead of discarding any of it, there was plenty of storage space at the new house, so I taped the box up and labeled it 'Noah'.

I'd already tossed his old work boots and tennis shoes; I couldn't imagine anyone wanting them. There were two sets of cowboy boots; one set loved and worn, and another set almost new. I didn't recall him buying new boots lately, and when I studied them, I couldn't help but wonder if they were the ones he'd worn when we got married.

I brushed them off and packed them in a box to take. I could always store them in one of my extra closets. When I pulled them out, I saw a wooden box I'd never seen before, and curiosity got the better of me. Inside was a small tin box with his father's old badge, and what must have been his parents' wedding rings. I closed the tin and picked up the old Bowie knife we gave Sam one year for Christmas. Its steel blade needed polishing, and the brass cross guard had tarnished and turned green. The leather sheath was dry and needed to be oiled. Old silver dollars and a paper bag filled with Indian head pennies sat atop a stack of old papers—and the box smelled like old paper. I found Noah's birth certificate, some of his old report cards, and his first driver's license.

The envelope with his father's name on it caught my attention more than anything. Inside were three birth certificates. Noah told me his father, Ben, had been adopted, but he'd never shared any of the details. So it came as no surprise to see the extra documents.

The one on top listed his father as Benjamin Joseph Keller, with Rachel Keller as his mother; there was no father's name on record. On the second one, the names had been changed to Rachel Keller Chambers, and a father's name had been added; Samuel Chambers, which must have the man she eventually married. Benjamin Keller had become Benjamin Chambers.

But when I saw the third one, I caught my breath and my hands started shaking. It was Ben's original birth certificate, listing his mother as none other than Celeste Williams, the famous actress from the 1940s. Noah had told me his father was adopted, and that he'd never had a desire to find his birth mother. How could he have felt that way after reading who his birth mother actually was? It wasn't my place to interfere, especially now that Noah and his father were both gone.

I don't know how long I sat there, trying to figure out what to do, if anything.

I took the dogs outside, and we walked the property. I hadn't realized I felt clammy until a cool breeze brushed my skin and gave me a chill. I watched the dogs playfully biting at each other and chasing after imaginary critters.

"Tucker! Cooper!" I called when I was ready to go back in.

They caught up with me and rushed past me until something else caught their attention. It was nothing, and they barked to urge me back into the house.

Once we were back in the cabin, I set the envelope on the dining table, and made myself a promise not to look at it or think about it, but I knew doing either was going to be a challenge.

I wrapped the wooden box in a blanket and set it in another box marked 'Noah'.

Within forty-five days, I'd made seven trips to the thrift store, and had everything else packed up; I scheduled a mover to take it all down the hill and store it until I was ready for delivery to Prescott.

It was a madhouse when the movers came, and as the moving van pulled out of the driveway, I stood there hugging myself. Even though it was warm outside, I felt a chill and my skin was sticky with sweat. I looked around and the empty cabin was desolate. Everything that meant something to me had been packed and taken away, and I wanted to put it all back. Suddenly, all the excitement and anticipation of my new life left me. The rooms were hollow, and my sense of loss was almost overwhelming.

I placed the last bag of the bag of nuts out on the deck by the kitchen door, and I left a note for the new owners to be sure to feed the squirrel.

I forced my feet to move—my legs felt like they weighed two hundred pounds each and the more I moved, the slower I went. I eventually found myself at the front door.

I made a last look around to make sure I had left nothing behind and then I took a deep breath and said, "You can do this."

I closed and locked the front door behind me.

"Damn it," I said aloud.

I'd forgotten to keep out a spoon or something I could dig with. I went down one of the gravel paths until I found a small tree branch; I brought it back to the front of the house and then dug a hole under the dogwood tree by the front door.

I read the note one more time before I buried it.

"Dear Noah. You were my life and my heart. I'll always love you."

Once the cat was in his carrier, I called to the dogs to get into the car. I'd already said my goodbyes to Sara and Josh, but I had one more stop before I headed back to Prescott. I drove around to the north side of the lake, where Hudson and Candace Fisher lived. I parked a couple of doors down. I purposely hadn't called to let them know I'd be coming by, and I wanted to make sure no one was home. After what seemed like forever, I took the envelope out of my purse.

It was déjà vu all over again. When Alyce Murphy came up to the cabins so many years ago, she wanted to see if she could figure out why her father did what he did. But too many years had passed, and there was no way seeing an empty cabin where he hung himself would reveal why. After she'd gone home, Sam discovered the note her father had left. I wasn't sure I wanted to send it to her, but Noah and Sam talked me into it. I didn't really expect to hear from her, and I didn't. The note never really explained why her father did what he did; I had no idea. It just confirmed it.

Just like I'd done then, I knew I had to deliver the envelope I found to Hudson Fisher. The only thing I'd written on it was "In case you're still looking for the 4th sibling."

It would make perfect sense to him.

There was no mail slot to slip in into, so I tucked it under the doormat.

Part Three

CHAPTER TWENTY ONE

Phillip and I met at Peregrine, the local bookstore. I was looking for something new to read and by chance we were in the same aisle.

"I've not seen you here before," he said. "Are you and your husband visiting?"

"No. I moved here a little over a year ago, actually."

"I own the antiques store next door, and when I need a break, I like to come in for a few minutes. One day they'll start charging me rent since I don't always buy something."

I laughed.

"I'm Phillip," he said.

"Annie."

"Well, if you like antiques, come in to see me after you're done here."

"I do, and I will. I'm constantly at the bookstore, and I've actually bought a few things from your store, but I don't think I've ever seen you."

"Sorry I've missed you. I do have a gal who comes in when I have outside appointments. See you later, then?"

"Yes."

I found a book by one of my favorite authors, Jodi Picoult, and then I searched for titles by Carrie Davis, a former design client from up in the mountains. There was one I hadn't read, so I picked it up as well.

"I know her," I told the clerk.

"That's always fun."

I took my bag of books and left the store. When I stood outside on the sidewalk, I saw there were two antique stores, one on either side. I went to the one on the right first, and when I peeked in, I saw Phillip rearranging something on the counter. I spent a few minutes looking in his store's window and thought, "He could use some merchandising help," before I went inside.

"Well, hello again," Phillip said cheerfully as I entered. "I see you found reading to keep you busy."

I showed him both books and said, "Carrie Davis was a design client when I lived in Lake Arrowhead. And I've discovered it gets pretty quiet around here at night."

"You're a designer?"

"Yes, but I retired and moved here to be nearer to my mother."

"I'm retired as well." He looked around the store. "Oh, this is my hobby. I had an auto dealership in Orange County. In California."

"I know where you meant. I was from Long Beach."

"Well, that was silly of me. I think everyone knows where Orange County is, don't they?"

"Yes, I think you're right."

I thought I detected a slight flush in Phillip's face.

"Do you like antiques?"

"I do. I've worked with them forever, and my own personal style is pretty eclectic, traditional with a mix of mountain—taxidermy and such."

"Well, I might have something just right for you—oh, do you have a house here? I should have asked."

"Yes, I do. I bought it last year and took my time getting situated."

"Well, here you go," he said, leading me to an enormous set of deer antlers.

I studied them for a moment and then said, "These are wonderful. I have a set now, but you can never have too many of them."

"Do you have someone to help hang them?"

"I don't, actually."

"Well, I could stop by on my way home and you can tell me where you'd like them."

"Let me look around for some more things. *Like I really need anything else.*"

By the time I was finished, I'd found some uniquely shaped gourds, some roe deer antlers on carved wood backs, a bronze antler table lamp, and a wonderful pair of pheasants mounted in flight.

"I see you've found quite a bit. When will you be home?" Phillip asked.

"I usually have dinner with my mother, so if you're thinking tonight, I should be home around seven-thirty, if that's not too late. We can always eat earlier..." I bit the inside of my cheek in thought. "We'll eat earlier tonight and I'll be home by around six-thirty if that works better for you."

"I'll take you up on earlier, so it's still light enough for me to find you. Just jot down your address on the invoice, and, oh, put your phone number down as well."

"Are you a wine drinker?" I asked.

"I've been known to imbibe."

"Then I'll have a bottle ready for us, *after* you finish hanging the antlers. I don't want you falling off the ladder."

He smiled, and I smiled back.

The dogs heard Phillip drive up before I did, and they raced to the front door where they stood wagging their tails.

"Some watch dogs you are," I said.

When I opened the door, they stood at my side for only a few seconds before they rushed to greet him, barking with delight to have company.

"I hope you like dogs," I said, as Philip waited for them to calm down.

"I think this one actually smiled at me," he said, setting his toolbox down and reaching down to pet both of them.

"That's Tucker. Cooper is the kisser, so just push them both away if they annoy you."

"If I'd have known, I would have brought treats," he said, making his way in to the entry.

"I've found the perfect place for the antlers," I said, snapping my fingers to get the dogs to come in. "I didn't think I had much wall space left, but I think we can squeeze these in."

"Great. I'll just get my ladder and meet you back inside."

The moment he came back inside, Tucker looked at me for permission, but before I could give it, he nudged Phillip's hand for a pet.

"You're bad," I said.

"He's fine. I like dogs. When I got a divorce, my wife kept ours."

"I have a cat too, but he hides when someone new comes to the house."

After Phillip hung the antlers, I asked if he minded hanging the pheasants and in no time, he was putting his tools away.

"I hope you like red," I said, uncorking a bottle of merlot.

"My favorite."

I poured, and we toasted.

"To a new customer, and hopefully a new friend," he said.

"Yes, that would be nice."

We talked comfortably.

"I'm divorced," he said.

"I lost my husband almost two years ago."

I wasn't sure why I just blurted that out. But to my surprise, Phillip didn't flinch.

"Oh, I'm sorry," he said, touching my hand.

"Do you have children?" I asked.

"Yes, a daughter. And you?"

"No. It wasn't in the cards for me."

Phillip frowned.

"Oh, it's all right. I'm a workaholic, it turns out."

"So was I."

"Do you like it here?"

"I do. I wish I would have done it sooner, but I was still building the dealership. And my daughter was still home until she went away to college. What about you?"

"My parents moved here years ago, and when I needed a change of scenery, this seemed the perfect place to come. It reminds me so much of Lake Arrowhead, although it's a higher elevation. I love the weather. And I wanted to live somewhere where there's a small town vibe; where everyone knows everyone."

Phillip raised his eyebrows and teased, "Well, that can be bad if you're trying to keep a secret."

I guessed him to be in his late fifties, and he was not only charming, but pleasant to look at. He had a full head of thick gray hair and I wondered if he'd grayed prematurely.

Noah had only recently started graying at the temples before his accident. And then it felt almost laughable even thinking about the comparison between the two. I wasn't looking for a new man in my life.

Before we knew it, it was eleven, and Phillip needed to be off.

"I don't open the store until ten, but I *do* need my beauty sleep," he said lightheartedly. "And I've really enjoyed tonight."

"So have I. I'll have to come back in and buy something else so you can hang it."

I couldn't believe I'd just said that.

"It's a deal. Or just stop in the next time you're at the bookstore. You don't have to buy anything."

"Thanks, Phillip," I said honestly.

"Thank *you*, Annie," he said, touching my shoulder.

The next day when I called my mother, I told her how our evening had gone, and she playfully said, "You're not looking for a new man yet, are you?"

There's always some truth in a comment spoken in jest, and for some reason, I was slightly on the defensive.

"No," was all I said.

"Oh honey, I was just kidding you," she quickly said. "I think you'll find someone when you're ready, if that's what you decide to do. Please don't be offended."

I changed the subject.

"You'll have to see the new antlers I bought from him the next time you're over."

A week later, Phillip called and asked if I wanted to have dinner with him.

"No pressure," he was quick to add. "I just enjoyed your company and thought if you haven't been to the new restaurant in town, I'd like to try it."

I'd been thinking about him. I wasn't sure in exactly what capacity, for I couldn't wrap my head around being with someone new after being with Noah for so long.

"In fact, since you're usually with your mother, the invitation is open to her as well," he added.

It was almost like asking a single mom to dinner and having her bring her kids. It sounded safe.

"Let me see if she'd like that. She may be getting tired of me."

"I don't see how she could be. It's the other way around. Mothers love their children forever. Or so I'm told."

Mother and I met Phillip at The Uptown Café and had a wonderful evening. He was entertaining, and I could tell Mother liked him instantly. The conversation was relaxed and comfortable, and the meal was delicious. Phillip shared how he wound up owning an antique store; he was looking for something to occupy himself, and always loved hunting for unique and interesting objects. He collected for about a year before opening the store, so he'd have plenty of merchandise to fill it. In no time, people came to him with things they wanted to sell outright or put on consignment, and he frequented estate sales in the surrounding areas.

I could understand his passion.

He talked about his daughter who still lived in Orange County, and then he quietly spoke about losing his young son many years ago. He'd been hit by a car while riding his bike to school. It surprised me how he seemed to feel comfortable telling us this, but while he talked, I notice his face paled. After a sip of water, his color returned.

Mother talked about being married to a Taiwanese man, which in their time was a rare occurrence. She talked about how my father's family disowned him when he married her, but after *his* father's death, his mother and brother welcomed our family home. She also talked about Loni, which I thought was interesting, for she was a very private person and I'd never heard her speak about my sister to a stranger.

I talked about David and coming up to the mountains, meeting Noah, divorcing David and then eventually marrying Noah. I found I could talk about his death; it surprised me that with time, it had become less uncomfortable for me.

We wrapped up the evening with a promise to dine again soon.

"He's a very nice man," my mother said when we got in the car.

"He is, isn't he?" was all I said. I wasn't quite sure what to think.

Phillip and I were friends for over a year. The three of us had dinners at one of our local favorites, or on the weekends, if a new restaurant opened, we'd try it out. Sometimes he cooked for us, and if he'd had a full day and was tired, he'd go get something and bring it home. He always had dog biscuits in his pockets, and he taught Tucker and Cooper to shake hands and dance.

On a much grander scale than our Memorial Day Festival, Prescott celebrated Frontier Days around the Fourth of July weekend. The streets were lined with American flags, and half circle bunting flags hung from almost every store front. On the day of the parade, people brought their chairs and lined up early for the best views of what was to come: the cowboys dressed in all their regalia, and the Clydesdale horses pulled a wagon with the town's mayor and cowgirls of all ages in western gear. Vendors set up tents selling everything from flags to belt buckles, and people along the Whiskey Row bars were lined up outside.

Phillip got us tickets for the rodeo; Mother and I had never been to one, and it surprised me how entertaining it all was. There was bareback riding and tie-down roping where the rider catches a calf and ties three of its legs together. The most exciting was the classic saddle bronc riding; the cowboy had to keep both feet in the stirrups and one hand on the bronc rein for eight seconds. Phillip whooped and hollered along with all the other spectators, and I had to laugh at him, dressed in his boots, jeans, cowboy shirt and hat.

He made a fine-looking cowboy.

He turned to me, as if knowing what I was thinking, and took my hand.

The closest we'd gotten to being romantic was us hugging or him giving me a gentle kiss goodnight. Even then, I could sense a hidden passion in me as well as in him.

I felt like we were a very prim and proper middle-aged couple. Even my mother asked when we were going to do something more with our relationship.

But what I truly loved about Phillip, before I ever acknowledged that I did indeed love him, was that he loved me as a person, and he wasn't looking for someone merely to have sex with. I knew the day would eventually come when we'd spend the night together, and part of me dreaded having someone see me naked. Another part worried about letting my emotions show, and the last part wanted to speed the process up.

The first night we spent together was at my house, which made me feel most comfortable. It wasn't like some crazy movie scene where the man and woman rip the clothes off each other, but it was a slow and gentle undressing of each other (with the lights off) and then laying next to each other on my bed.

I knew the moment I saw my mother the next day, she'd figured it out, and all she said was, "It's about time." It reminded me of when Noah and I first came in to Ginny's as a couple, and one of the waitresses said the same thing.

The next year, Phillip and I were married at the Hassayampa Inn in Prescott and, from the rooftop of the hotel, we drank champagne and watched the desert sun disappear into the horizon. There were just a few of us; my mother, of course, Sara and Josh, and Toni and Todd who lived nearby. Phillip's daughter Caroline came with her husband and children, and afterwards we had dinner downstairs in the courtyard.

We both loved our individual homes, so we did something different after we were married; we spent one month at my house and one month at his. The dogs loved it, and the cat, being a cat, wasn't thrilled, but he soon learned to roll with the punches. It was almost like having lots of mini-vacations.

After Noah died, I'd sworn I never wanted to get to know another man, especially one who came with baggage and possibly bad habits I wouldn't be able to break. I was pleasantly surprised with Phillip. Early on I'd kept my eyes open to any red flags, and while there were a few things, like not folding a towel and putting it back where it belonged, or putting the toilet seat down, there was nothing he did that I couldn't live with. I was certain there were things I did that surprised him, but throughout our entire time together, he never mentioned any of them to me.

When the gift store around the corner came up for sale, I asked Phillip how he felt about me buying it. I recalled how I'd sometimes made spontaneous decisions before telling Noah I wanted to do something and I knew it caused tension between us.

"I think it's a great idea. It'll give you something to do, and we can grab a bite on the way home after closing the stores."

I brought in some of Phillip's antiques to make my displays more interesting, and I'd always loved buying, so now I could do it again.

I called Toni, who only lived about twenty minutes away, to see if she was interested in coming to work a few days a week, and I was pleasantly surprised when she said, "I'd love to pick up where we left off."

We had new wills drawn up. Mine was simple; everything I had would go to Phillip, except for the commercial building I still owned with Sarah and Josh, and a small amount of cash that would go to Sarah's two children, Robert and Ava. Everything Phillip had would go to me until I died, and then it would go to his daughter Caroline.

I always called her by her proper name, Caroline, but Phillip called her Sissy, which I was certain was because his son had done so when they were both young. Caroline and I became very close. I'd call her and bring her up to date about what we were doing, and she'd call to let me know what was going on with the grandkids. When they came for a visit, the children would ask, "Which house do we get to stay in this time?"

Life with Phillip was comfortable and loving. It was a mature love; one with passion, but calmer, more relaxed. Phillip read the newspaper while we ate breakfast and I always had a current novel on hand. The stores kept us busy during the day and we still had dinners with my mother on the way home. He was so kind to her, which was easy for him. My mother looked to him if she needed help with something. True to his easygoing nature, he was always more than willing to oblige. We rarely took time away from the stores, but when we did, we included her. It was like he understood she was part of me, and she became part of him, too.

We ate breakfast every morning at Lucy's Café in town, and two times a week I'd work in his store merchandising it, especially if he'd purchased an estate. I tried to set up a few vignettes to look like someone's home. Just like in my stores in Lake Arrowhead, I secretly hated it when someone bought something that changed the look of the vignette. I had Sarah design a nice sale tag to put on items he no longer wanted, and she made up a new logo for business cards and personalized bags for customer purchases.

"You're making me look too fancy," Phillip teased when he opened the bags, but he winked at me when he said it.

CHAPTER TWENTY TWO

Just before I turned sixty, my mother died in her sleep. Her answering machine picked up the two times I'd called her that morning, which was unusual. It was around eleven when I called her neighbor to check in on her, and he was the one who found her still in her bed.

I called 911, and we closed the stores. When we got there, a police car with lights flashing was parked in front, and the coroner was on his way. I didn't want to wait, so I went inside. Aside from the police radio, the house was eerily quiet. When I went into the bedroom, my mother looked like she was sleeping. Sitting beside her on the bed, I touched her cheek, and I couldn't help but cry. When they brought her out on the gurney, I took her icy hand in mine and gently kissed it. I couldn't believe I'd lost my dear sweet mother.

It surprised me when the cause of death was listed as cardiac arrhythmia. I hadn't known she had any real heart issues. Later, when I checked her medicine cabinet, I saw among the typical collection of medicinal remedies, half filled bottles of amlodipine, for high blood pressure, and Lipitor, for cholesterol, but I took those also.

Either Phillip or I always took my mother to her doctor's appointments since we didn't want her driving, so I wondered if she'd instructed the doctor to not talk about anything if we were there with her.

Sarah and Josh came out for the funeral and the moment I saw them, I knew something wasn't right. Josh didn't look well, and although they went through the motions of being a couple, something was off. It was just like Sarah to clam up when I asked her what was going on, so I dropped it. Phillip and I were staying at his house, which left my house for them, and I hoped she'd talk to me before they went back home. No matter how many times I tried to pull her aside, she insisted everything was all right, so eventually I had to let it go.

Todd and Toni drove in too, as did Caroline and her husband. It was surprising my mother knew so few people other than her neighbors at the park, so the chapel was only about a quarter full. It reminded me of what Sarah had said about how only a few people attended her mother's funeral. I couldn't help but think it would be that way for *my* service when my time came.

I was a little nervous before I got up to speak, but Phillip took my hand and kissed it.

"Thank you for coming today. Unless you have a terrible childhood, you always think your parents are not only invincible, but the best people you know, especially your mother, who nurtured you and kissed away your pain.

"As most of you know, my parents were unique. My father came from Taiwan to make a better life for himself, and while at college, he met my mother. In those days, it was unthinkable for some to have two people from different cultures who loved each other, to marry and have children.

"My sister and I grew up knowing we were just different enough that we stood out from everyone else. When I was young, that bothered me. But as I matured, I understood my parents' love for each other, and I discovered that what people thought wasn't important.

"Of course, today almost anything goes, and the reason I even bring this up is that both my parents raised us to be honest, to be color blind when we chose our friends, and to care about others.

"I know I'll get over some of the emptiness I feel right now, but I don't want to ever forget how much I loved my mother."

Sarah spoke next.

"I was one of those children who *didn't* have a great childhood, and without Annie and her mother, I think I would have starved to death."

The people in attendance laughed.

"Mrs. C., as I called her, worked in the food program at our school, and she knew more than I gave her credit for. She and Annie made sure I had something to eat for breakfast. And I always thought I was pulling something over on her when I went back into the cafeteria line and said, 'I dropped my cookies.' She'd say, 'Oh, honey, here's another one.'

"I don't know that I ever thanked her for watching out for me; I hope she knew how much I appreciated her.

"I'll miss you too, Mrs. C. And I love you, Annie."

Sarah and Josh left the next morning, and I never had a chance to find out what was going on. I thought about when she first came up to the mountains, and kept to herself about what was going on in her life. Eventually she opened up while we sat under umbrellas in the Adirondack chairs outside the cabins. I thought we had a summer rain that day, though it really didn't matter—it was one of the many times we sat and talked—we watched Jezebel and Socks tip toe out on to the rain soaked pine needles and leaves, then dart back inside. I'd been telling her how I loved the smells of the mountains, and she'd said, "I could stay here."

I said, "Why don't you?"

And she did.

It was inevitable I'd lose my mother one day, and as I'd watched her age over the years, I always told myself she had plenty of time. She was so gentle and had grown more innocent with age. I hadn't anticipated losing her so unexpectedly. I was lost. My world had taken another wrong turn, and I felt an acute sense of loss. For weeks, I would lie in bed at night, with images of her being taken away on that gurney, until eventually, I could free my mind enough to fall asleep.

Phillip and I went through her personal things, and I kept her wedding rings and most of our family's pictures. I saw she had some of the same photos I did; of me and Loni in our Easter dresses and those awful school photos with us missing our front teeth. Of course, she'd kept all our baby photos and tons of us growing up; some I hadn't seen in years. In her wedding album, she and my father looked so young and hopeful; they'd been fortunate in their love for each other for so many years. I sorted through Loni's wedding book and only kept a few photos of her.

And then I saw it; at the bottom of the drawer, my mother had kept my wedding album from when I married David. My heart skipped only a few beats before I quickly set it in the pile to be discarded. My parents never cared for him, and she'd probably forgotten she had it.

Then there was my wedding to Noah. I already had my own album from that beautiful April day we married, but even if it was a duplicate, I knew I couldn't just toss this extra one aside. I'd find a place for it with all the other photographs.

The smaller album with photos of me and Phillip was a duplicate too, but I'd keep it also, along with everything else.

I glanced through the scrapbooks she made from our trip to see my father's family in Taiwan, and from the time we spent up in Lake Arrowhead. I would treasure these forever.

When we were finished, I called a woman's shelter to come in and take what they could use and we donated the rest to one of the thrift shops.

I had the interior of Mother's mobile home painted and carpeted before we put it up for sale. It took almost a year because prospective buyers had to go through hoops to qualify; not for a loan, but to agree to all the restrictions. No overnight guests under the age of fifty-five, only two pots with plants out front, no parking in front of the home, no loud music, and prospective buyers had to present a year's worth of bank statements to prove they had sufficient income to retire there. Talk about discouraging prospective buyers!

I was grateful I had my gift shop, for when I found myself grieving for my mother, I could change my thoughts, focusing on things I needed to do. Both our stores kept me busy. My mother lived a full life, and that knowledge should have made me feel a little better, but she was still gone. I'd grown so accustomed to being with her, I felt emptiness even when Phillip tried to comfort me.

He'd lost his parents years ago; first his father and then after we were married, his mother. But he never seemed to suffer from the same sense of loss as I had. I knew most men handled grief a lot differently than women did. He'd broken down at hearing the news about his mother, but only once, and then he remained composed throughout the funeral. He'd paid little attention to details, where his daughter Caroline insisted everything be perfect. She selected the flowers, chose the music, selected the pallbearers, and went through family photos so she could make up storyboards.

I met Phillip's first wife at his mother's funeral. She was an attractive woman, all dressed in black, including a small hat with a net covering her face. I hadn't thought to dress so chic; I wore a black dress with matching stockings and shoes.

Caroline came to us and welcomed me.

"Mother, this is Annie," she said, greeting me with a kiss on the cheek.

"Sorry to meet you under these circumstances," I said, although I couldn't think of any circumstances other than a wedding or funeral where we would have met.

"Me too," she said. "Oh, Phillip, luncheon will be under your name at the club in case you get there before we do."

"That was rude," Phillip said once we were out of earshot.

"She's just marking her territory," I said.

"Well, I don't like it."

"It's fine."

"She's probably put us at the children's table," he said.

I laughed.

"You're funny. If she has, then look at it on the bright side. We won't have to sit with her."

It was almost as bad as that. We got to the club before anyone and Phillip checked the seating arrangements, and we weren't at the family table at all. He quickly exchanged his card with hers, and when she finally drifted into the room, we were already seated.

She was furious.

"Good one, Dad," Caroline said.

"She was *my* mother, after all," was all he said.

Six months after I lost my mother, Sarah called to tell me Josh had passed away.

"I'll get a flight out as soon as I can," I said.

"I'll fill you in when you get here," was all she'd say.

Phillip offered to go with me, but both of us couldn't be gone from the stores, and if I was honest, I was almost relieved he wouldn't be joining me. Not that I didn't love his company, but it would be the first time I'd been back up the mountains since I'd moved away. I didn't trust my emotions, and if I was by myself, I didn't have to pretend my nerves weren't shattered.

Sarah picked me up at the airport and after we hugged and got teary-eyed, I loaded my suitcase in to the back seat and we headed back up the hill. The call of the mountains was almost as strong as it had been when I first came up as a child, and then later when I came up to decide what to do with my life. I couldn't think of the word at first, but then it came to me; it was bittersweet, and I felt the same peacefulness I'd felt so many years ago.

We drove past the design store and At The Cabin on the way to her house. I hadn't wanted to stay there, knowing her children and their families might stay with her too and I truthfully would have felt more comfortable in a hotel. But she insisted, and I wanted to know what had happened. Sarah still lived in the same cabin she and Josh bought after they got married, and when we drove up, I could see it had been well cared for over the years.

"Soon," she said when I gave her my raised eyebrow look. "We can talk after dinner with the kids. They're looking forward to spending some time with you. We've already made all the funeral arrangements, so now we can take a breath. Until tomorrow, that is."

"Are you sure there's enough room?" I tried to sound upbeat, but I wasn't sure it came across that way.

"We'll be snug as bugs. The kids will have their old bedrooms, the grandkids can camp out in the living room, and you can sleep with me."

Although there was a new owner, The Cowboy Bar was still there, and Sarah suggested we go there for rib eyes. Even driving up to the building, my stomach flipped, and it was worse when we walked inside. Truthfully, I couldn't understand why Sarah would want to go back to our old stomping grounds.

"Robert and Ava wanted to bring everyone here," Sarah said, as if reading my mind.

The minute we opened the door, the old musty smell of beer and stale cigarettes transported me back to what seemed like a hundred years ago; to when Noah and I first fell in love, and also to the beginning of Sarah's and Josh's relationship. The music hadn't started yet, so once we rearranged tables and chairs to accommodate us all, we were able to get a little caught up.

Ava had become a physical therapist, and she and her husband, a pharmacy tech, lived with their two children in Palm Desert, near Palm Springs. Robert, a computer geek, as he called himself, worked for a national payroll company and his wife was a special education teacher in Los Alamitos.

Of course they knew I'd remarried, and I told them about Phillip and how we stayed busy with our stores. They told me they were both sorry to hear about my mother, and I gave them a weak smile to acknowledge their condolences.

Sarah talked about Josh's kidney disease.

"It started when I made him go to the doctor. He was diagnosed with high blood pressure and diabetes, and he pretty much didn't take care of himself."

"Mother," Ava whispered.

"Well, it's something you kids need to know. You need to take care of yourselves before you get to a point where nothing can be done."

The table was silent except for the kids who were oblivious to any of our conversation, and I, for one, could tell Sarah felt bitter about it all. I made the decision to wait until we were alone to learn more, but only if she would talk to me about it.

"Anyone for dessert?" I asked, changing the subject.

Once we were finally in bed, I made Sarah tell me what was going on.

"It's pretty simple," she started. "I knew there was something wrong with him, and he wouldn't go to the doctor. We'd started growing apart, as a lot of couples do, just having different goals, and he thought I worked too much. I love working with clients, and hearing their stories, even if they can be bizarre. You know that more than anyone.

"No matter how much I tried, he continued to drink soda and eat the wrong foods, and honestly, Annie, after a while, I just gave up. And of course, that made things between us even worse. It was almost as if the sicker he got, the more angry I was with him. Everything he did got on my nerves, and to tell you the truth, I still feel angry, but mix that with feeling guilty for giving up? Well, the combination was really hard for me."

I was at a loss for words. I could only imagine what Sara was going through, knowing what I struggled with when Noah died. And I hadn't been angry with him.

"I'm so sorry," was all I could think to say, and I didn't know what to do.

Before I could comfort her, she rolled over and turned her back on me.

I had a difficult time sleeping. Not only was I in a bed Sara shared with Josh, but sleeping with someone other than Phillip was awkward. I wanted to grab an extra blanket and sleep on the sofa, but when I peeked out the bedroom door, young adults were sleeping everywhere. I tiptoed back to bed and hoped I hadn't woken Sara.

When I finally drifted off, Sarah's quiet sobs woke me throughout the night.

When I got up, I was so physically and mentally exhausted I didn't know how I was going to make it through the day. I'd come up to support Sarah and yet I somehow felt like I wasn't going to be any good to her or her family. I waited in line for the bathroom and eventually brushed my teeth and had my shower. When Sarah came out of the bedroom, she was red eyed and congested from crying all night.

I hugged her.

We all voted cooking was not an option, so we had breakfast at the old Ginny's, which had changed hands again and was now called Julia's Kitchen. We had some time to kill, so we headed over to the Village to sit and look out at the lake. A gift shop now sold duck food, so we bought a couple of bags, and the moment we opened them and stood at the railings, the ducks knew we were going to feed them. Dozens swam over and several sets of ducklings obediently followed; watching them learn to eat without immersing their heads deep into the water made me smile.

I waited for everyone on the old bench still outside the gift shop, and as I raised my face towards the sky, the sun felt good on my skin. I was grateful for a cool breeze. Out of the corner of my eye, I saw a butterfly land on the bench next to me. Mesmerized, I watched its wings slowly open and close, it too seeming to rest and sun itself.

"Did you know when they extend their wings like that it's a way to camouflage themselves from birds?" Robert's son said, quietly coming to stand near me. "Their wings can also match leaves and bark."

"Well, how did you get so smart?" I asked.

"I don't know. I read about them, and I guess it stuck," he said.

"Well, now, it looks like I've just learned something new too," I said.

"Ready to head over?" Robert finally asked. "I think we're it, and Dad's probably getting anxious."

His wife gave him a twisted smile.

He thought it was funny and just shrugged his shoulders.

We had a late lunch at the Sports Grill. I'd been in a hundred times when I still lived in the mountains, but the minute I walked into the front door, I couldn't help but think back to when I first officially talked to Noah. It was there. I hadn't recognized him when he came up to my table until I saw his work boots, and then I realized he was the man who'd been standing in the doorway when I was checking into the cabins with Sam.

They too had a new owner, and yet everything looked the same. The large painted map of Lake Arrowhead was still on the wall, although someone had touched up the paint from years of cleaning, and each television was broadcasting a different sport; baseball, hockey, and reruns of old basketball and football games. Usually when a new owner kept the old menu, things just tasted different, but I ordered my old standby, their signature chicken club sandwich, and I was surprised it was as good as I'd remembered it.

After we ate, I wanted to see my old stores, so we waited for traffic to slow down, then we paraded across the street, the kids much like the ducklings, following their mothers on the lake. I saw that a new realtor had opened next door to the design store, and I paused to check out the listings they advertised in the window. A woman within waved to me, and it turned out to be Beth, the realtor who helped me process the sales of Noah's cabin and the cabins on the highway.

"You've changed offices?" I asked when she came out.

"I thought it was time. My old boss isn't very happy about it, but I think it's a good move."

"Wow, prices have really gone up," I said, looking back at the listings in the window.

"It's great if you're selling," Beth said, holding her arms out for a hug. "I know why you're up, and I'm really sorry to hear about Josh."

Sarah caught up with us and gave Beth a quick hug, too.

"I wanted to see the old place before I headed home," I said.

"It's good to see you, Annie," Beth said as she turned to go back into the real estate office. "We've missed you. Safe trip back."

When I got to the design store, everyone had already gone inside, and I had to wait to get in. In a way, everything looked the same, but different. I noticed some updated sample display racks and new merchandise filled shelves. Sarah had done a great job of keeping everything in order.

"It looks super," I said genuinely.

I pulled her to me, although she tried to pull away. She nodded slightly—it seemed only to acknowledge me—and it was obvious she wasn't handling Josh's death any better today. Her dull eyes scanned the store, and then when she looked back at me, I almost thought she was going to burst into tears. But she maintained her composure. My eyes filled just looking at her and understanding the pain she was feeling.

"We can still talk before I leave, you know," I said.

"I'll be fine. I'm actually looking forward to having the house back to myself. Not that I haven't appreciated everyone, but I need the peacefulness I love about this place."

I understood, but from experience, I wanted to tell her that the peacefulness probably wasn't going to be as tranquilizing as she hoped it would be. Maybe the silence would be more comforting to her than it ultimately was for me.

I could tell both Robert and Ava were anxious to get the kids rounded up, and I wondered if they were going to try to head home tonight. I knew I was ready to get back, but I'd committed to staying with Sarah for as long as she needed me.

When we returned to the cabin, the kids packed everything up, and once they pulled out of the driveway, I had to admit the quiet of the cabin was welcomed. I saw it in Sarah as well. Neither of us was very hungry for dinner, so we made popcorn, drank soda and had Oreo cookies and Doritos. I knew I was going to feel like crap in the morning.

"Do you want to talk about it?" I asked once we turned off the TV.

"I'm good. I just need time to sort through it all," Sarah said.

"Well, I'm here."

She said, "Now that we have the cabin to ourselves, I won't be offended if you want to sleep in one of the kid's bedrooms or on the sofa."

"I think I'll take you up on that. For some reason, my back is killing me."

It was, but not because I'd slept in Sarah's bed. It was from the stiffness of constantly tensing my muscles. I slept better that night, but in the morning, I felt like crap from eating so much junk food. A quick shower gave me a new lease on life, and I wanted to help Sarah start sorting through Josh's things.

"Only if you're ready," I said. "Everyone does things at their own pace."

"I'd love the help. I've been collecting boxes from the store, and we can start in one of the other bedrooms. That's where Josh had been staying, so a lot of his things are already there."

That one caught me by surprise.

"Once he started getting sicker, it was easier for him to sleep in the other room. For both of us," she added.

"Then let's start there," I said. "Give me some boxes."

I was hoping Sarah and I would have talked again, but I remembered how I'd felt when I was dealing with Noah's death, and I offered to be there if and when she wanted me to be.

"Since we're hitting all the old stomping grounds, can we go to the Saddleback Inn for dinner?" I asked. "I don't know when I'll be back up, and I'd hate to leave without eating there one more time."

The minute we were seated, I ordered a bottle of wine and we toasted, "To one day at a time," I said.

"Yes, I can do one day at a time."

"I don't think we made a very big dent," I said.

"Actually, it's the opposite. I was able to start. I think that's always the worst part—just starting."

I found a flight out the next day, and I didn't realize just how much I missed home until I saw Phillip at the airport.

"I've missed you," I said, kissing him on the cheek.

"Not nearly as much as I've missed you."

Poor old Cooper was now our only dog, and he rushed—in his own way—to greet us at the door. I couldn't help but think there was nothing quite like the love of an animal to welcome you home. Once he settled down and I sat in my favorite chair, Dillinger, the cat, poked his head into the family room, and then sauntered over to sit on my lap. He looked back up at me—as if saying 'I'm glad you're back,' before he made himself comfortable enough to nap.

That next fall, Phillip and I hired people to work our stores, and we flew back to New England to see the fall colors and to go on a buying trip. I'd always wanted to do something like that, and since he'd been once before, he knew just where he wanted to go.

We had four seasons in the mountains and in Prescott, but nothing like the fall on the east coast. As the air got crisper, the leaves changed color, and the landscape was transformed into reds, oranges and golds.

I loved stopping in all the stores and warehouses, and I couldn't get over how much more there was to choose from than any of the stores I'd been to in California. And the prices were a lot more reasonable, which meant it would be easier to ship everything back and still make a profit. We'd decided neither of us wanted to rent a large truck and drive it back to Prescott.

To make bookkeeping easier, Phillip purchased everything for *his* store, and then after we returned and when the truck arrived with our treasure trove, we'd priced it all out, and I could choose what I wanted to put on consignment in my store. While we waited, I put sale signs on everything we no longer wanted, and I cleared areas in both our stores for the new merchandise. When the truck arrived, we paid the drivers extra to help us bring it in and help us place everything where we wanted it.

CHAPTER TWENTY THREE

We kept our stores until we were both in our seventies and grew tired of schlepping things around. I only wanted to deal with one store closing at a time, so I put mine up for sale first. After about six months, I found a buyer, and Phillip helped me do an inventory. The new buyer wanted about fifty percent of what I had in stock, so I made a separate list of what was left and if Phillip didn't want it, I donated it to the Boys and Girls Club thrift store. They were delighted, and I got to write it off.

Phillip sold his store next. The new owner hadn't been an antiques shopper and wanted a full store, so he bought almost everything, which was a godsend. Phillip was more attached to his merchandise than I was, and he hated selling it all in bulk. We set up a sale area in the store for everything else, and when escrow closed, we had the Boys and Girls Club back out to take away a truckload of the rest of the small items.

By then, instead of alternating houses, we mostly stayed in my house since it was the larger of the two. The upkeep on both houses was getting to be too much for us, so we had Caroline and her children out one last time before we put Phillip's house on the market. I knew he still loved his home, and part of me felt selfish the few times I tried to sway him, gently pointing out how it was the best thing to do. No one ever wanted to get to an age where they made decisions based on the stage of their life they're in, and that's how he felt.

Dear Noah

For the most part, I was silent as he gallantly went room by room, listing everything he wanted to keep. In between déjà vu—having images of David and me doing the same thing almost fifty years ago—I made a mental note every time he wrote something down, trying to determine if I would have to change out something I already had to fit it in to my house. I wished we still had one of our stores so we could at least try to sell some things, but that wasn't how it was to be.

Secretly, I was glad it took a while for his house to sell; if it had gone quickly, I think it would have devastated him. As it was, he went over there almost every day to see if any realtors had been by and left their card. Almost three months later, a new family wanted the house, and Phillip made sure he met them before he accepted their offer. He gave his daughter and grandchildren most of the proceeds.

We figured no matter who died first, we were set for the rest of our lives.

We all have seasons in our lives, and I was in my wintertime when I decided to write about living in the mountains. In fact, I'd just celebrated my eightieth birthday, which some would think was too old to even take on such a challenge. But by then, I'd had plenty of time to look back on my life—time had brought me much happiness and had healed most of my sorrows and disappointments.

When Sarah died, I insisted on traveling by myself back to New York to attend her funeral. Phillip had a bad knee, and I knew he wouldn't be comfortable sitting on a plane for hours, and I knew I could have someone at the airport help me if I needed it.

She'd never remarried after losing Josh so many years ago, and in a way, I didn't blame her. Her son Robert had transferred out of state, and when her daughter Ava divorced and remarried a man from upstate New York, Sarah sold the stores and the commercial property we owned together, and she moved back east. She'd sent me photos of the charming cottage she lived in on their property, and yet I still couldn't believe she'd move away from the mountains where she'd started a new life. But when Phillip and I traveled back to see her one fall, I understood why;

we loved everything about the place. Her house was nestled into a copse of trees where two dogs frolicked, and she'd even planted a garden.

I didn't know why I was surprised she'd do that; until I saw how happy she was. And, after all, that's what I did after Noah died. Sometimes you have to move away to really begin the healing process.

Now, outside the chapel, I saw Sarah's son Robert first. He was greeting everyone as they entered the chapel, and he looked so handsome in his suit. Just like a miniature of his father, Josh. It made me think back to the day Sarah and he got married under the gazebo on the cobblestones of Noah's cabin so many years ago.

"Auntie," he sighed as he enveloped me in a bear hug.

"I don't know what to say," I said dumbly. "We'll miss her."

His two sons stood near us. "You remember Auntie," he said to them, encouraging them to greet me. Of course, they couldn't have remembered me. They were in their forties, and I hadn't seen them in over twenty years. They were so handsome standing there in their suits; my heart brightened to think that Sarah had had such a lovely family. And then I saw Ava.

"Oh, Auntie," she said. "I was afraid you weren't going to make it after all."

When I held Ava in my arms, I closed my eyes and pictured me hugging Sarah. When the children were born, she'd given me several choices of what I wanted to be called; Aunt Annie didn't sound right, and Auntie Annie was too sing-songish, so I decided on just Auntie. As they grew older, I noticed when I spoke with them they'd dropped the Auntie, and started calling me just Annie. But not that day.

"Wild horses couldn't have kept me away," I said. "I wish I could have been here sooner, you know, to help you pick out the casket and make the arrangements. I can't tell you how many times your mother was my strength and moral support when I needed her. I wanted to come out a day earlier, but I couldn't get myself a flight." I was babbling. And of course I wasn't telling the truth.

Ava hugged me again. "You're here now," she said soothingly.

I could have made it work. I just couldn't bear to say goodbye to my friend.

"And I had plenty of support from my husband and my children. In fact, here he is. John, you remember Annie."

Suddenly, it sounded strange to hear her call me that again.

Once inside, I looked around at those gathered there, and I felt the same way I did when Sarah and I talked about the funerals we'd attended over the years—how the crowds were sparse—and it reminded me it would be the same for me when I died. I cried, as I always did at funerals and weddings, and when Ava spoke, it broke my heart to hear how much she loved her mother. I should have had the courage to get up and talk about Sarah like she had done when my mother died, but I hadn't prepared anything, and Ava hadn't asked me.

Sitting behind her, when the service was over, I was among the first to get up and acknowledge the family before stopping at Sarah's casket. I wished they wouldn't have had it open. I hated seeing my friend looking so old. And I never remembered her wearing such a dark shade of red lipstick. It was, indeed, a somber day—for Sarah and I were the same age, and her death meant mine couldn't be far behind.

As soon as I returned home, I started writing my story.

I was ten when my parents bought the house in Lake Arrowhead. We called it The Pine Cone Lake House. The moment we drove up, I saw the shimmering water of the lake and the second my father turned the car engine off, I took off in a run. He was quick to stop me.

"Help us unload the car first," he called.

The lake house was larger than any house I'd seen, and after a quick glance at the downstairs, I rushed up the stairs and found what was to be our bedroom. When I saw the built in bunk beds, I knew we had to call it The Bunkhouse. For once, my sister Loni agreed with me. Or at least a shrug of her shoulders gave me her approval.

Even at a young age, old classic homes fascinated me. When my mother would finish reading her decorating magazines, I'd sit for hours looking at them, imagining what it would be like if we lived in something so wonderful. Of course, these homes were nothing like what normal people lived in. But even so, if I liked a page, I'd tear it out and add it to my scrapbook. I'd already filled two books, and at the rate I was going, I'd need to ask my mother to take me to the dime store so I could buy more.

The first time I saw the Pine Cone Lake House, I felt it was worthy of being in one of those the magazines. It was grand. I knew Loni never felt that way about it; I could tell by the way she treated it. She'd leave her clothes scattered on her half of the bedroom floor, and no matter how many times I reminded her, she'd leave open bags of chips and empty soda cans on her bed and around the room. One time she spilled milk and never told anyone. When we came back up almost a month later, our room smelled so bad, we couldn't sleep in there until my mother washed all the bedding and aired out the room.

Loni and I were like that all our lives when I think back on it. Opposites. We looked similar, with our dark hair and eyes, and our slender builds when we were young. She would sass my parents when they weren't looking, while I did what I was told, and rarely did I get in to trouble. I wasn't perfect, mind you, but I didn't seem to have that same restlessness Loni did. I used to envy her her friends. Boys and girls alike seemed to gravitate toward her, where I found it harder to meet new people.

There were other girls in our neighborhood that I could have walked to school with, but most of them walked with someone else and over the train tracks. I was afraid to walk by myself, so my mother, who worked at the school, drove me every morning.

I'd seen Sarah a few times, but she was from a different part of the neighborhood, and she was one of the kids who crossed over the tracks. We both lived in a middle class neighborhood, but my environment was safe—her home life was disturbing. Her parents drank, had wild parties, and she and her sisters were not allowed to have outside friends.

Once we started driving Sarah to school, my mother, who was a saint, would make sure she had something to eat every morning on the way. Because my mother worked in the cafeteria, Sarah would often get an extra serving of the lunch special of the day. With Sarah, I never felt better than her, but I learned at an early age to be grateful for what I had.

Having Sarah as my friend completed me. She'd sworn she was going to leave and go away to college the minute she could. And true to her word, she bought a bus ticket to Las Vegas and left the day we graduated from high school. She went away to go to college, and I stayed home.

Looking back on my life, Phillip and I have had many good years together, and I still think he's a terrific guy. While not as devoted to animals as I am, he's grown to tolerate and love the menageries I've brought home to share our bed. At first, he tried to break both me and whichever dog (or cat) we had at the moment from that habit, but we outvoted him every time; he's actually referred to me as "momma" when talking to them. I bought him a lint roller to keep near his reading chair so he could quickly remove pet hair from his pants when one of them sat on him.

"An outfit is not complete," I once told him, "unless it has pet hair on it."

I couldn't help but observe him over time, as I'm sure he has me too, and I've hoped his eyesight worsened when it came to seeing how much I've changed; it might have, for he's had nothing but complimentary things to say to me over all these years.

We've had medical issues that come with aging, and we've tried to change our lifestyles; but it's not that easy when you get older. You're set in your ways and, for me at least, I've wondered if changes would make a big difference if I didn't do what my doctor said. I remember an older friend being told by her doctor what not to do; 'don't have ice cream, don't have any desserts, don't eat too much, and lose weight.' Her attitude was if she'd lived to be the age she was, what difference would it make if she kept on eating and enjoying food the rest of her life? I tended to agree.

When I turned eighty, I realized there were only a few things I'd never done in my life; one was to have a ranch, and the other was to write a book. Owning a ranch was out of the question at our age, but writing a book might be something I could do.

So I asked Phillip how he felt about it—the book idea, not the ranch. Since it would be from a time when I hadn't known him, I wanted to have his blessings. Once he gave me the go ahead, I decided to write about my life before and after I moved up to the mountains.

I've tried to look back on my life, especially as I'm writing my books, and understandably, I've had some regrets.

One is that I never stood up for my sister Loni; we both had issues with our mixed heritage, but she internalized hers more than I did. We were both hurt when people teased us for looking different, but I had Sarah to defend me. I wasn't sure who Loni had.

Throughout my life, I only criticized her and got angry with her for drinking; I never stopped to ask her why she started. Had she simply hung out with the wrong crowd? I don't know if she would have talked to me about it even if I asked her to. I don't recall us ever having a serious conversation about anything. There was a lot I didn't know about her. She must have wished she was someone else, but I think I always wished I was her.

When she died, I regret not being more empathetic towards my parents. I had no idea what it was like to lose a child, and I should have done a better job being there for them. Loni and I had grown further apart over the years, and being busy with my own life, I didn't miss her like they did.

I felt I let my mother down again when my father died. I don't think children ever understand until it's too late how their parents could have ever been in love. It was just different. It was almost impossible to think of them in romantic terms; your parents were always old. I should have been there for my mother, but I was fortunate; I had a chance to make up for it when I moved back to Prescott. I found time for my own life, but I made time for hers, too.

I regret having an affair when I knew I loved Noah. He'd gone off on one of his tangents, and I was determined to do what I wanted to do. He took me back even after I broke his heart. To this day, I still feel a sorrow deep inside me when I think about it; I'd betrayed someone who loved me.

I was given a second chance with Noah, too, for I committed myself to making him happy during our marriage, and by being the best wife I could be. I know at times I pushed the envelope and frustrated him with all my ideas and adventures, but I also didn't feel I needed to apologize for them either. They were part of me, and therefore, I figured, they were part of what he loved about me.

I still regret that I can't remember if I told him I loved him when I sent him off on his hunting trip.

I regretted letting a thread break between us when Sarah moved away after high school. I still loved her, but it wasn't the same as her being there at home. Over the years, we'd both gotten married, and while my life was busy, I still thought about her often. As it does, time had a way of slipping by and then I realized I hadn't kept in touch with her as much as I wanted to. That all changed when she came up to see me in the mountains and stayed.

AUTHOR'S NOTES

As always, thanks to all my readers for following me along the journey of the cabins and their stories. The Guest Book Trilogy started out with three books, beginning when Annie turns eighty and decides to write about a period in her time that was important to her.

Once I finished with the stories about the cabins, I was curious to discover the story about the woman who owned the cabins *before* Annie bought them; that's when I wrote Book Four, *The Maidservant in Cabin Number One, the Beginning*.

Then I couldn't help but wonder what happened in Annie's life from her 40s until her 80s, and that's where the idea for *Dear Noah* began.

I'd like to thank my wonderful support team who were there for me in the beginning; Myrt Perisho, Pat Aldridge, Susan Denley, Sue Jorgenson, Joan Barkdull and my editor, Pam Shepherd. Thanks also go out to readers like Ferne Knauss and Diane Streich who have pointed out things I should have caught before going to press: I can't thank you enough for that! Along the way, I've met some wonderful readers who faithfully post when I have a new book out, and of course thanks to my special Lake Arrowhead community of ladies (and gents)! Four friends, Maria & Joel Harmon, and Toni & Todd Paul, actually let me use them as characters in this book.

And last but not least, I need to thank my wonderful husband Larry, who, when I struggle, always tells me to write what I want to write.

If you enjoyed reading the series, please tell a friend, and take a minute to leave me a review on Amazon. If you ever want to chat, email me. I always reply.

chrysteenbraun@gmail.com

chrysteenbraun.com

Dear Noah

All the places I've written about are real, but I've taken liberty with some dates (in history) so that it works for my story. I've thoroughly enjoyed researching the places and events I've included, but what I found very interesting was that in high school, I didn't have the patience for, or interest in, doing research for any papers I wrote. I had several sets of encyclopedias and the National Geographic back then that I "borrowed" from for my extra credit reports.

INTERESTING FACTS

In October 2003, 80,000 Lake Arrowhead and surrounding community residents were forced to evacuate while firefighters fought a 91,281 acre fire which destroyed 993 homes and caused six deaths. The fire was finally contained November 2, with the help of rain and snow. They estimated the final cost of fighting the fire at over 42 million dollars.

The cause of the fire was arson; witnesses saw a man throw a lit flare into the brush along the side of the road.

Two months later, another storm caused a mudslide that surged through a campsite in Waterman Canyon, causing additional deaths.

The 2003 fire had a devastating impact on Wildhaven Ranch, a wild animal preserve, destroying most of its buildings and structures. Volunteers were able to move all the animals off the mountain to other wildlife facilities, but because the structures weren't considered permanent, insurance only covered 50% of the cost to rebuild. Through grants and donations, the animal enclosures were rebuilt.

They were also deeply affected by the 2023 snowstorm, nicknamed Snowmageddon, that caused a tremendous amount of damage. Thankfully, no animals were lost or injured, but their habitats were again seriously damaged or destroyed. To this day, Wildhaven depends on donations and grants to maintain the facility and feed the animals, and they are one of my favorite charitable organizations. If you love animals and you'd like to be involved, you can make a donation by contacting wildhavenranch.org.

(The portion of my story about Noah and Josh building and doing repairs was what they would have done if they were actual people.)

In 2007, **the Slide Fire and Grass Valley Fire** destroyed over three hundred homes in the mountains. Our cousins lost their home when it burned its way down the mountain. When they were finally allowed back in to survey the damage, everything was gone but a statue of a small boy holding a soccer ball and a few pieces of her mother's china. Some families chose to forgo rebuilding, but our cousins loved living in the mountains, so they met with an architect and general contractor and rebuilt the home of their dreams. They've lived in Lake Arrowhead for over fifteen years.

Ice Castle, Lake Arrowhead

In 1988, Carol and Walter Probst built an indoor skating rink in Lake Arrowhead and established it as an international training center, where Olympians Michelle Kwan, Robin Cousins, Irina Rodnina and others trained. They purchased a nearby compound with cabins where athletes and their families could stay, attend lectures, and dine.

Olympian Anthony Liu bought the property in 2002, but in August 2013, the small rink closed. The mountains have missed it ever since.

Crestline, California

As you travel up to Lake Arrowhead, Crestline is the first town off Hwy 18. Historically, like most of the other towns up in the San Bernardino Mountains, Crestline was known for hunting, fishing, timber cutting, plus nut and fruit harvesting.

The mountain's first inhabitants were Native Americans coming up from the desert and valleys, and in the 1850s Mormons settled in San Bernardino. They logged up the mountains, traveling up over the crest, and it eventually became known as Crestline.

In the 1920s, Arthur Gregory of Redlands built a sawmill near Crestline, and he donated eighty acres of land to create Lake Gregory. In 1946, George. C. Goodwin Sr., son-in-law Bill Fuller, and son George Goodwin Jr. opened a small general store. Over the years, Goodwin's Market would grow to almost twenty thousand square feet until their 42,500 sq. ft. supermarket was opened.

In the 2023 snowstorm, Goodwin's roof collapsed, and the store was closed for rebuilding. It's now been rebuilt.

Customers from all over the mountain would stop in and say hello and shop at Goodwin's Oak Trunk store, which carried yarn, fabric, crafting supplies, fudge and ice cream, and holiday décor. In 2018, it closed.

The Stockade, Whiskey and Grub, Crestline, California
Originally established in 1954, from the outside, the Stockade looks like it belongs in a western town, with its old wood front. Inside, it's decorated with hundreds of autographed $1 bills on the walls and ceiling, along with taxidermied deer heads, a buffalo, and pictures of John Wayne. New owners, Chip Anzalone and Kyle Lake, have restored the restaurant, and when we were at a book club signing in Crestline, we couldn't resist giving the place a try. Plus, Chip and his family bought our original cabin, aka Noah's Cabin, in Sky Forest, along with our commercial property where our store, At The Cabin and The Hungry Bear Deli were, on the corner of Kuffel Canyon and Hwy. 18. You might say, we're family!

Catalina Island
For over 7,000 years, Catalina has been inhabited; it's said that Santa Catalina Island has been a stop for gold diggers, pirates, hunters, the Union Army, missionaries and smugglers.

In 1892, the island was sold to the Banning Brothers, who established the Santa Catalina Island Company, and they began building hotels and roads, as they turned it into a resort destination. They built the Pleasure Pier, which still stands today in Avalon Bay, along with developing the beach areas. In 1915, a fire burned half of Avalon's buildings, and in 1919, chewing gum magnate William Wrigley Jr., bought the island and almost every share of the Island Company. He built a reservoir, the first theater designed to show talking motion pictures and the famous Catalina Casino, which boasts the world's largest circular ballroom.

Until 1951, Avalon was the spring training home of his beloved Chicago Cubs baseball team. During World War II, the island was closed to tourists, as it had become a military training facility. In 1975, Phillip Knight Wrigley and his family deeded 42,000 acres of the island to the Catalina Island Conservancy, making it the oldest private land trust in Southern California.

In the 1930s, 40s and 50s, Catalina was a popular spot with Hollywood's elite, and has become a popular location for movies, documentaries and commercials.

Some facts about the Catalina Bison (according to a tour guide and Wikipedia): Bison aren't native to Catalina; they were originally brought over for a movie in the 1920s. At one time, the herd had grown to almost 600, and in a 2003 study, it was recommended that between 150-200 would be an ideal size and less ecologically damaging to the island. Over the years, Bison have been sent to the mainland for auction, and have been relocated to Native American reservations.

Prescott, Arizona
Prescott was once the territorial capital of Arizona until Phoenix officially became the capital. Other little-known facts, if you're not from there, for a small town, there are 809 buildings on the National Register of Historic Places. Whiskey Row is the home of The Palace Restaurant, originally built in 1877. After fire destroyed it, it was rebuilt and is now the oldest continuous business in the state.

Famous people who lived there include Wyatt Earp and Doc Holliday. The bar-room brawl scene with Steve McQueen (in Junior Bonner) was filmed at The Palace.

About the rodeos: One of Prescott's claims is that they're the world's oldest rodeo since they began charging admission in 1888. But Cheyenne, Wyoming, Winfield, Kansas, Deer Trail, Colorado and Pecos, Texas, all had what was considered "bronco-busting contests" as early as 1869.

Flagstaff, Arizona
Fires plagued early Flagstaff like so many frontier towns, and in 1897, building ordinances required buildings to be built from stone, brick or iron. John W. Weatherford built the first such building; it was a general store with living quarters above. A few years later, when he realized tourism was a growing industry, he began building what was to become The Weatherford Hotel, whose guests included William Randolph Hearst, and the novelist Zane Grey.

Oatman, Arizona
Originally, Oatman was a small mining camp that at one time boasted a population of 3,500 during the gold rush in 1863. Per the 2020 census, the population was down to 102. In 1924, the United Eastern Mines permanently shut down its operation after producing about $13.6 million worth of gold. They left the burros behind.

Today, Oatman is famous for its free roaming burros. On any given day, you can find them milling about the streets, looking for treats, and when we were there, a newborn calf was walking with its mother. The burros are protected by the locals, who make sure they're fed and cared for.

Burros and Donkeys
What's the difference between a donkey, a burro and a mule? All burros are donkeys. They derive from the African wild ass or *Equus africanus*, and have been classified either as a "subspecies thereof, or as a separate species" according to Wikipedia. Burro is Spanish for donkey.

Mules are a hybrid between a male donkey and a female horse.

Sedona, Arizona

Sedona's first people were known as the Sinagua. They built adobe structures—some capable of housing hundreds of people. After hundreds of years, the Sinagua mysteriously disappeared. Some believe they migrated north to the Hopi Mesas and some believe the holy men saw the coming of the white man and realized it was time to go. Either way, it's one of the biggest mysteries of the Southwest.

Next came the Spanish, and by the 1800s, the white man. Early settlers were farmers and ranchers. Some parts of Sedona didn't have electricity until the 1960s.

At about 4500 feet above sea level, Sedona is known for its gigantic canyons, desert areas, incredible rock formations and volcanic mountains. Redwall Limestone, which was formed between 300 and 340 million years ago, sits at the base of the famous Colorado plateau.

Tlaquepaque, (ta-la-que-pa-que) Sedona, Arizona

In the 1970s, Abe Miller, a Nevada real estate developer who loved art, began coming to Sedona for vacations. He found the perfect creek side property to create an art colony like those he'd seen in Mexico. After several years of trying to convince the property owner he'd not remove the beautiful sycamores on the land, but build around them, he built Tlaquepaque which combines art galleries and living spaces. From the Aztec people, Tlaquepaque means "best of everything."

The Mission Inn, Riverside, California

I've mentioned the Mission Inn when Annie and Laura (her friend and hairdresser) meet for lunch in a previous novel, but I wanted to have Annie and Noah spend some time there for their anniversary. It's a wonderful old hotel and is a natural historic landmark. Many famous people have stayed there including, Amelia Earhart, Albert Einstein, Helen Keller and John Muir. Movie stars Clark Gable, Tom Hanks, Barbra Streisand and James Brolin, and presidents Theodore Roosevelt, Herbert Hoover, John F. Kennedy, Gerald Ford and George W. Bush have all dined and relaxed there. Richard and Pat Nixon and Ronald and Nancy Reagan spent their wedding nights there.

During the holidays, more than four million lights illuminate the Mission and the grounds. Traditionally, The Festival of Lights is from mid-November until the first week in January. If you haven't been there, it's incredible.

Alaska

If you remember your history classes, in 1847, the United States purchased Alaska from Russia for $7.2 million (or approximately 2 cents per acre). It was then known as Russian-America. Until the gold rush in 1897, the land was so far north that to many, it was considered unusable and uninhabitable, and it was nicknamed Seward's Folly, (after then Secretary of State William H. Seward) who negotiated the purchase.

The Klondike gold rush was short-lived, and many gold seekers died from either hypothermia, malnutrition or avalanches along the route before they could make their fortunes.

The once popular name Eskimo, is now no longer used, and the people of Alaska are referred to as Alaska Natives or First Nation.

Chrysteen Braun

Continue to read an excerpt from Chrysteen Braun's novel,
Family Portrait

Coming soon…

My name is Vasiliki but I go by Vaso. For many years, I've I wanted to write this story about my family, and now that everyone is gone, I finally feel the freedom to do so. Part of me always feared what people would think about some of the things I did when I was younger, but I wanted you to know the person I was then, and the person I became. I believe it's those very things people do when they're younger that make them the person they ultimately become.

Better or worse.

In my case, better.

I've left nothing out.

But first, I want you to meet my family—to have them tell you their own stories— so that you'll know them not just from my point of view, but from theirs.

1980

If this was the beginning of a movie, in the background, while the credits were rolling, the members of my family would be making an attempt to assemble on my grandmother's front porch for a portrait. The patient photographer would be doing his best to organize us by family. But he would be contending with someone who didn't want to follow the directions of hierarchy. That would be my uncle. Even though he was the youngest of the siblings, since he was the only surviving male—and the only college graduate, and the only pompous attorney, and the most married and divorced—did I say all that aloud?—he wanted to stand closest to my grandmother with his family seated in front of him, right in the middle of us all.

"Psst!"

Yia´ Yia's whisper was barely audible as she tapped his shoulder. But I heard it. And so did Stavros. "Stand where he tells us," she said.

His face immediately turned beet red, and he glanced about to see if anyone else had heard her. Then he gathered his current wife, Kelli, and his daughters, Emma and Sophie, and moved to stand next to my mother, who was already in place with my father and brother.

I could see Uncle Eddie's mother, Auntie Bessie, awkwardly waiting to find out where she would stand, since she technically wasn't part of our family; and then my Aunt Cynthia made room for her to stand next to her on Yia´ Yia's right.

Chrysteen Braun

The standing arrangement was supposed to be much like our family tree:

My grandmother Yia´Yia (Pronounced Yi´ Ya)

My parents,	My aunt Cynthia,	My uncle Stavros
Kate & Nick,	with her husband,	with his current wife
with my older brother,	their children	and his children
his wife and children,	and their families	
and me, Vaso,		
with my family		

That's the way it should have been; my mother was the eldest, my aunt in the middle and my uncle, the youngest.

"Enough!" Yia´ Yia finally said, impatiently tapping her cane on the porch step. She didn't use her matriarchal influence on us often, but when she did, we came to attention and responded accordingly. In other words, we all fell into place.

It was a perfect day for the photo, although it meant the photographer stood facing the sun in the heat of the afternoon and we were testing his good nature. He pulled a small towel out of his bag and wiped his forehead before he called us to final attention.

In a few clicks, he was done.

Finally, the director would call "Cut!"

Afterward, Aunt Cynthia stood smoking one of her cigars and said, "You know, this will be the last photograph of all of us together."

Part of me wanted to say, "This is also the *first* photograph we've ever had," and "can you please put that awful thing out?" But I didn't.

Then she added, "I read the coffee grounds with Mother this morning, and soon, some will no longer be with us."

Only my cousin Kaylee heard this dire prediction, and we caught each other's eyes. I thought what Aunt Cynthia said was troubling. It made sense though, since Auntie Bessie was in her eighties, my grandmother was in her late seventies, and her three children were in their fifties. But my aunt was known for saying what she thought, and my older brother especially adored her. After all, they were both kindred spirits.

In other words, they were both rebels.

Aunt Cynthia had predicted our fate accurately. Everything changed. A year later, Auntie Bessie died, and then, several years later, Uncle Eddie died of prostate cancer. My Uncle Stavros, my brother, and my cousin Kaylee got divorces, and to make up for those we lost, my other cousin, who already had four children, had twins.

My mother and grandmother had had their portraits framed, and even though my uncle and brother remarried, for years, my mother hung hers in the hallway amid other family pictures and my grandmother kept hers on a table in the living room until she died almost twenty years later. I put mine in a drawer with other photographs and memorabilia, and who knows what everyone else did with theirs.

THE MAN IN CABIN NUMBER FIVE BOOK ONE

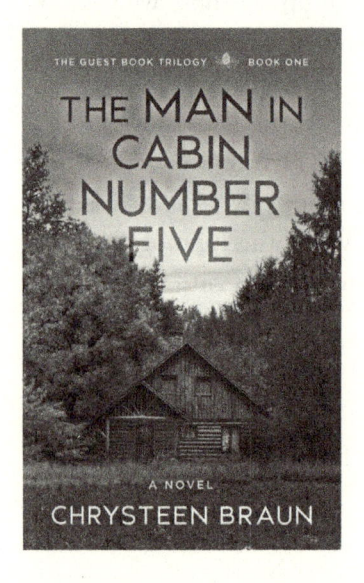

When Annie Parker discovers her husband's infidelity, she doesn't let it destroy her. She packs her bags and heads to Lake Arrowhead, California, the mountainside town where her family used to summer. Immersing herself in the restoration of seven 1920s-era cabins, Annie begins to put the pieces of her life back together. But starting over is never easy.

Alyce Murphy needs closure. When she discovers her father did not die from a heart attack, as she's been led to believe for the last 30 years, but in a murder/suicide, she is determined to uncover the truth of his death. But when she visits the cabin where her father ended his life, Alyce has to accept she may never know the true story.

Annie is looking toward her future while Alyce needs to put the past to rest. In parallel stories, both women are drawn to the rustic mountainside cabins as they search for the missing pieces—but they soon discover that the cabins have their own stories to tell.

THE GIRLS IN CABIN NUMBER THREE, BOOK TWO

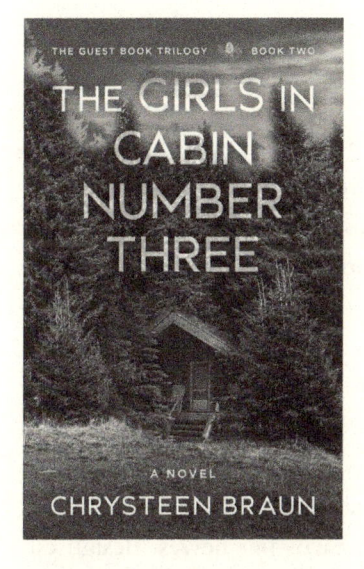

In book two of the Guest Book Trilogy, eighty-one-year-old Annie Parker recounts taking on, against the wishes of her new love Noah, an out-of-town design project that leads her down a path that is more than she bargained for.

Back in Lake Arrowhead, California, a long-awaited mystery is buried in Cabin Number Three. Annie meets Carrie Davis who wants to update her childhood home on the lake and feels a tie to Annie's cabins. Apparently, Carrie's parents stayed here during the Roaring '20s when Bugsy Siegel ran an underground speakeasy and distillery. Unconvinced, Annie decides to investigate and finds their names in the old guest books—Elizabeth Davis and Thomas Meyer. As exciting as that sounds, it's only the start of a winding tale that Carrie and the new man in her life uncover. The pair unravel a family history filled with gangsters, working girls, and a surprising twist to a family tree.

The Girls in Cabin Number Three combines women's fiction with romance, cozy noir mystery, and suspense—all wrapped up in the majestic environs of this lovely lakeside haven.

THE STARLET IN CABIN NUMBER SEVEN, BOOK THREE

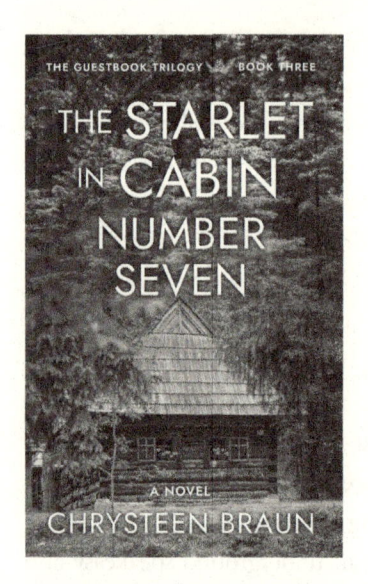

Return to picturesque 1980s Lake Arrowhead, California where another cozy cabin sheltered amongst the sweeping pine-lined vistas holds a long-buried secret, waiting to be divulged.

In this third installment of The Guest Book Trilogy, a young Annie Parker is struggling to overcome her grief over the recent loss of her sister, when a childhood friend unexpectedly turns up seeking refuge from an ill-fated marriage. It would have been easy for Annie to sink deeper into sadness, but when she learns her newest design client, Hudson Fisher, is the son of the late film actress Celeste Williams, her curiosity is peaked. As it turns out, the Roaring 20s starlet was no stranger to the Lake Arrowhead cabins—and this revelation sparks the unraveling of a scandalous story from Hollywood's bygone era. Did an illicit romance between this leading lady and her dashing costar take place in Cabin No. 7? What really went on behind-the-scenes during the filming of that silent picture? Will discovering a piece of the past bring closure to Annie's present?

A heartwarming tale of friendships, forgiveness, and a touch of old Hollywood glamour, *The Starlet in Cabin Number Seven* will have readers captivated from beginning to end.

THE MAIDSERVANT IN CABIN NUMBER ONE: THE BEGINNING, BOOK FOUR

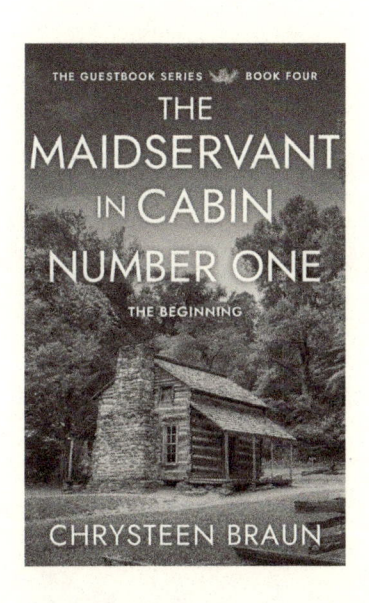

After her father's death in 1923, when Ruth Ann Landry is just ten, she joins her mother as a maidservant for a wealthy Seattle family. The hours are long, the rules are strict, but she and her mother desperately need her wages to survive.

By the time she's seventeen, they've moved into the house, and she's become a mistress to her employer. While accompanying the family on vacation, she sees an opportunity to start a new life, and leaves. Ruth eventually finds solace in the mountain town of Lake Arrowhead, California, where she stays in one of the cabins owned by a man who becomes part of her future.

The Maidservant in Cabin Number One is the beginning of the story of The Guest Book Trilogy, and of Annie Parker who eventually comes to own the cabins where Ruth Landry stayed.

Made in the USA
Las Vegas, NV
27 May 2025